DEATH *of an*

AMERICAN BEAUTY

DEATH *of an*

AMERICAN BEAUTY

Mariah Fredericks

Minotaur Books
New York

First published in the United States by Minotaur Books,
an imprint of St. Martin's Publishing Group

DEATH OF AN AMERICAN BEAUTY. Copyright © 2020 by Mariah Fredericks.
All rights reserved. Printed in the United States of America.
For information, address St. Martin's Publishing Group,
120 Broadway, New York, NY 10271.

www.minotaurbooks.com

Designed by Devan Norman

Library of Congress Cataloging-in-Publication Data

Names: Fredericks, Mariah, author.
Title: Death of an American beauty / Mariah Fredericks.
Description: First Edition. | New York : Minotaur Books, 2020. |
    Series: A Jane Prescott novel; 3
Identifiers: LCCN 2019048853 | ISBN 9781250210883 (hardcover) |
    ISBN 9781250210890 (ebook)
Subjects: GSAFD: Mystery fiction.
Classification: LCC PS3606.R435 D42914 2020 | DDC 813/.6—dc23
LC record available at https://lccn.loc.gov/2019048853

Our books may be purchased in bulk for promotional, educational,
or business use. Please contact your local bookseller or the Macmillan Corporate
and Premium Sales Department at 1-800-221-7945, extension 5442, or by
email at MacmillanSpecialMarkets@macmillan.com.

First Edition: April 2020

10 9 8 7 6 5 4 3 2 1

In memory of Sue Gilmore
"Yaya and Shoo"

Acknowledgments

I had an enormous amount of support while writing this book. Many people responded to my questions with generosity and insight. The first is my editor, Catherine Richards, who went above and beyond, gently pushing for change where it was needed. I also thank Nettie Finn for her invaluable perception and for tidying up the mess I made with skill and grace. Eternal appreciation to my agent, Victoria Skurnick. Big bouquets of thank-you to Kayla Janas and Allison Ziegler, David Rotstein for the gorgeous cover, production manager Cathy Turiano, and production editor Chrisinda Lynch. Last but never least, copyeditor India Cooper and proofreader Laura Dragonette, who caught my errors before they made it into print! I thank the entire team at Minotaur for the title.

Several people and organizations were invaluable when it came to research. Among them:

Elizabeth Kerri Mahon for her early read and kind correction on fashion history, which saved me from looking stupid. (If you haven't read her book *Scandalous Women*, please do so now.)

Leontine Greenberg for putting up with my endless clothing questions and providing invaluable research assistance.

Eric Peterson, who talked through music issues with me.

Reverend Mark Fowler, who reviewed points of religion and language choice.

The Schomburg Center for Research in Black Culture.

Among the many excellent works consulted for this book are *1913* by Florian Illies, *The Light of Truth* by Ida B. Wells, *Harlem* by Jonathan Gill, *Jazz: A History of the New York Scene* by Samuel B. Charters and Leonard Kunstadt, and biographies of Irving Berlin, especially Philip Furia's *Irving Berlin: A Life in Song*. I am also indebted to *They All Sang* by Edward Bennett Marks for the title "Piano Tuners Benevolent Euchre and Whist League." Allyson Compton's "The Breath Seekers: Race, Riots, and Public Space in Harlem, 1900–1935" provided enormous insight into the issues of public space during this time. Otelia Brooks's life passion was, in part, inspired by the glorious exhibit of Mae Reeves's work at the National Museum of African American History and Culture.

Deep gratitude is due my comrades in the mystery-writing profession, especially the ladies of the Queens Writers Group. Most of all, I'm thankful to Josh and Griffin Weiss for their amazing support through this stage of my career.

And lastly—the readers! Thank you all for listening to my stories. I appreciate it more than you will ever know.

Something is wrong with the world. These men know.

—JAMES A. STILLMAN ON THE ARMORY SHOW

What is, or should be, woman? Not merely a bundle of flesh and bones, nor a fashion plate, a frivolous inanity, a soulless doll, a heartless coquette—but a strong, bright presence, thoroughly imbued with a sense of her mission on earth and a desire to fill it.

—IDA B. WELLS

DEATH *of an*
AMERICAN BEAUTY

The Princess of Wales has had a son.

Beyond that, I'm not sure.

My eyesight is not bad for someone of my age, but by any other measure, it is not good. Reading the newspaper has become a challenge. My glasses must be fixed at a precise point, the light sufficient, and the room quiet because I cannot read the words if I cannot hear them in my head. My daughter says this makes no sense, but they're my eyes and it's my head.

Raising the paper, I peer at the print, which I swear they've made smaller. The young man who shot the president has been found not guilty because he is insane. Apparently the would-be assassin wished to impress a famous young woman. I think of all the things one might do to impress such a woman. Killing the president is not one of them.

The same thought occurred to the jury; they found the young man's reasoning so flawed, they decided it constituted insanity. They must have felt he was sincere; I might have thought he was lying. That he tried to kill the president not because he wanted a young woman to think well of him, but because he wanted to think well of himself. If he found it splendid to kill, she would also find it splendid and reward him.

Perhaps if the prosecutor had pointed out this level of self-interest to the jury, they might have told the young man and others like him that you cannot kill because you have come up with stories about women that are not true. No matter how alluring those stories might be. Helen of Troy was probably an ordinary-looking woman who had gotten bored with her husband and vice versa. But would we remember the heroes of the Trojan War if the Greeks were simply land-hungry? No, much better to say it was the face that launched a thousand ships. A woman's face.

I wonder if this jury would have declared Achilles insane. Or if they might have understood that he had a compulsion to kill and Helen's face was simply the excuse.

Or maybe the Greeks disliked that she ran away. A woman at liberty—that could be provocation enough.

I feel a curl of unease, a memory unfolding. A face.

For a moment I can't breathe. Even after all these years, I can feel the vicious grip of those hands on my neck. There are days when I feel unsteady. I feel it now. A sense of falling, flailing . . .

I hold my head at the correct angle. Try to focus on the newspaper. The princess. The young man. But still I see that other face.

A woman's face. Taken apart. Put back together.

And the scars, so many years later.

1

"*Four score and seven* years ago . . .'"

I looked up from the script. "I'm sorry, Mrs. Tyler. That's the Gettysburg Address. You're meant to be reciting the Emancipation Proclamation."

"Am I?" Louise exhaled fretfully. "Oh dear."

"'That on the first day of January . . . ,'" I prompted.

"'. . . first day of January . . .'" Remembering the rest of her line, she rattled off, "'In the year of our Lord one thousand eight hundred and sixty-three . . .'"

"'All persons held as slaves . . .'"

"'. . . slaves . . .'"

"'. . . shall be then, thenceforward, and forever free.'"

"'Forever free,'" Louise echoed, and removed her stovepipe hat. "What does thenceforward mean?"

"From now on, I suppose."

"Well, why didn't Lincoln just say so?"

As a lady's maid, it wasn't for me to defend the stylistic choices

of the martyred sixteenth president. But while Lincoln had been
eloquent in the face of civil war, congressional opposition, and the
pistol of John Wilkes Booth, he had probably never faced a salon
of society ladies, as Louise was preparing to do. In fact, he rarely
visited the city, which had twice refused to vote for a Republican
seen as insensitive to the commercial benefits of the slave trade.

However, it was the fiftieth anniversary of the Emancipation
Proclamation, and New York had embraced its commemoration
with gusto. Which was how Louise found herself balancing a
makeshift stovepipe as she struggled to recite Mr. Lincoln's great
speech.

Bored by the traditional dinner parties, the city's great ladies
were keen to display their artistry in different ways. *Tableaux
vivants* and amateur theatrics were the rage. One might enjoy
Mrs. Halsey's Brutus on Monday, Mrs. Foster Jenkins's selections
from *Die Fledermaus* Tuesday, and on Wednesday, Mrs. Fortesque's torrid attempts at Apache dance. And so, led by Dolly
Rutherford of Rutherford's department store—the newest and
most ostentatious of the ladies' shopping paradises, which billed
itself as the place "Where every American Beauty blooms!"—
my employer Louise Tyler and others were to perform "Stirring
Scenes of the Emancipation" in a week's time.

Being tall and willowy, Louise had been chosen to play the
Great Emancipator himself. This was an honor that one might
have thought due the hostess. But Mrs. Rutherford was round of
figure and short of stature. At one point, it was suggested she play
Harriet Tubman, but in the end, she had accepted the almost
equally, *if not more*, important role of Mary Todd Lincoln. (The
part of Harriet Tubman went to Mrs. Edith Van Dormer. Having
died earlier that month, Mrs. Tubman would be spared that performance.)

Now Louise sank into an armchair and gazed out the window

at the mid-March morning. The calendar might say spring, but the chill air and dull skies showed that winter had not yet loosened its grip. A fire burned nicely, and the remains of Louise's breakfast tea sat on the table beside her. The townhouse in the East Twenties was quiet, as William Tyler, her husband of eight months, was in Washington with Louise's father, Mr. Benchley. There were rumors that Woodrow Wilson was working on a new sort of revenue system, a tax on actual income. The more one earned, the more one paid. Some considered this a monstrous assault, including Mr. Benchley, who had many friends in Washington and had gone to urge them to fight the president's plan. He had taken his son-in-law and newly minted attorney with him, leaving Louise on her own and at the mercy of Dolly Rutherford.

I blamed myself for Dolly Rutherford. William Tyler's mother and I had, between us, successfully shepherded Louise through her first six months as a New York matron. The senior Mrs. Tyler had introduced the junior Mrs. Tyler to the ladies she ought to know, warned her off those she should not, while I had polished her appearance and bolstered her confidence. When the elder Mrs. Tyler went to visit her daughter Beatrice, now husband hunting in Boston, she said to me, "I leave Louise in your capable hands, Jane."

Mrs. Tyler had been gone but a day when I came down with gastric flu. With her mother-in-law away and me indisposed, Louise had fallen into the clutches of one of the city's most limber and exhausting social climbers. Dolly Rutherford let it be known that she refused, just refused, to be idle. "To be idle is to be bored and to be bored is to die." Her passion was the transcendent, especially in the arts. If it hung in a gallery or danced, sang, or declaimed upon the stage, Dolly Rutherford would lure it into her salon and display it, "flayed, dressed, and pickled," as one critic put it. She might have been ridiculous except for two

assets: a will worthy of Genghis Khan and her husband's fortune.
Stronger women than Louise Tyler had been pulled into Dolly's
orbit. I felt guilty nonetheless.

As the clock on the mantelpiece chimed nine, I hoped Louise
would remember what today was before I had to remind her. But
she noticed my glance at the clock and said, "Oh, it's time, isn't
it?" Rising, she held out her hand. "What will I do without you?"

"You can reach me at the refuge anytime."

"It's your holiday, Jane—why don't you go somewhere nice?"

"I want to see my uncle. And I have other plans as well."

"Oh, and what are these plans?"

"I'm afraid some of them are shocking."

"Jane!" Smiling, Louise put a hand to her chest. "Well, all
right. Go and do your shocking things. But I'll miss you at French
lessons. And rehearsals. If Dolly Rutherford shouts at that poor
seamstress from her husband's store one more time, I'll have fits.
Still, I suppose it's something to do."

With a small sigh, she looked around the sitting room as if
hoping distraction would present itself. Or her husband: I knew
she was missing William. That much could be said for the Rutherford Pageant: it was a diversion.

With as much speed as was polite, I went upstairs to change.
When William and Louise had moved to their new home, I had
been given a spacious room on the top floor.

Taking off my daily outfit of plain skirt and shirtwaist, I pulled
on a high-necked blouse and a dark skirt of jersey wool I'd made
myself. Then I added a long navy jacket that had been left behind
by Charlotte when she went to Europe. Then I put on my new
hat, black felt, turned up at the front with a dark red rose at the
side and a handsome velvet band. Finally, I put on my new coat, a
present from the Tylers this past Christmas. It was also dark wool,
but the cut was exquisite, with a hobble skirt, large baggy pockets,

a wraparound bodice that buttoned daringly at the bosom, and a high collar. Looking in the mirror, I decided that while I was not quite Lillian Gish, I needn't be ashamed to be seen in her company should she turn up at the International Exhibition of Modern Art.

For that's where I was going, to mark the start of my vacation, the scandalous art exhibit known as the Armory Show. The exhibition of twelve hundred works by three hundred American and European artists had descended on New York in a blaze of sensation. It was the talk of the city, so popular that people went again and again, just to be seen. On one day, you might see Caruso sketching in a corner. On another, former president Roosevelt. Cartoonists depicted landmarks from the Statue of Liberty to the Brooklyn Bridge in the shocking new style dubbed Cubism. The artists had been lampooned as "nuttists," "dope-ists," "topsy-turvists," and "toodle-doodlists." Even official critics were uncertain as to the Cubists' merits, asking, "Is their work a conspicuous milestone in the progress of art? Or is it junk?"

I was fairly sure I wouldn't be able to decide either. But that wasn't important. All that mattered to me on that cold March day was that the Armory Show was the most fashionable place to be in New York City and that I, Jane Prescott, would be there.

In service to absolutely no one but myself.

* * *

The 69th Regiment Armory was only a few blocks from the Tyler home in the East Twenties. Designed along elegant, modern lines with curved arches and a French mansard roof of limestone, the Armory welcomed visitors with a banner hung above the entrance: INTERNATIONAL EXHIBITION OF MODERN ART. Limousines were already lining up outside, creating traffic jams as they disgorged their stylish passengers. As I joined the line to get in, I heard a man ask, "How does a minister's niece come to be at this tawdry spectacle?"

I turned and saw Michael Behan. I had not seen him for several months, and an art exhibit was not where I expected to find him. "What on earth are you doing here?"

"I am paid to be here," said the reporter. "Which is the only way you'd get me near the place. Are you going in?"

"I am."

"Well, let the *Herald* pay your fare. Come on, I'll give you the guided tour."

As we sailed inside and past the guards, who seemed to know him well, I said, "Don't tell me you're now an art critic."

He shook his head. "There are only so many ways to say bunk, garbage, con, and hooey, Miss Prescott. These fellows make P. T. Barnum look like an honest man. No, I'm here to cover the local color angle. Reactions of the average man and woman, with a bit of gossip about the famous who wander through."

He handed our coats off at the coat check, then turned to me. "Now then, average woman. What would you like to see first?"

I gazed at the bustling, well-dressed crowd. I had dreamed of this for weeks, and now I was actually here. Thrilled to feel both free and in exactly the right place, I said, "I want to see every last bit of it, Mr. Behan."

"Shall we start at the Chamber of Horrors?" This was the nickname for Gallery I, where the Cubists were displayed.

"Let's."

I had last seen Michael Behan at the time of William and Louise's wedding. It had been an uncertain time for me. I had not been sure of my place with the Benchleys, and just before the wedding, a young woman I knew had been murdered. The sudden end of her life had made me look at my own in a different light.

In such a mood, seeing Michael Behan, who was both good-looking and married, had been complicated. I realized now, I had let myself get caught up in all sorts of stupid ideas, taking letters he had written to me for something beyond what they were. Thankfully, I hadn't made a fool of myself, and I could now be in his company without a trace of confusion. Yes, I was pleased to be seen in smart new clothes. But if women couldn't take pleasure in having their attractions noted, a lady's maid's career would not thrive.

Gallery I was by far the most crowded. Craning to see over shoulders, I asked, "Where is *Nude Descending a Staircase?*" The painting by a Frenchman named Marcel Duchamp was said to be the most shocking of the entire show, and I was in a mood to be shocked.

"Right over here," said Behan. "And I'll give you a dollar if you can see anything remotely resembling a human being."

The painting was mobbed, and it was a while before I could get even a glimpse of it. I confess, my first thought was *Mud*.

"Stunning, isn't it?" said Behan. "Puts me in mind of a dropped book."

I peered at the canvas, determined to see that nude. There was a briefest flash of comprehension—*Oh, it's like that, isn't that astonishing?*—before a beefy man elbowed me to one side and I was back to seeing muddy trees.

The reorientation of my eyes held enough that when we moved on to a sculpted head that looked made up of triangles and rectangles, I said truthfully, "That's beautiful." But I felt my face go red when we approached a black-and-white image of a nude woman. The strokes were rough and unlovely. She was well fleshed, her belly sloping, legs open. Avoiding Mr. Behan's eye, I went on to *Woman with Mustard Pot*.

Here, you could see the person clearly: a woman sitting, rather bored, her head leaning on her hand. Her face was all angles, slashing cuts of black, orange, gray, and yellow. I wasn't sure I liked it; it felt almost cruel to take a face apart like this. But it was also mesmerizing. Nearby a matronly woman declared that if her child ever made art like this, she would smack it.

We wandered through to another room, where Mr. Behan admired a painting of boxers—all muscle and epic struggle—and we both smiled in recognition of a painting of three young women drying their hair on the roof of a city building.

Then I heard a high, excited voice call my name. I turned to see Louise's young sister-in-law Emily Tyler weaving her way through the crowd, catching the eye of several gentlemen. This was not surprising; she was tall and lively, with the reddish-brown hair of the Tylers and mischievous brown eyes all her own. What was surprising was her presence in the city. She was supposed to be at Vassar College.

As she reached us, she said, "Is Louise here, or are you on your own?"

"On my own," I informed her. "It's my holiday."

"Me as well," said Emily happily. "Not officially, but yesterday, I just decided that if I had to read or write one more word, my head would burst. So—here I am."

Notebook at the ready, Behan inquired, "And what do you make of the exhibition, Miss Tyler?"

"Well, there are an awful lot of naked people," she said, dimpling.

"Miss Prescott?"

"I like it," I announced. "It's a new way to see things."

Behan took this down; I knew how he'd write it. My views would be given due respect. But Emily would have the last word.

"Do you cover the arts, Mr. Behan?" Emily asked.

"Just the life of the city, Miss Tyler. Art, crime, the human drama . . ."

"Oh, well, you should talk to Jane. Her uncle runs a home for prostitutes on the East Side. That's just full of human drama."

Her voice had risen on the word "prostitutes," and Michael Behan's brow quirked. He might write about tawdry subjects, but he was conservative in some things, and young women shouting about prostitutes was apparently one of them. Making his excuses, he left me to manage a wayward college girl avid for experience.

I asked, "Does your mother know you're here, Miss Tyler?"

"She does not," said Emily, gazing at the black-and-white nude. "And don't you tell her. Not a word to William or Louise either."

I was about to say she had one week to enjoy my discretion when we heard "Emily Tyler!" and turned to see Mrs. Dolly Rutherford. She embraced Emily in the manner of an old family friend, even though they'd only met once or twice before.

"Have they released you from that purgatory in Poughkeep-sie?"

Like most socially ambitious women, Mrs. Rutherford had an excellent memory. Small and blond, she gave the impression of a woman who cannot imagine being unable to charm anyone into anything. She had a beautiful rose complexion and a ready smile. But the ringed fingers that set themselves on Emily's arms were white at the knuckles, even as she kept a sharp lookout for anyone more important.

I was certainly not that person. Nor was I a great fan of Mrs. Rutherford's, so I stepped tactfully away and examined the next painting, three undressed women, painted by someone named Seurat. I wasn't sure what to make of it, so I listened in as a bearded gentleman lectured a pink-cheeked young man, saying,

"See the tiny dots of color? It's called Divisionism. You don't mix the paints into one muddy slosh, you let each color stand separate and of itself. But next to it, you put a contrasting color just as bold, and the two side by side give so much more light and life."

I was thinking that was rather marvelous when I heard Dolly Rutherford reproving Emily for speaking with a reporter.

"Oh," said Emily, with mock regret, "but he was a very *handsome* reporter. And anyway, now he's run off. I don't think he cared for what he was seeing. Much preferred the earlier pieces." She twinkled at me. Had she not been William Tyler's sister, I would have thrown a glove at her.

Dolly Rutherford adroitly moved the topic back to a point of interest: herself. "Mr. Rutherford can't abide this sort of thing either. I said, George, this is the most important art event of the year, you must see it. But the poor dear took one look, said he felt ill, and went back to his office."

"He's announcing the next Miss Rutherford's soon, isn't he?" said Emily, referring to the annual contest in which young ladies vied to be the face of Rutherford's department store. "I'm wild with curiosity as to who it will be."

Dolly Rutherford smiled briefly. "Yes, that will be announced at the conclusion of my musicale, 'Stirring Scenes of the Emancipation.' Your dear sister-in-law has deigned to take part, and I have a feeling she will amaze us all!"

Well aware of Louise's shyness, Emily giggled. Mrs. Rutherford then suggested Emily join her at Rutherford's celebrated tearoom, the Orientale; the store was only a short distance, and they could take the car. In the tradition of students since time immemorial, Emily sensed a free meal and accepted on the spot. To me, she gave a wave of the fingers, which she then drew across her lips, urging silence. And I was free to wander the exhibition on my own.

Which I did for a very enjoyable hour. But I was getting tired, my head overfull of images, when I stopped in front of a black-and-white etching. It was a city scene, a group of buildings at night. In one window, a woman, not quite dressed, put her wash on the clothesline to dry. There was a man behind her; her husband, presumably, but she felt vulnerable, unaware of being watched. In another window, a woman stood in just her underdrawers, arms above her head as she pulled her hair into a knot. She seemed to be enjoying her nakedness, taking in the air on a sweltering summer night. But a shadowy figure on a nearby roof was gazing at her. This vision of the city was both jarringly realistic and something out of a storybook, and it unnerved me.

"That's grisly," said Michael Behan behind me.

I wheeled around. "You deserted me!"

"I certainly did. What *is* it they're teaching at ladies' colleges these days?"

"Oh, that's just Emily Tyler. She likes to be shocking."

"She succeeds."

He said I had the look of a woman in need of a cup of tea, and I said I was exactly that. The day had started as exhilarating, but now I felt exhausted. I simply could not look at another thing.

I said as much to Michael Behan as he set two mugs of tea and a plate of seed cake on the café table. I expected him to tease me, but he said, "I don't much care for it. Cutting up the face, shoving it this way and that. As if it's a . . . thing. Not human. Hits you in strange ways. I'll be happy to be done with this assignment, to tell you the truth."

As he cut the cake in two with a fork, he added, "Although it does get me home in time for dinner."

In the past, Mr. Behan had worked long hours; this, I sensed, had caused domestic quarrels. "How is Mrs. Behan?" I asked.

"She is very well, thank you. Actually, I do thank you, as it's partly down to you."

"Me?"

He nodded. "You remember telling me that Mrs. Behan's mood might improve if I hired a day girl?"

"And you did?"

"Not exactly. But her father died"—I was about to offer condolences, but a quick shake of the head told me Mr. Behan did not mourn his father-in-law—"which left our fortunes somewhat improved. Also, my mother-in-law in permanent residence. Which has its . . . charms. But it's put us in mind of family, so I'm working a bit less and home a bit more often." He sipped his tea. "Those who aspire to posterity must work to achieve it, or some such pablum."

He was shy as he said it, and I understood that future Behans were now hoped for. Knowing he liked children, I said sincerely, "I wish you great success."

"Well, thank you."

For a moment we smiled at each other, and I thought how nice it was to be friends with a gentleman. Michael Behan would have fat, handsome babies, and I would knit something for them. A hat.

"Where is it you're off to after this? Is all this"—he waved a finger at my new jacket—"for your uncle? Or has that milkman finally found his nerve?" Behan liked to spin yarns about various suitors who were yearning to approach but had yet to find the courage.

"We have a new milkman now, and I never see him. Nor the policeman nor the butcher, baker, or candlestick maker. But I am off to the refuge."

Apparently, Emily's impulse to shock had rubbed off, because I added, "We're having a dance tonight."

"A dance."

"Yes, it's an annual event. The Southern Baptist Ladies' Cotillion." I sipped my tea. "Or, as some of the women prefer to call it, the Whores' Ball."

Behan leaned back in his chair. "Now, this I might have to see. How does one get invited to this soiree?"

"You don't, Mr. Behan. No men are allowed."

The cups were empty, and only crumbs were left of the cake. As we got up to leave, he said, "You'll be doing their hair, I suppose."

"Oh, I'll be dancing, Mr. Behan."

"Will you?"

"I happen to dance very well."

"Do you?"

"I do."

We collected our coats and made our way outside. After the overheated air of the crowded Armory, the chill and damp were refreshing. As we walked out of the tunneled exit, I decided this was a very satisfactory start to my vacation.

By now the crowds were much larger, and for a moment we were trapped at the gates, buffeted by people eager to get inside. There was a screech of tires and a wet thud. Then someone screamed. My immediate thought was that a person had been struck by a car, a driver making a sudden dash around the traffic and running into someone. But then I saw people gathering by the wall of the Armory, heard cries of "Revolting!" "Who would do such a thing?" The sound of retching.

Drawn by instinct, Behan had pushed his way through the crowd and was trying to get a look over hats and shoulders. I saw his neck go rigid, and he stepped back.

"What is it?" I asked, looking even as I heard him say, "Don't."

A cat—the tail and stiff paws told me that right away. The

staring eyes, bulging entrails. The poor head, hanging by a sinew, spoke of deliberate cruelty. And the red, spreading in the gray snow, that wide gaping slash in the belly . . . I swallowed, tasted bitter tea and bile.

"I hope that's not the *Herald* critic's review," said Michael Behan, guiding me away. "Come on, let's find you a cab."

2

The Southern Baptist Ladies' Cotillion was the creation of Otelia Brooks. Her blood could still be seen on the carpet in the entry hall of the refuge if one looked hard enough. It had been cleaned many times—often by Miss Brooks, who was frustrated with herself for losing consciousness when she arrived. That she had made it to the refuge at all was providential. But she was a woman who demanded the miraculous of herself. Only such a woman would have attempted to get my uncle to host a dance at the refuge— and succeeded. The cotillion was the most festive day in the Gorman Refuge calendar, and I smiled in anticipation as I walked the last blocks to the place I had once more or less called home. But my mood changed abruptly as I turned onto Third Street.

They were back.

The refuge had once been a brothel, but in the 1890s the owner, Mrs. Gorman, turned it over to my uncle to start a place where women could learn skills that would result in less professional peril. Over the years, there had been some in the neighborhood who objected to a home for former prostitutes in their midst. But beyond the occasional drunken serenade and self-exposure from men on their way home, the refuge had been left alone.

Until recently. In 1909, a reporter had published an article called "The Daughters of the Poor," which argued that prostitution was no longer a business of women but of men who saw profit in selling them. Many took up the cause with moral fervor: committees were formed, investigations launched. No vast network of villains was revealed, only venereal disease and a lot of poor women who found prostitution paid better than other work.

Still, the danger of losing a generation of men to syphilis gave rise to organizations such as the American Vigilance Association and the American Purity Alliance—as well as the zeal of Clementine Pickett. Mrs. Pickett had been obliged to move to the Lower East Side a year ago, following a loss of income with the death of her husband. Already prickly over that misfortune, she had been dismayed to discover that she now lived "mere blocks from a bawdy house." Not only her home but the morals of her son, Orville, were in jeopardy. My uncle and his supporters had met with the lady several times in an effort to persuade her that their mission and hers were the same: fewer women engaged in the business of prostitution. But the widow Pickett was of the opinion that any house occupied by women who had once sold themselves was a brothel and that the man living with such women was a procurer. She wanted them out of the neighborhood.

To that end, she had organized several of her friends and associates to stand in front of the refuge and harass anyone who went in and out. They prayed loudly, sang hymns, and bellowed shame at any woman who crossed the threshold. Mostly, they were a nuisance. But in recent weeks, they had gone beyond prayer and singing. One or two of Orville's friends had gotten close enough to the women to offer personal insults. Dog feces were left on the steps. Two weeks ago, a rock had come crashing through the second-story window. My uncle had called the police, and since then it had been quiet. But it was an uneasy truce. And the dance tonight might be enough to break it.

At first I was relieved to see that Orville, not his mother, was on duty this evening. Mrs. Pickett was a sharp-tongued interrupter; I found her too enraging for politeness. At thirty and nearly six feet, Orville Pickett was a slab of a man, overgrown but soft and immature. The reddish hair on his egg-shaped head was thinning, and his cheeks were flushed. Away from his mother, he seemed to have no real meanness to him. Out of the corner of his eye, he saw me and raised his hand ever so slightly in greeting. I nodded back, hoping that our tentative friendliness might facilitate peace.

Peace was not the goal of the Duchess of Damnation, however, who stood across the street with her ladies in waiting. For the Duchess, it was surrender and withdrawal from the field of battle or nothing. Known at one time as Jennie Bullotte, the Duchess was one of the most notorious madams on the Lower East Side. Fiercely protective of the honor and welfare of her trade, she took offense at the Lord's judgment delivered by people "who ain't got no more pull with Him than I do." So when the Purity Brigade took their position, she showed up with her girls to respond. Not above five feet, with a tower of black hair trimmed in silk butterflies, she was a skilled saleswoman who knew that parading her ladies along the block opposite Mrs. Pickett's brigade made a pretty—and provocative—contrast. Through the drone of hymns and prayers, the Duchess and her ladies would chant things such as "On our backs or at the tills / working women pay the bills!" When Mrs. Pickett read from the Bible, the Duchess read from her own price list for a wide array of services. In one tour de force, they had bent over as one to reveal a splendid lineup of scarlet underdrawers.

As for Mrs. Pickett's group, we seemed to have only the stalwarts this evening, huddled together against sin and chill winds: Orville, Mrs. Hilquit, and Miss Cobb, who read from Deuteronomy in a quavering voice.

And then I saw Bill Danvers.

The women drawn to Mrs. Pickett's cause were devout, fearful, or bored to varying degrees. Most of the men were similar. I suspected some were paid. But Bill Danvers was different. A rangy man with a chicken neck, he wore his dark hair slicked close to his scalp. His teeth were crooked, the canines pointed. His ill-fitting "respectable" clothes hinted at the hand-me-downs of redemption; his cheeks were newly shaved, and his mustache trimmed of all vanity. But I suspected his piety went no deeper than his shirt and was just as easily shrugged off. He had already had a fractious encounter with the Duchess, and his eyes glittered at any young woman that passed. I felt fairly sure it was he who had thrown the rock and left the mess on the steps, and whenever he was around, the group was agitated, bolder. As I approached, I saw his tongue flick across his lips. And knew he had wanted me to see it.

I did not want Bill Danvers around during the cotillion.

"Good evening, Mr. Pickett. You shouldn't read in this poor light, Miss Cobb, it's bad for the eyes."

She glared. "'And if thy right eye offend thee—'"

"I'll be sure to pluck it out, thank you. Mr. Pickett, may I speak with you?"

Orville glanced uncertainly at the group. But as I had suspected it might, the chance to talk to a girl overrode his anxieties, and he followed me a little way from the refuge.

"Mr. Pickett, do you really think women of Miss Cobb's and Mrs. Hilquit's age should be out in the cold like this?"

"God doesn't care about the cold, Miss Prescott."

Seeing I couldn't talk him into a temporary cease-fire on account of the weather, I asked, "Who will be here tonight?"

"Tonight? Me, Mrs. Bailey, Mr. Danvers . . ."

As he listed the names, I made a hasty decision. A lie was in order.

"It's just that it's my birthday, Mr. Pickett."

"Oh." He blinked. "Happy birthday."

"Thank you. We're having a party at the refuge. There will be some music and dancing. Innocent, of course. There will be no men present."

"Your uncle will be."

"No, he won't. He has business elsewhere this evening, and he doesn't care for dancing. It will just be me and the other ladies. But it's the sort of thing a less honorable mind might misinterpret, and I wouldn't want any trouble. I know Mr. Danvers is a friend of yours, but he hasn't got your . . . self-discipline."

Almost no one can resist an appeal that rests on the premise that they are better, finer people than their friends. Orville Pickett was no exception.

"Maybe it would be better if Bill went home early. The cold does make him ornery."

"Thank you, Mr. Pickett. I'm so grateful." The hymns would be loud, I thought, but it would be better than dung on the stoop or rocks through the window.

★ ★ ★

Whenever I went home, I liked to speak with Berthe Froehlich first. Except for my uncle, no one had been at the refuge longer.

Most women left in a matter of months, a year at most. But Berthe's face had been badly scarred by acid in a suicide attempt; she was also over six feet tall. No matter what her skills, life outside would have been difficult. So she became the cook, as well as doing a hundred other jobs that might have fallen to me had I stayed. She not only knew everything that went on at the refuge but, unlike my uncle, was willing to talk about it. And so I went straight to the kitchen and sat while Berthe brought me up to date. She told me about a new woman who just arrived two days ago and was struggling to stay off drink, the jobs found by three women who had left, a leak in the roof, beds that needed new mattresses, and her trials with Sadie Ellis.

Sadie Ellis had arrived at the refuge four months ago. When she came, her eye was swollen shut, the brow purple and ballooning. Her lip bulged grotesquely, cut and bloodied by broken teeth. Even her bright auburn hair was tangled and matted with blood. Her gait was unsteady, and she mumbled odd answers to Berthe's questions.

She had been brought by her friend Carrie Biel, who had left the refuge a year ago. Carrie had known the moment Sadie took up with Joe McInerny that he wasn't in it for love. But even she had been shocked by what he had done to Sadie for what he called "acting up."

At the refuge, Sadie recovered her spirits. She had the vivacity of the intensely self-absorbed, and she made many friends at first. Each new friend was her savior, her wise counselor. But as each friend found, Sadie really only had one interest: Joe. Yes, he had lied to her, beaten her, and loaned her out to other men so he didn't have to find work. But she missed him. Or at least, she missed a life where she did not have to sit in a classroom all day and work at things she found dull. She'd start by saying she would never see Joe again and end by remembering that sweet thing he had said or a trinket he'd bought her. The women lost patience with her soon, and these days Sadie had few people left to listen to her. Lately, she had started to "wander," leaving the refuge without permission. And Berthe was fairly sure she was meeting Joe.

Now Berthe said, "She don't want to stay put, don't want to learn. Just wants to get back to the man who sold her and beat her up. Your uncle should let her go for good."

"How can you let a girl go back to a man who did that to her?"

"If she's foolish enough to want to, who can stop her? At least he's stopped coming around here."

When Sadie had first arrived, Mr. McInerny had turned up drunk several times, bellowing to be let in or for Sadie to come out. He would go from remorseful to frustrated and then enraged, threatening to kill her the first chance he got.

I said, "I suppose I should present myself to my uncle."

"Tell him he needs to do something about Sadie. She's making trouble, and I don't need more of that." She nodded toward the street. "Not with the Bible thumpers and stone throwers."

Just then Sal Karlsson looked in. "There's a phone call for you, Miss Prescott."

"Same as before?" asked Berthe.

"Think so," said Sal, who was a girl of good humor and better sense. "She sounds kind of desperate."

Knowing immediately who the caller was, I said, "Thank you, Sal," and went to take the call.

Anna Ardito was my oldest friend—and closest, although we were very different people. I toiled for the rich; Anna fought for their destruction, currently with the Industrial Workers of the World. Her work was the sole focus of Anna's life; she had no other interests or passions. But at the moment, she was finding the object of her devotion a headache. Anna had done many things for the cause. Now the IWW had asked her to do a task she not only found morally repugnant, but for which she was extremely ill-equipped: fund-raising.

The silk workers of Paterson, New Jersey, had been on strike since late February. The New York press's apathy about anything that took place across the Hudson was no doubt intensified by the discomfort of newspaper magnates at the thought of labor unrest so close to their doorstep. So as far as Manhattan was concerned, the strike was not taking place. Remembering the impact of the children's parade on the sympathies of New Yorkers during the Lawrence strike, Mabel Dodge, a lady with keen tastes for beauty in spectacle and radical young men, suggested the strikers be brought before the public. Why, the strikers could tell their own stories! Just as actors might! Why not, everyone agreed, make it a real show? And so on June 7 the Pageant of the Paterson Strike would be performed in Madison Square Garden.

Taking up the front desk phone, I said, "Hello, Anna."

"I was thinking"—Anna was not one for time-wasting niceties—"maybe your uncle would like to bring some of the women to the pageant."

"My uncle has no money for pageants. But I'll be there, I promise."

"Maybe you could bring a friend? Two friends? Ten friends?"

"I don't have ten friends, Anna. I have you." Briefly I thought of Michael Behan, but it was not appropriate to ask him, and his review would be scathing.

"What about your boss? It would be very educational for her."

"I'm sorry they're making you sell tickets," I said gently. "You're an excellent comrade."

For a moment Anna was silent in defeat. Then she said, "I saw those lunatics outside your building. Why don't you throw a piss pot over them?"

I glanced out the front window. "Tempting, but provocative."

"You should get rid of them," she said, suddenly serious. "Religious fanatics are no joke."

"It's calmer now," I said. "I think the police scared them."

"People obsessed with heaven don't scare easily. But I hope you're right. Happy Cotillion Day."

As I climbed the stairs to my uncle's office, I thought how I might phrase Berthe's concerns about Sadie. My uncle valued Berthe's opinion. Although he had never said so; he was not the sort of man to make his affections plain. I sometimes doubted whether he had affections.

When I was three, my father left me on the street with my uncle's address pinned to my coat. Summoned to the police station, he had said, "Well, now. I am your father's brother. He has gone, so you will come and stay with me."

Then he held out his hand and I took it. And that was the most we had ever spoken about our connection. If he resented the burden his brother left him, he never said so. If he ever tried to reach my father, he never said that either. I don't remember what my father looked like, so I cannot say if the brothers resembled each other. My uncle was a small, compact man with bright blue eyes and thick gray hair. He reminded me of a terrier, stern, bushy browed, and once set on something, difficult to dissuade. As I knocked on the door, I hoped I would not have to argue with him about Sadie.

I got a smile as I entered, but he finished his letter, signing it with a quick, brief stroke before coming around the desk and accepting a kiss on the cheek.

"So," he said, sitting down again, "you're here for the week."

"I would never miss the cotillion. I see Mrs. Pickett and her group are still with us."

"As sleet in February. Predictable, persistent, and chilling."

"The Duchess livens things up, I suppose."

This was followed by a pause, common in conversations with my uncle. I thought there was more to be said on a subject; he did not.

And so I changed it, saying, "The weather doesn't seem to bother Sadie Ellis."

My uncle frowned as if he could not place the name.

"Berthe says she's been leaving without permission."

"This is not a prison. We don't keep the women under lock and key."

"Of course not. But while the women are here, they're meant to be focused on their future. Berthe thinks Sadie's sneaking out to see Joe McInerny. You saw what he did to her."

"I'm sure she'll settle eventually."

This was vague—and unlike my uncle.

"It's been four months. She's fully healed. If she doesn't want to be here, why not let her go? There are other women who would gladly take her place."

"She's never told me she wishes to leave."

"But if staying here comes with conditions and she's unwilling to meet those conditions—"

My uncle took out his watch and consulted it. "You have been here for less than an hour, and yet you're telling me how to run an organization I have managed for more than two decades."

My choice to leave the refuge and work in service had always been a sore point with my uncle. He had never said outright that having taken me in, he might have reasonably expected some years of free work when I was old enough to be useful. Or that employment as a lady's maid, helping wealthy women be attractive, was less worthy than helping poor women find their footing in the work world. But then . . . he didn't have to.

"I'm sorry," I said. "But I hate seeing Berthe troubled."

My uncle waved his hand. "If we only helped those who were

easy to help, our work would have no meaning. Miss Ellis is young. She may need more time than others to see her future clearly. If you find her so misguided, perhaps you might make an effort. Make her feel she has a place here, that she's welcome."

As if every woman at the refuge had not already listened to Sadie's woes. Still, I said, "Very well. She can help me with the cotillion."

That got a brief nod of approval.

"And where will you go this evening?" I asked him. My uncle adhered strictly and gladly to the rule of no men at the ball. "Will you be dining with Mrs. Forbes or the Reverend Endicott?"

"Neither." Then, taking up his pen, he said, "I'll say good-bye before I go."

Leaving his office, I wondered if all men of the cloth managed to make people feel that they had failed to be pleasing in the sight of God or whether it was a particular skill of my uncle's. Feeling deflated and dissatisfied with myself, I went to the front parlor. The women were already getting the room ready. The dining table had been moved out, the chairs set against the wall, and now garlands were being hung on the walls. Next to the piano was a new addition: a phonograph.

Then I spotted Sadie. She lolled by the window, foot swinging as she gazed out. Remembering my uncle's request, I asked her, "Have they gone away?"

"Who?"

"The Committee for Moral Rectitude or whatever it is they call themselves."

Sadie giggled. "Oh, no, they're still there. Dried-up old Mrs. Hilquit and that Bill Danvers, too. He's always looking at me. The other day, I said, Mr. Danvers, you need to bring me flowers or something, you come here so much. He told me I was going to hell. I said, Well, to hell with you, then."

The giggle made me realize the truth of what my uncle had said: Sadie was young. "Sadie, would you help me with something? I don't know much about the new dances." She nodded sympathetically; I was, after all, five years older. Senility would have set in by now. "Would you show me? And maybe some of the other women?"

Her face darkened. "They don't care about me."

"They do care, Sadie. That's why they want you to break with Mr. McInerny."

It was a mistake to mention him. She flared at the criticism, saying, "Joe wants me back. A neighbor told me he'd been round to the house, asking for me."

There was an obvious, cruel reply to this, but I said, "Of course he wants you back. You're very pretty, and you were good to him. But he wasn't good to you."

"He wasn't *so* bad. Me seeing men, that was my idea. He didn't really like me doing it, I think."

Then why did he beat you up when you refused a man he owed money to? Why did he stand out in the street, howling that he would kill you if you didn't leave the refuge that night?

But I bit my tongue and said instead, "Do you remember how you felt, the night you came to the refuge? What you saw when you looked in the mirror?" Sadie frowned. "He did that to you, Sadie."

"I didn't want to come," she said. "My friend Carrie made me."

"Are you sorry she did?"

"Sometimes," she said defiantly. "No, I don't mean that. Only I wish there was a way I could be here *and* have Joe."

She posed it as a serious question, clearly expecting me to give in. Taking her hand, I said, "Come. Let's pick a song for the dance."

At the phonograph, I chose the first record I found, and in a moment we heard the first tinkling sounds of "The Peachtree Rag." The other women paused in their work to glance at one another, excited at this early break into frivolity.

A letter writer to the *Times* once bemoaned ragtime's immoral influence, especially on the young: "Songs that are clearly immoral are being issued with unabated energy—even sung by little girls on their way to school."

The pompous gentleman was right in one thing: ragtime was about energy. The waltz might have been scandalous in its day, but its elegant orchestral sounds were a bit grand for girls who moved faster and more heedlessly through the world than their mothers had. They swapped the swooning strings for the bounce and beat of the piano and a sound called ragtime, for its ragged syncopated style. Hard, bright, and a bit cheap, ragtime's rhythms bypassed the brain and worked directly on the sinews. *You're young*, it said, *you've got no business being still, get up. Get up and saunter right into the future.*

The music seemed to take Sadie out of her mood. "Do you know the Grizzly Bear?" she asked me.

"I do not," I said, and held up my hands.

Animal dances were all the rage, with the Fox Trot joined by the Bunny Hop, the Turkey Trot, the Squirrel, and so forth. The Grizzly Bear was said to imitate a dancing bear, so Sadie and I circled each other, arms, or rather paws, up as we stepped to the music. Sadie was surprised at the speed of my feet, taking the revelation that I was not entirely decrepit with a smile and a "Say, you're good!"

"I have a good teacher," I called over my shoulder.

With my uncle upstairs and Berthe occupied, the other women in the room joined hands and began polka-ing around the parlor.

Someone turned up the phonograph. Women twirled, bumped into chairs, caught one another, and, laughing, launched back into motion. Some sashayed, one hand to their hair, the other on their hip. Others leapt like ballerinas. Hair fell, blouses came untucked. At one point, a shoe went flying, to much hilarity.

Then somebody cried, "Is that the door?" and I stopped to listen. Yes, there it was, the bell. Gesturing that we should turn the phonograph off, I went to open it. And found Orville Pickett standing on the step, a bunch of flowers in his hand.

"For you," he said.

Bewildered, I took them. "Thank you, Mr. Pickett."

"And I wish you a very happy birthday."

Curious, the other women had come out from the parlor, still breathing deeply, their cheeks pink from dancing. They were flushed, disheveled, and happy. Orville Pickett stared.

Aware that my own blouse had come loose from my skirt, I was about to thank Orville and shut the door when Sadie piped up, "But it's not your birthday."

I hastily assured her it was. But Orville Pickett had the keen sensitivity of the often mocked, and his eyes narrowed. "You said there was a party . . ."

"Oh, that's the Whores' Ball," said Sadie provocatively. "We're going to dance, Mr. Pickett. 'That Scandalous Rag.' 'Everybody's Doing It.' 'The Syncopated Boogie Boo.' You watch. Never know what you might see."

I gave her the flowers. "Would you take these to the kitchen, Sadie? Thank you." She headed down the hall, more slowly than I would have liked, the other women parting to let her through.

Reaching the kitchen door, she gave a backward glance to Orville Pickett, then kicked her right foot up, briefly showing a plump, stockinged calf before she disappeared inside.

Turning back, I said, "I'm sorry, Mr. Pickett."

I meant to apologize for Sadie's behavior, but Orville gazed at me until I said, "I truly am sorry."

Then I closed the door.

★ ★ ★

That evening, the Duchess and her ladies went off to work, while Mrs. Pickett's Puritans stood sentry outside. But I was relieved to see that there was no sign of Bill Danvers, and those that stayed behind couldn't kill the excitement that hummed through the rooms and halls of the refuge. In deference to my uncle, everything was kept quiet until we heard his footsteps on the staircase, the creak of the door, and the metallic snap of the locks as it shut. One woman raced downstairs to put on a record while several other women scrambled into chairs, ready to be styled for the evening. "The Frog Legs Rag" floated upstairs as I went from woman to woman, styling their hair. It took longer than I hoped, but I had lost my assistant. Sadie was nowhere to be found. I had given her some sharp words after the incident with Mr. Pickett, and it seemed she was still sulking.

By tradition, the ladies descended the stairs in a line when everyone was ready. Applause and cheers greeted each lady as she came down. The parlor, restored after the romp earlier, looked lovely. Berthe had set out small sandwiches and punch, and the chairs were arranged at the edge of the room. Every year it was the same: some of the women elected to sit patiently, waiting to be asked to dance, while others took the floor with gleeful abandon the moment the first note sounded. The more high-spirited women usually managed to get the shyer ones dancing. Sometimes the ritual of invitation, refusal, and acceptance took on a feeling of courtship.

Berthe did not dance, but I did. For an hour, I fox-trotted, polka'd, and waltzed. Then, out of breath, I stood to the side and gave thanks to Otelia Brooks, wherever she was, for persuading my uncle to have the cotillion. But as I enjoyed the women's happiness, I realized one woman was missing.

"Where's Sadie?"

Struck by my tone, the women stopped dancing. She wouldn't have gone upstairs, I thought. Everyone was down here, and Sadie hated to be alone. Still, I sent Sal to check.

"She's wandered off again," said Berthe grimly.

That was my fear—confirmed when Sal called from the stairs, "She's not up here."

Going to the hallway, I took my coat off the hook and said, "All of you stay here. I'm going to look for her."

In an instant, Berthe was beside me, shrugging on her battered overcoat. "You're not facing that hag Mrs. Pickett and her lump of a son alone."

But as we hurried down the icy steps, I was dimly aware of a quiet absence. It seemed the Purity Brigade had decided on an early night: no cries of shame rang out; no quavering hymns strengthened at the sight of us. It was a foggy night, and it was difficult to see even across the street.

"Where do you think she goes when she wanders?" I asked Berthe.

"Back to the man who beat her, I would guess."

"They lived on Allen near the park, didn't they?"

She nodded. "But you can't be getting between them. That man's dangerous, even if she's too big a fool to know it."

"I don't think she's been gone long. Maybe I can catch up to her."

I started in the direction of Jefferson with Berthe close behind.

After a few blocks, she said, "What if she is with him? What will you say?"

"Sadie thinks she can have the refuge and Joe both. I'll explain she has a choice to make."

"She'll make the wrong one, if I know her."

I turned my head to answer, and that's when I saw it. Them. Legs. Stockings down, skirts flung up. Pale, helpless, lifeless legs.

She lay in an alley behind a factory, a deserted place. Half in shadow, lower half exposed to the streetlight. At first I had the mad thought that perhaps the woman had passed out, even though the odd, rag-doll fall of the legs told me otherwise.

It was the shoes that told me it was Sadie Ellis, the battered leather boots she had danced in earlier. Her hand lying across her middle, her head turned slightly, she resembled nothing so much as an exhausted child who has finally collapsed. But, oh, the face. She had been . . . carved, and in the chancy light of the street, it seemed she had no face at all, merely a blood-soaked mass of split skin and sodden hair.

She would have suffered, I thought numbly. Every cut, every slash. How could he do such a thing? I found myself wondering. This wasn't murder; it was butchery.

Looking again at her shoes, I thought, Something is wrong. Off balance. Then I realized one dark stocking was gone, the laces of that shoe untied, the shoe itself hanging from her foot. I was dimly aware of Berthe wailing behind me. Her howls became words—"Police! Someone call the police! There's been a murder!"

My uncle had said Sadie was young, that she needed time to see her future. She had spent her last day on earth gazing out the window, looking for it. Spent her last hour hurrying down the street toward it. I could see her: giggling at her naughtiness, defiant as she picked up her skirts to go just that bit faster, looking back to see she wasn't followed. At some point, I thought, she had seen him, there on the street, her Joe. Her future.

And now that silly, laughing, dancing girl was gone. Cut to pieces and left in an alley for strangers to find and wonder who she might have been.

3

The police did come. But the newspapers came first. And the ghoulish and judgmental beat them both to the scene. Berthe, wild with grief, kept them at bay while I stood with my arms uselessly extended across the alleyway to give poor Sadie some measure of privacy.

"Who is it?" one woman called. Followed hard by "What's her name?" and "Who did it?"

"Go home," I told them. "It's cold. There's nothing you can do for her."

That prodded some of them to wander off. But then I heard another voice in the fog. "Was she one of yours?"

"What?" I blinked at the strange question.

A man stepped—or shambled—into the patch of weak light from the streetlamp. He was large, belly straining the buttons of his overcoat, beefy arms stuffed into the sleeves. The coat was grimy and had seen better days. His hair and scruff were blond. His face was reddened by cold or drink. One look at the writing hand emerging from his pocket told me this was a reporter.

"One of yours. From the refuge."

"She was a friend. Can you step back, please?"

"How'd you know her, this friend?" His voice was a lazy growl; he would find it all out, sooner or later. But the little eyes were sharp.

"We share an interest in thoroughbreds—step *back*." I had thought I was too exhausted for anger; apparently I was wrong.

Then someone yelled, "Oh, look who showed up."

The police. I felt the crowd tense as they approached. Then I saw Mrs. Pickett walking behind them and felt myself tense in turn.

Clementine Pickett was deceptively small for a woman who had the capacity to bring a crowd to silence or screaming madness. Widely spaced gray eyes dominated her face; her nose was narrow, her mouth a thin pale scratch across the face. She wore a drab dark coat, and the hat resting on gray curls was functional. She had not been put on this earth to smile, laugh, eat, or enjoy. Her mission was to see *all*—and to judge that which was unworthy. I would have liked her to be stupid, but she wasn't. She was intelligent, quick in argument, and knowledgeable about the world beyond the Bible. In short, formidable. I was not happy to see her.

Briskly, she pushed her way through the crowd. The sight of Sadie brought her up short. She gasped, her hands fluttering to her face in shock. Then, closing her eyes, she offered a brief prayer.

I said to the policemen, "Please tell these people to go home. They don't have to be here. We knew this woman—"

"We knew this woman, too," said Mrs. Pickett, gesturing to the crowd. "We know what she was."

Sensing they had a defender, the crowd rumbled in support. Motioning Berthe over so she could stand guard over Sadie's body, I approached the more senior-looking of the patrolmen. He had a graying mustache and slack cheeks, and he rested a hand on his stomach as he tried to catch his breath. I could not say he looked ready to take charge. Still, he gave me his sympathetic attention, introducing himself as Officer Nolan.

"My name is Jane Prescott. My uncle is the Reverend Tewin Prescott. He runs the Gorman—"

"He runs a house of sin," pronounced Mrs. Pickett.

"You shut your mouth," said Berthe.

The reporter drawled, "He runs a refuge where whores can get a bed they don't have to put to professional use. Or so I'm informed."

The junior policeman piped up, "She was one of the reverend's girls?"

"She lived at the refuge. She was not *his girl*," I said. "She wasn't anybody's girl."

The older policeman nodded toward the alley, and his partner approached, keeping a safe distance from Berthe. I could tell the moment he laid eyes on Sadie as he clapped a hand to his mouth and stumbled backward.

"What was she doing out on the street?" The reporter indicated the cold drizzle. "Not an especially nice night for a stroll."

I looked up at the surrounding buildings. Why had it happened here? There were few houses on this block; it was mostly factories and warehouses. I gazed up at the vast windows and saw they were dark. It was the slow season, so they were not occupied at night. Breathing in, I caught the iron tang of blood and sharp stench of bleach. There was a slaughterhouse nearby. No one would be surprised by the sight of blood on the streets here.

But why meet here on the Bowery, blocks from their home?

There were no saloons around. Perhaps without Sadie's income, Joe had lost their rooms. The Municipal Lodging House was uptown on Twenty-Fifth Street. And you had to work five hours a day hauling stone to stay there. I couldn't see Joe McInerny signing on for that.

Or perhaps, as it was late, Sadie had asked him to meet her close to the refuge. That made more sense. Meeting on the Bowery, they would have headed home together. Maybe they had argued, the fight grew violent, and Joe saw his chance with the alley. I looked at the ground up and down the block. No stretch of blood; Sadie had been killed where she was.

Or had Sadie been going the other way? Had she refused to stay with Joe and he caught up to her here?

"She was going to meet a man," cried Berthe, and her savage tone implied this was the gravest mistake any woman could make. "She was going to meet a no-good bastard of a man who hit her and sold her and now he's butchered her."

Officer Nolan looked to me. "Do you know the man she's talking about?"

"I do. And when you've cleared this crowd, I'll tell you who he is."

As the policemen began waving people off, Mrs. Pickett called out, "You might ask the reverend where he's been this night."

At that, the crowd slowed. Heads turned. I stared at Mrs. Pickett, wondering if she had lost her mind.

"I think you know that my uncle would have nothing to say about this."

"I do not know that," she said.

Her calm conviction that she was in the right cost me my hold on my temper, and I took a step toward her, fist clenched. Officer Nolan stepped between us, saying, "We will want to speak with him, Miss Prescott."

"But my uncle has nothing to do with this."

He nodded toward Sadie. "You said she lived with him."

"She lived at the refuge. As do many women."

"Many women," echoed the junior policeman. I was glad to see Nolan give him a warning look.

"The man you need to talk to is Joe McInerny," I said. "That's who Sadie was going to meet. He's hurt her before. He threatened to kill her. Look at her face." I saw the officer was in no hurry to do so. "Go look. And then tell me if you think that's the work of anyone but a madman."

So urged, Officer Nolan had no choice. Stepping carefully— ostensibly to avoid the blood—he gazed at the body a long moment. His expression turned grim, and he yanked his colleague back into place as sentry.

Striding back to me, he said, "You're going to take me to your uncle."

Alarmed, I glanced at Mrs. Pickett, who looked satisfied by this demand. "What about Joe McInerny?"

"You know where he lives?" the officer asked.

"Allen, near the park. I don't know the building."

"Maybe your uncle does." He took me by the arm. "Let's go."

I removed my arm from his grasp; I would go, but I would not be pulled. "You stay with Sadie," I told Berthe.

On the walk to the refuge, I offered up a prayer: Let my uncle be home, let my uncle be home, let my uncle be home. Behind me, I could sense the crowd, led by Mrs. Pickett. They followed at a distance as if they were going home as Nolan had told them to. But I knew that when we reached the refuge door, I would stop and so would they. I glanced at Nolan to see if he understood this, but his face told me nothing.

I looked down to see the faint traces of red on the pavement. There was blood on the soles of my shoes; I must have stepped too close. How long before people started to clean the streets? How long before they came for Sadie's body? Burial, we should think about burial. Did she have family to do it? I could not remember.

Let my uncle be home, please let my uncle be home.

But he was not at home. Instead I was greeted by Sal Karlsson, who broke away from the other women who had stayed downstairs to hear word of Sadie. The punch bowl and plates were still out, the decorations hung on the walls. But the phonograph was silent, the mood of the room fractured and anxious.

Sal began to cry the moment she saw the officer. When she was ten, she had come back from work to find the neighbors gathered outside her home. That's when she knew this was not ordinary bad, but "something real bad, something you don't go back from." The door to her apartment was open, the neighbors clumped together. Everyone, she said, was in the wrong place. She knew before they told her that her mother was dead and her father arrested.

Officer Nolan asked if the reverend was home, and the women slowly shook their heads. My arm around Sal, I said, "He'll be back soon, I'm sure."

His eyes stayed on the group of women. "Any of you know where Miss Ellis was going tonight?"

They glanced at one another; the faces went blank, arms folded. Answering a policeman's questions was not an easy thing. They had been tricked too many times, led into implicating friends or lovers, or sometimes arrested for providing a policeman with a service that, once he was finished, he remembered was illegal. Eyes slid to Ruth Renehan, who was a little older and more assertive than some; she was chosen to speak.

"I think . . . we all thought . . . she went to see that Joe she always talked about."

"That would be Joe McInerny?" Nolan asked me.

"Yes," I said, thinking he would be halfway to New Jersey at this point.

There was an eruption as the crowd outside began shouting. I heard Mrs. Pickett calling for calm, of all things. Then the door opened and my uncle stepped into the foyer with the words "Jane, why is this door not locked?"

Then he noticed the policeman. "Officer."

It was my uncle's habit never to say more than absolutely necessary; he neither asked the reason for the officer's presence—that would come—nor offered his assistance. I could see Nolan resented it.

Nolan tried to regain the upper hand, saying, "Are you the Reverend Prescott?" My uncle nodded. "Did a young woman named Sadie Ellis reside at this address?"

I thought I saw something flicker in my uncle's eyes. Not wanting the women to hear the blunt details of Sadie's death, I said, "Maybe we could continue this conversation upstairs. The hallway isn't the place."

My uncle glanced at the women as if he had just noticed they were there. "Yes. Will you come upstairs, Officer?"

When we were in the office with the door shut, I said, "Sadie's dead, Uncle. She went to meet Joe McInerny, and—"

Officer Nolan didn't let me finish, asking, "Where were you this evening, Reverend?"

"I am afraid I cannot tell you."

"Can't remember?"

"My memory is fine, thank you. No, perhaps I should have said, I will not tell you."

The officer's eyes slid in my direction. "If it's a matter of your niece's sensibilities . . ."

"Her presence makes no difference to me," said my uncle.

My uncle was not a sentimental man, but this was offhand

even for him. He was angry, I realized. Angry to be questioned by the police, angry that Sadie had disobeyed, angry that she was dead. Or . . . angry that it was late and he wished to go to bed, who could tell. But he had to stop this game, and if my leaving would help, so be it.

"I'll go," I said. "Then you and the officer can talk."

"About what?" my uncle wondered as I left the room.

Berthe was back. I found her in the kitchen. The lights were off, but she was kneading dough in the moonlight, throwing it with concentrated rage onto the counter. She did not look up as I came in, but she sniffed harshly and knuckled her eyes to keep back tears. Pulling out a chair, I sat down at the table and pressed the heels of my hands hard into my eyes. Dear God, what McInerny had done to that poor girl.

When had she realized, I wonder? That the man on whom she put all her hopes was going to kill her? She had once said there were two Joes, the nice one who talked sweet and bought her presents, then the other—who you had to be careful with. The one who snarled at her for the littlest thing, punched her, then hit her again harder when she screamed *Don't*. Yes, they would catch Joe, and they would put him in jail or give him the chair and it would all be one big waste.

Berthe's voice came to me in the darkness. "He's talking to the police?"

Startled, I said, "I think so. I hope so. Did he tell you where he was going tonight?"

The briefest pause. "No."

I took a deep breath, gazed at the table's edge. "He's not wandering again, is he?"

Berthe turned, I think about to speak. But then Officer Nolan knocked and came through the door. His eyes were bruised, his shoulders slumped, his aspect disappointed. Some policemen trifled with their job, thinking their mere presence—drunk or sober—deterred crime. But if you did not think that way, policing would be a thankless, heartbreaking task.

"Would you like some coffee, Officer?"

"No." Manners beget manners, and he added, "But thank you."

"My uncle told you where he was, I hope. I would imagine it was Mrs. Emmeline Roberts or maybe Mr. . . ." The name did not come, and I was left gaping.

"No. He wouldn't tell me." He took a seat at the table, glancing briefly toward the window to see the crowd still gathered outside, as if he did not relish having to walk through them when he left.

"Joe McInerny," he said. "What can you tell me?"

"Not much," I admitted. "The only jobs Sadie ever mentioned him having were ones he'd lost. Docks, factory work, a tannery, I think. He didn't sound like a man who got on well with others." The officer grunted, familiar with the type. "She said it made more sense for her to work; it was easier for her."

"Can you remember any of the places he worked?" I shook my head. "What he looks like?"

I looked to Berthe, who said, "Short, blue eyes. Bald. Bandy legs. Puts you in mind of those fighting dogs they bet on."

I added, "Carrie Biel—she was a friend of Sadie's. She might know more about him."

"Is she here now?"

"No, she left about a year ago. But I think I can find her. I'll have to. She was one of the few people who cared about Sadie."

At the thought of having to tell Carrie what had happened to her friend, the tears returned and my throat felt tight. "Joe Mc-Inerny threatened to kill Sadie for leaving him. And you should have seen her when she came to us. Her face . . ."

I was about to say he had cut her before. But I realized, in my tiredness, I was confused. I thought of Sadie's battered, swollen features and realized the cut I had seen so clearly . . . was not hers. It was a different face, from long ago.

Before I could decide whether this was knowledge to share or just exhausted confusion, Officer Nolan said, "We'll find McInerny. But you tell your uncle to account for himself."

He looked pointedly at the window, and I understood. Those people—none of whom had cared a jot for Sadie when she was alive—wanted her killer. And they hated my uncle. It was a dangerous mess of emotion. The sooner the police caught McInerny, the sooner we'd be rid of the mob outside.

I walked Officer Nolan to the door and let him out. As I locked it, I could hear the shouts of outrage as he emerged alone. Curses against the police who showed up late and then did nothing. Degenerates, criminals, and troublemakers left among them because they were poor and didn't matter. Who would protect *their* daughters? *Their* men? Keep the streets clean of whores and vice? Didn't they have the right to live decent? And how could they when the city pushed all its crime and filth into their neighborhood?

I jumped as I heard glass shatter. Someone had thrown a bottle. A thud as something else landed against the door, then the sharp crack of another bottle breaking. I heard Officer Nolan ordering people home and waited, heart pounding. Then the clarion call of Mrs. Pickett: "Good people, we shall not take the law into our own hands. Let the police do their work. Let it be our task to make sure that they do."

So instructed by their leader, the crowd began to disperse. The pounding of my heart eased, and I gathered the nerve to go to the door to make sure it was securely locked. Then, before heading up to bed, I settled on the stairs a moment to mourn the happiness of just a few hours ago. And Sadie. Then I let my eyes rest on the old hallway carpet and tried to think of nothing.

Carpets are wonderful things. You can gaze at them endlessly. All the swirls and patterns, even in an old carpet where the colors are faded and the wool is threadbare in spots. That spot there, just where you step as you come in. Thinner, darker, marked with the grime of so many shoes . . .

But it was not grime, I realized. The shadow that spread from the worn and ragged center. It was blood. Old blood. Washed many times, but the stain still there.

Otelia Brooks's blood.

4

I was eleven the night she came to the refuge. She announced herself with a swift and frantic pounding at the door. I was not allowed to open the door at night; no one was, except for my uncle and Berthe. But that night, my uncle was out and Berthe had a head cold. The other women were upstairs. With no one to tell me otherwise, I had stayed up late. I had been sitting on the steps, wondering how many I could jump, when the knock came.

I looked up the stairs, thinking someone would come, but no one did. There was another burst of knocking, this time more urgent. I peeped through the curtain and saw a dark-skinned woman, her hand braced against the door for support. Her face was slashed, and blood ran from her cheek down her neck, soaking the collar of her shirt and shabby coat. Her head was down and her shoulders were heaving. Despite my shock, I still hesitated. My uncle had warned me that sometimes men used women to try to trick their way in.

There was another knock, weaker this time. An exhausted "Please . . ."

Undoing the lock, I opened the door slightly. The woman frowned, either surprised by my age or trying to focus through pain. The light of the hallway gave me a better look at her wound, which was so terrible it could only be real, and I opened the door fully, indicating she should hurry inside. She did, unsteady on her feet. She tried not to touch anything but at one point had to use the wall, leaving a bloody imprint. I stood, mouthing and useless, then remembered that I needed to lock the door.

By the time I had turned around, she was unconscious.

A nurse sympathetic to my uncle's mission was called. I was told to leave the room. But I heard the muffled screams and saw the clumsy stitches afterward. "No white man will want her now," said Rosa Lengler, whose mean streak had not faded in her time at the refuge. Still, several of the women agreed. Black women, they felt, were bad for business, and they didn't want her in any place they understood to be theirs.

Peace was important to my uncle. The refuge was too crowded to accommodate those who had succumbed to addiction or madness. Disruptive behavior was not tolerated, and the women made clear their opinion that Otelia Brooks's arrival was indeed disruptive. They would not turn her out while she was ill. They weren't unfeeling. But when she could stand, she would have to go.

When I thought about what should be done, I felt like two different people. One understood the women; the new arrival was . . . shocking. Different. And it felt strange to have her here. It was as if something would have to change if she stayed, although I couldn't think what. The other person in me kept seeing her gaze as she struggled to remain herself through blood loss and pain. What would it feel like to tell that person to leave? Small. It would feel very, very small.

"She can sleep in my bed," I told my uncle.

My bed, my uncle explained, was separated from his office by a curtain. It would not do to have any woman sleep there. For now, the residents would have to make do.

Two days later, I came down the stairs to find her scrubbing the carpet. I shrank in guilt; cleaning the floors was my job, and I said so.

She glanced up at me. "Come on down and do it, then."

Kneeling down, I set the brush to the rug and started pushing. But I was distracted by the sight of her stitches, clumsy black thread crisscrossing her face from ear to jaw. And by the hope she would say something more.

"It's not pretty," she allowed.

"It'll heal," I said. She met my eye, and I felt rebuked for foolishness.

I felt she would rather I go away, but as much as I wanted to please her, I stayed, half scrubbing, half listening for a chance to say something. When she winced and rubbed two fingers against her forehead, I said, "Does your head ache? My uncle keeps brandy in his cabinet."

"I don't take alcohol," she said.

Then, noticing my half-hearted scrub motions, she said in a gentler voice, "You're just working it deeper in. Here—"

Taking the brush, she showed me how to loosen and liquefy the stain, then gather it up with the bristles and rinse it clean in the bucket. I imitated her, with much better results.

I don't know why my uncle decided Otelia Brooks could stay. He never gave a reason, not to me and not to Rosa Lengler when she demanded to know. Perhaps he felt there did not have to be one.

Women settling in at the refuge were often on edge; they looked for opportunities to argue, take offense, do battle—both to prove themselves and calm their nerves. Miss Brooks was different in that way. She seemed to have no interest in either allies or enemies. When she took her place in the classroom, the women nearby ostentatiously moved elsewhere. Otelia Brooks took no notice of them—or of me when I sat down in the space next to her. I would like to claim that conscience drove me to it. But really, I was fascinated by Otelia Brooks. She had told me I cleaned badly, then shown me how to do it right. Her good opinion seemed worth having.

She struggled with cursive, and I struggled with her. But she had no need of the sewing class—her stitches were small and precise. Still, she took them and often sewed after classes were over. Over the next week, the curtains were all rehemmed, my skirts let down, dresses mended. Anything that might be improved with a needle and thread passed through her hands.

"You don't have to," I told her, puzzled that anyone would take on more work.

"I know," she said. "But it keeps me on my path."

I had never known anyone to speak of a path. I wanted to ask where hers was, where it had begun, where it would take her. But she was not an easy woman for questions. She didn't stay still, for one thing, beating rugs, gathering plates, working in the sewing room until we put the tables aside and set up the beds. Another time, I found her restless and wandering the parlor as if searching for something. Her hands twisted uneasily around each other. She sat down by the window, rocking, her hands between her knees. Then she stood and began draping the curtains so they fell more evenly.

If you wanted her company, you had to work alongside her, so I did. She had taken on the job of doing laundry, and I held the basket of wet sheets as she pegged them up on the line in the backyard. In a ploy to get her to talk, I said, "I like how you speak."

She smiled, mildly disbelieving. "That's Mississippi."

"Is that where you're from?" She nodded. "Will you go back there?"

She hesitated, then shook her head. "I brought everything I cared about here."

And now it was gone—that much was clear by her presence. Shy in the face of her loss, I offered the plan that made the most sense to my eleven-year-old self. "You could get married." She would have a house, I thought, and children. I could play with the children and keep helping her with the wash.

"I was married," she said, not looking at me.

My breath caught. I had forgotten a basic truth known by everyone at the refuge: simply because a man gave you a wedding ring—or promised one—didn't mean safety. Wanting to make amends for my ignorance, I blundered, "He did that to you."

She went still, then deliberately threw the pegs onto the ground before fixing on me. "You think my husband did this?"

I stepped back, knowing I was wrong, but beyond that not sure of anything.

"Let me be very clear with you. A white man did this to me. And he did it slow. You know why? Because he enjoyed it. And this was just the first cut. He meant to take his time. I know because he told me so. He breathed in my face, put his spit on me, and said those words. And in case you're wondering why my husband didn't stop him, it's because he's dead. You're a smart girl, I'll let you figure out what happened to him."

Shame, like bile; all day. I tasted it in my throat, felt it roil my stomach, sour and debilitating. I tried to throw it off, tell myself I couldn't have known, it was a simple mistake, she needn't have gotten so *angry*. And at me. It wasn't my fault. If she hated it here so much, she could just go. Never mind the fact that she'd never said she hated it here, although the other women had given her reason to.

That evening, my uncle remarked that I was in a bad mood. I opened my mouth, ready to complain. Then I realized my uncle would not respect my complaints. And that they didn't deserve respect.

The next day, I found Otelia sitting alone in an empty class-room. Her hands were placed flat on the desk in front of her, and she was very still. She breathed deeply, held it, then exhaled. For a brief moment, she lifted her hands; they shook. Putting them back down, she took a breath, shut her eyes, then let the breath go. Then she opened her eyes.

On the table in front of her, there were some scraps of felt, a needle and thread, and an overturned bowl. She began arranging the felt, pulling and folding, around the bowl until it started to take shape.

From the door, I asked, "Are you making a hat?"

She didn't answer right away, and I thought she was still angry with me. Then she sighed. "I'm not sure. Does it look like a hat to you?"

I came inside, shut the door. "It could."

"In my head it does. This felt disagrees."

I knew what it was to wrestle with fabric, wanting it clean or mended, and feeling it fight you. "It's too old. New felt would listen to you."

"Would it?" She smiled. "Well, we don't have new, so let me see if I can get this old stuff to listen. Miss Jane, could you fetch me some glue?"

I did, and sat while she carefully worked the felt. When she needed a ribbon, I offered mine. It was shabby and not wide enough, but you could see where it would lead. Discarded pieces of fabric from the floor expanded the hat's silhouette. She left off the traditional adornments but added flourishes in different places. It was and was not like any hat I had seen. Rough, misshapen, but with a halo of true potential.

Taking her hands away, Otelia Brooks looked at me and said, "Maybe?"

"I think it'll be wonderful."

Her body eased, and a small smile appeared. "Miss Jane, may I ask you a question? Do you always wear your hair in a braid?"

Embarrassed, I said, "It's the only thing I know how to do."

"I took your ribbon. How about you let me do your hair?"

Thrilled, I ran upstairs for my hairbrush and then sat down on a hassock in front of her chair. I heard her murmur, "All right, now . . . ," as she pulled my hair loose. "This is very pretty hair, Miss Jane. You need to let people see it. You also need to wash your neck because we are going to be showing this neck because it is like a swan's. You ever seen a swan?"

I shook my head.

"Oh, well, that's something you'll have to see someday, but for now . . ." She started to brush, keeping the strong fingers of one hand on my head as she did. She talked, partly to me but mostly to herself, low and intent, keeping herself company as she worked. I understood that I was like the classwork stitches, the curtains, and the hats; a way to occupy her hands. To stay on her path. Lulled by her voice, feeling her fingers in my hair, the way she gathered it into coils, winding it this way and that, I fell into a dream. So I cannot tell you how long it was before the two hands rested briefly on my shoulders and I heard, "Let's find a mirror."

There had been mirrors aplenty in this house when it served as a brothel, but my uncle had removed most of them. There was still one in the entry hallway that led off the front parlor, and when I stood before it, I did not recognize myself. I had always felt I had a drab face, the kind you saw behind a broom handle.

Features serviceable, nothing more. Otelia Brooks had made me look not just . . . nice, that foolish word . . . but like a *someone*. It was like opening an old packing case that sat in the cellar for years and discovering treasure inside.

"Can't speak? You're that ravishing?" she teased. "Well, I guess you do look pretty. What you need are ear bobs. You tell your uncle to get you some when you turn sixteen. But not before. See—"

"What do you think you're doing?"

Startled, I turned to see Rosa Lengler at the door. Then I felt myself yanked away from the mirror.

"You don't touch her."

"I don't believe I was," said Miss Brooks.

Other women gathered at the door, drawn by the sounds of an argument. I stood between Rosa and Miss Brooks, confused. "She did my hair . . . ," I offered.

"And *you* should know better," Rosa told me. "She's dirty."

At this, a short burst of laughter came from Miss Brooks. Followed by the crack of a slap. Miss Brooks went completely still. I saw something flare in her eyes, and I knew Rosa should step back. But Rosa lifted her hand again. This time, Miss Brooks caught it and jerked her arm down, twisting it so that Rosa cried out.

"You going to try that again?" Miss Brooks asked, whispering into her ear. "You think that's how this works?" She gave Rosa's arm a wrench and the other woman bent, grunting a filthy insult that made Miss Brooks's mouth twist in a brief, bitter smile.

Rosa spun loose and shoved. Almost exasperated, Miss Brooks shoved back. Enraged, Rosa started punching. The other women were shouting; I was shouting, too, what I don't remember. But when Berthe broke up the fight and sent both women to talk to my uncle, I do recall feeling that this was my fault. And that my uncle should know it was my fault.

I went up to his office to find the door closed. Standing as close as I dared, I heard my uncle say, "What do you think I should do, Miss Brooks?"

If there was an answer, I didn't hear it.

"It will be better if we speak freely."

"Will it?" said Miss Brooks.

There was an edge of impatience in her tone, and I could sense my uncle's surprise as he said, "Yes, of course." Then after a moment, "Please."

I heard a sigh. "What do you mean to do here, Reverend? With this place?"

"I would think you knew, having come here."

"I came because I needed safety. And I had heard you help women." There was a pause. "Do you think you do? Help these women?"

"I gather you think otherwise."

"I think sewing's fine as far as it goes. But you need to teach them about money. You're thinking these women are going to work for someone else, but why shouldn't they have their own business? Not like they didn't before. Don't misunderstand, I appreciate what you do. But you're helping these women be laundry workers, seamstresses, and they could be more. Some of them, anyway. I also think you need to let them loose."

"Loose?"

"I don't mean turn them out. I mean give them some rest. You make them sit in prayer when they wake up. Then they sit in class all day, sewing or staring at letters. Then there's chores. Afternoon, it's proper speech and handwriting. Back in prayer before bedtime. Whole day spent . . . tight. Silent. Scared they're going to make a mistake. Maybe you don't realize it, but you can be a heavy presence." I smiled at that. "No wonder they start shoving and screaming the first chance they get."

"People trying to change their lives need to be kept busy. I would have thought you agreed with that."

"I do. But they can't spend their days feeling bad about what they were, working hard to be a woman they can't even imagine yet. You have to let them be free sometimes. Otherwise all that energy turns sour. Ugly. Let them go outside, take a walk. They have those public dances at the church, let them go there."

"Some of these women have men looking for them. Should they go outside as well?"

Now it was Miss Brooks who let the talk lapse.

I heard my uncle say, "The man who did that, could you identify him?" She must have shaken her head. "He's not a man who should be on the street."

"No," she agreed, her voice strained. "He likes to hurt people and I imagine he'll keep on doing it. But I couldn't say who he was." Then, changing the subject back again, she suggested, "You know, you could let the women dance here if you don't want them going out."

"Here?"

"Why not? That front parlor's big enough. You have a piano."

As I listened, I thought how Miss Brooks's voice had changed since she first arrived. It had been so hard to get one word out of her, and those were stiff, almost stern. Now, arguing with my uncle, which no one ever did, she sounded relaxed. Almost as if she were enjoying herself.

"A dance. Here."

"A dance here," she echoed. "Just think of it: the Whores' Ball." My uncle must have glared, because she said, "Fine. Call it the . . . Southern Baptist Ladies' Cotillion. Call it what you want.

But let those girls dance. Let them feel pretty and hopeful and work out their nerves in a good way instead of hitting and scratching."

"Speaking of which. What shall I do about Rosa Lengler?"

I waited.

Miss Brooks said, "It's my understanding that anyone who disrupts the peace can't stay."

"That's correct."

"Well, then."

Rosa Lengler was gone the next day. And the first Southern Baptist Ladies' Cotillion was held the following month. Otelia Brooks did several women's hair for the occasion, and I was allowed to assist. But I was not allowed to go to the dance; my uncle had been quite clear on that point. From my bed, I listened to the sounds of the piano, the stomp of feet, and the shouts of laughter. In my childish way, I wondered if anyone was dancing with Otelia and worried they were not. Seized with the idea that they had left her out, I decided it was up to me to remedy the situation. So I crept downstairs and surveyed the parlor from the stairwell. I saw many happy women. But I did not see Otelia Brooks. Puzzled, I began looking in the classrooms and found her back in the sewing room.

As she had before, she sat with her eyes closed and her hands flat upon a table. When I shut the door, her eyes opened. "Don't let your uncle catch you out of bed."

I pulled up a chair and sat down. Unconsciously, I put my hands on the table in imitation. Smiling slightly, she touched my fingers with hers, and I understood that I had done a satisfactory job dressing hair.

"Where did you learn about hair?" I asked shyly.

"My mother taught me."

My first thought was disappointment that I would never learn, then, because I didn't have a mother. My second thought was of Otelia's mother. How she had learned hair, whose hair she had dressed, how she had taught Otelia how to dress hair different from her own. Math was not my best subject, but I could guess Otelia's age, and I could guess that Otelia Brooks knew how to dress hair like mine because her mother had been . . . property. I had images in my head of slavery, mostly drawn from old pamphlets kept by my uncle's abolitionist colleagues, but those images had nothing to do with the woman sitting opposite me.

I had not understood.

I had not understood at all.

In the following weeks, my uncle invited the foreman of a cannery and the owner of a saloon to the refuge. He asked his patron, Mrs. Armslow, to send one of her accountants to speak with Miss Brooks. Whether they were able to tell her what she wished to know about business, I don't know. I do know that she left that summer. She didn't say good-bye, but I found the hat she had been working on left on my bed. The rough old piece of felt had been cunningly molded into a fetching dark bonnet with a pale yellow ribbon on the brim and a wide white bow tied neatly at the back. With it, she had left a note: *It listened. Otelia Brooks.*

Years later, I asked my uncle if he knew where she had gone or what had become of her. But he said that once the women left here, they left their past as well. For all intents and purposes, the Otelia Brooks I had known no longer existed.

★ ★ ★

Falling asleep, I had relished the thought that I might not wake until noon. But the next morning, I felt a hand on my arm, heard the chatter of morning, and smelled coffee, and I knew it was not noon. Rolling onto my back, I saw Sal and groaned.

"Sorry, miss, phone for you."

I had a flash of hope that it was Officer Nolan, calling to say they had caught Joe McInerny. Swinging out of bed, I said, "A man?"

"Woman."

It couldn't be Anna, I thought, hurrying down the stairs. We had just spoken.

Picking up the phone, I was about to ask the caller to identify herself when I heard Louise Tyler say, "Jane, I'm so sorry. Really. I'm so sorry, I feel just terrible . . ."

Louise Tyler was a woman who apologized, frequently, sincerely—and often incorrectly. She once said "Sorry" to a man who had stepped on her foot; clearly, the foot had been where it shouldn't.

Out of habit, I said, "That's quite all right, Mrs. Tyler."

"No, it isn't, but I'm going to ask you anyway. I know it's your holiday. But can you come straight to Rutherford's? Something dreadful has happened."

5

Dreadful *can be a* relative term. An injury might be dreadful; so might a flower arrangement. Louise had not called me for a floral emergency. But the Brooklyn Bridge hadn't fallen either, and at first I wasn't sure who needed me more: my frantic employer or the women of the refuge, in shock over Sadie's death. Once here, they were supposed to be safe. To feel otherwise was deeply unsettling.

After breakfast, I told my uncle about Louise's request. I said that I was under no obligation to go; I could tell Louise I was needed here—if I were needed here. My uncle simply shrugged and said it was my holiday.

So I decided to answer the call of the one person who was not ashamed to say she needed me. Until we heard from Officer Nolan, there was nothing more we could do for Sadie. My uncle was determined that the refuge routine not be altered. For me, perhaps distraction would be beneficial. And I would at least get to see the famous Rutherford's department store.

As I took the trolley uptown to Thirty-Eighth Street, I thought, A man's home might be his castle, but for a woman, home was the only place she was promised a degree of protection and authority. According to the ideal, for a woman to venture beyond the home was to invite degradation, violence, and exposure to the sordid realities of life. Heavens, that was what servants were for. The ideal might be out of reach for most women, but inability to adhere to the norm did not mean you escaped the consequences. So while men might go to their place of business, stop in at the club, walk down the streets, travel by public transport, dine in restaurants, or . . . well, live, women were well advised to stay indoors unless they were accompanied by men.

Then the first department store opened its doors, and women had a place to go that was, for all intents and purposes, theirs. In this "Adam-less Eden," as Edward Filene called his Boston store, women could wander as they pleased, as long as they had money to spend.

For size and splendor, Rutherford's surpassed all other department stores. One did not go there simply to shop; that would have been vulgar. No, one went to dream. Passing through the brass-and-smoked-glass doors of Rutherford's took you into a palatial wonderland. As I made my way down the plum-colored carpet adorned with the majestic silver *R*, I felt I had entered an enchanted world of riches: scarves, gloves, earrings, shoes—and that was only the first floor. Hats alone took up half the second floor. Things, things, things—drawn from all four corners of the earth, and oh, how you coveted all those wonderful, magical things.

There were, of course, also mirrors. Small ones on every glass counter so a woman might judge the effect of a potential purchase, and panels of them, interspersed with polished wood. Because the most enchanting, fascinating thing in Rutherford's was the woman herself. Or what she could be, with a little help. With the right accessories, a dowager might become a temptress, a typist a Valkyrie, a maid an empress. The air was subtly perfumed, alive with the tinkle of laughter, soft cries of delight, and subversive encouragement. "Oh, you must have it, it's perfect!" "I shouldn't, really." "I won't let you leave without it, Aida."

The sumptuous surroundings were made that much more pleasant by the feeling of gratification in the air. Women could spend hours in Rutherford's, arriving for a fitting in the morning, stopping for lunch at the Orientale, where they served tea and champagne all day, then browsing the new arrivals in the hat department before taking a cup of restorative Lapsang souchong with a friend. As I stepped carefully among the customers, gazing here and there to sigh over a pair of gloves I would never wear or an elegant watch that would slip from my wrist the second my hand had to do anything more energetic than reach for a petit four, I wondered if some of these women never left the store. It would be hard to blame them. It was a woman's world. Men ran the elevators and waited tables at the restaurant upstairs, but they were otherwise absent. With one notable exception: George Rutherford.

Rutherford's was the creation of George Rutherford, a beloved tyrant of fashion. He was often in the store, greeting its customers, supervising the salesladies, even at times offering personal consultations to his wife's friends and other valued clients. These "chats" were said to be brutally honest, but all the more valuable because it was said he would never allow a woman to leave Rutherford's in something that did not suit her, and his candor—which some said bordered on crass—made a refreshing change for women used to outrageous flattery. "I can't help myself. When I see a lady out and about and she doesn't look as she should, I have to speak. I'm from Ohio and I value truth over couth," he once said, making an awkward joke at his own expense. These encounters had grown into the stuff of near-legend, as women reported them as a mark of special favor. "He told me my hat was at the wrong angle." "He said if he were my husband, he'd never let me leave the house in something so cheap." "He said maroon did not suit me—and he was right." Because, of course, he was always right. That was why the Miss Rutherford's pageant was cause for so much excitement. George Rutherford could look at thousands of girls without means and choose the most lovely, whirling them to a new life of splendor and good fortune. I did not believe the oft-repeated rumor that all the Miss Rutherford's had gone on to marry millionaires, but even I liked to think at least a few had.

In the lobby, I noticed two young women gazing hopefully at the swooping staircase that led to the second floor. No doubt waiting for the great Mr. Rutherford to appear and pronounce them perfection. Alas, that morning, George Rutherford was only present in the large oil painting of him that hung above the elevator bank.

One of the most famous parts of Rutherford's was the Crystal Palace, a grand hall that borrowed its name from the exhibition hall in London's Hyde Park. Located on the very top floor of the store, it boasted a magnificent ceiling of smoked glass and wrought iron. The store's biannual fashion shows took place there, of course. But it was best known as the spot where Miss Rutherford's was introduced to the world. In the weeks leading up to the announcement, the ten contestants, dubbed American Beauties as a group, were each photographed and interviewed by the local papers. Newspapers breathlessly speculated on the girls' prospects, and odds were placed on the likely winners. Prevailing wisdom had it that it was down to Hattie Phipps, telephone operator from Sunnyside, and Gertrude Walsh, waitress at Rector's, although there were those who insisted that Eleanor Gosnell, typist, would take the crown. Louise and I had a friendly bet; she was backing Gosnell, but I had defiantly put my money on a long shot, Celeste Dwyer, who had enormous eyes, enjoyed the fox trot, and worked at a lace factory. At any rate, all would be revealed a week from now, directly after "Stirring Scenes of the Emancipation."

Briefly I thought of Sadie. Just yesterday, she had boasted that she could beat both Hattie Phipps and Gertrude Walsh simply by rolling out of bed. At the time, her arrogance had irritated me; now I wondered why I had been so ungenerous.

Some had wondered why Mr. and Mrs. Rutherford had decided to combine the events. Mrs. Rutherford had informed the *Times* that she felt the Miss Rutherford's contest was in danger of becoming shallow. To truly represent the store, a girl must be an American Beauty both inside and out. Therefore, they wished to present the young ladies in a more serious light; throughout the pageant, each of the girls would step forward and recite one amendment in the Bill of Rights. Then together, they would recite the Thirteenth. Some applauded this high-mindedness; others snickered that Dolly Rutherford simply wanted to keep an eye on her husband around so many young lovelies.

The Crystal Palace was on the sixth floor, which meant I could take the famous Rutherford's elevators, paneled in marble and edged in malachite and red jasper. Every operator was specially trained to greet you with an admiring but entirely proper "Welcome to Rutherford's, miss." Even though I knew the operator had said it a hundred times in the past hour, I still felt I was the prettiest girl ever to step into his elevator. When we arrived at the sixth floor, he wished me a very good day.

But as I entered the Crystal Palace, I saw it would take more than his wishes to ensure a good day. The Rutherford's seamstress recruited to do the costumes for the pageant had been berated once too often and walked out. The precipitating event? That was hotly debated. Either the seamstress was incompetent or Mrs. Fortesque, playing John Wilkes Booth, had put on weight. The latter being unthinkable, the former was obvious—at least to everyone except the seamstress. Dolly Rutherford accused her of stinting. The seamstress wondered if perhaps Mrs. Rutherford were going blind. Mrs. Rutherford upped the charge to theft. The seamstress replied that she would be an inept thief to steal such cheap goods. Her willingness to overspend called into question, Mrs. Rutherford fired the seamstress. Or the seamstress quit. Again, there was debate as to the time line. The long and short of it was, the seamstress was gone and Mrs. Fortesque's costume still didn't fit.

There were other problems as well. Mrs. Van Dormer was unhappy with her kerchief. Also, Mrs. Fortesque's mustache itched. The sleeves of Louise's topcoat seemed to have been cut to Mr. Lincoln's actual measurements, and the makeshift stovepipe had been badly dented. In short, there was a lot to do.

But the Crystal Palace lived up to its name, and I admit to a giddy thrill of excitement as I walked in, head tilted to take in the miraculous ceiling. A full stage was on one side of the room, a piano nearby. Four long rows of chairs lined either side, and there were balconies for extra seating. During the contest or one of the fashion parades, the ladies would make their debut on the stage, pose decorously, then promenade down the aisle so they might be examined up close. As this was only rehearsal, the gorgeous carpets and elaborate floral arrangements were not yet out. But I was sure they would be there in a week's time. The Miss Rutherford's contestants were not here; as most of them had jobs, they would only be called in to rehearse at the very end.

When I arrived, Louise described the disasters of that morning. Some of the ladies had been tardy to rehearsal and unwilling to give up their conversations when asked to. (Mrs. Lonsdale and Mrs. Tallworthy were particular offenders.) Vocal auditions were being held in an effort to weed out the poorer singers. Some of the ladies were being asked to simply mouth the words, and among the designated mouthers, there were whispered accusations of favoritism and smugness on the part of those chosen to sing. Mr. Rutherford was furious with the set designer. The White House kept collapsing, and the curtains wouldn't stay still. And the pianist had disappeared for a time, which brought Mrs. Rutherford's temper to a boiling point.

As Louise gestured helplessly at the room of bickering, dissatisfied ladies, I asked, "Where should I start?"

She looked first to Dolly Rutherford, who stood grim-faced by the piano, still dividing the competent from the tone-deaf. As the *la-la-la-la-las* rang through the air, Louise looked at a tall man with light, thinning hair and said, "I suppose you could speak to Mr. Rutherford."

Only someone as shy as Louise Tyler would fail to appreciate the challenge of addressing a man as powerful and influential as George Rutherford. To Louise, the world was full of George Rutherfords, intimidating and impatient people given to harsh punishment of anyone seen as wasting their time. Her mother-in-law was George Rutherford; so, too, Monsieur Lafitte, her French master, and the waiter at the Hotel Astor tearoom. But since I was always exhorting her to be brave, I couldn't show myself a coward now. Even if the prospect of speaking with one of the most notoriously difficult tastemakers of the day made my stomach jump.

"Very well," I said, and headed in the direction of Mr. Rutherford, who stood at the right side of the stage, which had to be styled to serve both the Emancipation pageant and the reveal of Miss Rutherford's. Even from a distance, I could hear every word as he berated the carpenter. The carpenter looked about to lose his breakfast from nerves. George Rutherford motioned that he should follow him. The men climbed onto the stage while I sidled along at the foot, hoping to catch the Rutherford eye. Rutherford marched left, I slid left. He drifted right, I moved right. He walked to the back, I drew closer. No luck.

When he had found six things that were unacceptable, five things that were grotesque, three dangerous, and two that were simply an affront to decency, he left the carpenter and stormed down the stage-left stairs. At which point, I decided I had no choice but to place myself directly in his path and make my presence felt by the man who decided what American Beauty was and was not. Here was New York's high priest of fashion, and like any priest, he had an air of the ascetic about him. He was slender, well groomed. The graying blond hair was styled to conceal a lack of volume, his skin smooth, his nails clean and trimmed. As he approached, I caught a discreet waft of expensive eau de cologne.

I was met with a curt question: "Why are you in my way?"

I indicated Mrs. Rutherford. "I was told—"

"Who are you?"

I gambled. "Do you really want to know?"

"No. Continue."

"The costumes."

"They're a disaster."

"I'm here to fix them."

For a moment he assessed me; was I up to the task?

Then he barked, "Do it!" and pushed on.

Rude, no doubt, but there was something propulsive about George Rutherford that made me ready to do almost anything to get the job done. The gargantuan drive that made mincemeat of niceties was contagious. Climbing onto the stage, I shouted, "Ladies! If you need your costume changed . . ."

But my voice got lost in the hubbub of the room. I could see

Louise trying to get people to listen. I had also attracted the notice of the piano player. I tried again, "Ladies! Ladies!" But to no
avail.

Raising his hands, the piano player brought them down hard
on the low notes; a chord both commanding and doom-laden re-
sounded through the room. When the startled crowd looked to
him, he gestured to me on the stage.

"Thank you," I told him. "Ladies, I am here to fix the
costumes . . ."

Within minutes, I had an endless line of complainants and several baskets full of work. I was given a chair behind the piano where
I could sew and commiserate with the ladies who wanted changes.

The costumes being on hold, Mrs. Rutherford decided to rehearse the closing number, "Battle Hymn of the Republic." As
she was playing the wife of the slain president, it was felt—exactly
by whom was never established, but it was felt, and strongly, too—
that Mrs. Rutherford should begin the song solo. Then the rest of
the cast would join in as she knelt to an ascendant Louise.

While undoubtedly stirring, the "Battle Hymn" is something
of a mouthful. Some of Julia Ward Howe's loftier lines do not
make sense, and words that don't make sense are hard to remember. Then there was the fact that Mrs. Rutherford could not
sing—even the lines she did remember. I saw the pianist wince
as she cracked on "fateful lightning of His terrible swift sword."
He was a show in and of himself. He was about my age, and not
much taller, with dark hair that was thick, almost springy. His
large eyes were brown, with pronounced brows. His mouth had
a fullness that was in contrast with the leanness of his frame. He
struck the keys quickly and instinctively, with a sort of desperation
that was understandable. Many people try to insulate themselves
from the currents of feeling around us, but he seemed to let it run
right through him—the tension, the comedy, the embarrassment,

all of it played across his face in leaping eyebrows, gritted teeth, and desperate smiles that seemed to say, *Oh, Mrs. R, you almost had that note! Try again, you never know . . .*

He put me in mind of the time when Mrs. Armslow had switched her Newport home from gas lighting to electric. Watching as the electrician installed the wiring, I was nervous at the thought of threads of fire running through the walls; surely the house would burn down. He explained to me that the energy passed through a commutator, which controlled the fire, allowing it to give light and power safely. As I listened to the barely constrained energy bursting on the keys, I decided the young pianist was a human commutator.

Mrs. Rutherford ran afoul of the lyrics again, and the music ground to a halt. The chorus, having been denied its entrance one too many times, began making suggestions. Perhaps, suggested Mrs. Byrd, Mrs. Rutherford could hold the lyrics sheet? Or someone else could hold them written on large cards. Or someone else could sing the first verse . . .

With this politely offered heresy, conversation reached a point where it was clear no singing was going to be done by anyone for some time. As the battle raged onstage, the pianist sulkily picked out the first notes of the hymn with one finger, then struck several wrong notes on purpose so the mighty anthem collapsed in vulgar cacophony. Then his fingers rippled over the higher keys in imitation of Mrs. Byrd's cajoling. Dark low notes echoed Mrs. Rutherford's increasingly strained response. Hapless, random chords stood in for the ladies striving to mediate. Clever, I thought, and smiled over my sewing.

I heard a few tentative notes, which led into a jaunty assertive rag. It was less dazzling than Mr. Joplin's, but I found my head bobbing along to its rhythm.

"You like it?" he asked.

I did and said so. "Is it Mr. Berlin?"

"It is not," he said, annoyed. "It's the 'Pickle Barrel Rag' by Hirschfeld. Leo Hirschfeld."

He seemed to be introducing himself. I said, "Prescott, Jane Prescott."

"Let me guess," he said. "You committed a terrible crime, but the jails were full, so they sent you here."

"I work for Mrs. Tyler." I nodded toward Louise, who was indeed trying to maintain the Union. Her overlong sleeves flapped helplessly as she tried to get the ladies' attention.

"Lincoln? I like Lincoln. Can't sing. Knows she can't sing. Just mouths the words. Her humility is a wonderful thing."

"It is a wonderful thing, actually." I finished off the seam; there, now Mrs. Fortesque would be able to breathe. "What brings you here?"

"My mother," he said gloomily. "She works in the delicates department. No one sells underwear like Mrs. Ida Hirschfeld. I'll take you over sometime. She'll give you a discount."

I had the feeling that offer had been made to many girls before me, but there was something cheerfully forthright in his flirtation that made it impossible to take offense. His grin seemed to say, *I'm a handsome fellow, as I'm sure you've noticed. You won't mind if I notice you're rather attractive yourself.*

"That still doesn't explain why the illustrious composer of the 'Pickle Barrel Rag' is playing for Mrs. Rutherford's pageant."

"Because to date, the 'Pickle Barrel Rag' has earned me all of two nickels, and my mother worries. So anytime one of her customers is having a party, she says, 'My son plays the piano. You should hire him!' Naturally, when the boss's wife needs a piano player, Ida Hirschfeld is only too happy to help."

"Why don't you get a job? That way your mother can't hire you out."

"I have a job, thank you. Several. Sundays, you'll find me at the Union Square nickelodeon. Mondays, I play piano for a show because the regular pianist is still drunk from the weekend. Tuesdays and Thursdays, I play auditions for a theatrical agent. Wednesdays and Fridays, I sing."

"You're a performer?"

"No, I'm a waiter."

"And Saturdays?"

The eyebrows jumped. "Depends what happens on Friday. No, that's when I write. You watch, one day, my songs will be famous. I'll have my own show." He hit the keys. "Three shows. Five shows. All Broadway will be one big Leo Hirschfeld production. And I'll have a publisher who doesn't take eighty percent."

With this bold prediction, he made a comic flourish on the piano, which became "The Peachtree Rag." This happened to be the song I had danced to with Sadie, and it put me in mind of her surprised compliment—*say, you're good!*—that impudent flick of her ankle . . . and then her poor lifeless legs.

It became a strain to keep smiling, and I concentrated on my sewing. After a few minutes, I heard a funereal melody and looked up.

"Sorry, from your expression, I thought it was a better match for your mood."

"Oh, no—"

"No? You're happy?" Striking the keys, he began to play "Ballin' the Jack." I smiled slightly. "Better? How about this?" A baroque version of "Pop Goes the Weasel." I laughed. "Ah, I knew you were a woman of sophisticated tastes . . ."

I could sense some of the ladies looking in our direction, and I nodded a warning. Without breaking stride, his fingers sailed into a blandly soothing piece.

"Why are you sad?" he whispered when the women had gone back to their negotiations.

I took up Mrs. Unger's blouse, which would be livened up with a swath of vermillion. "A friend of mine died last night. Well, not so much a friend, I didn't even like her very much. But she didn't deserve . . ." I swallowed at the memory of Sadie's ruined face. "The last time I saw her, she was dancing to that song."

"Oh." He had no joke, and I liked him for that. "What happened?"

"She was murdered by her . . ." I didn't know what to call Joe McInerny, so I just said, "It was very cruel."

He frowned. "Was this on the Lower East Side?"

"Yes."

He reached under the piano bench to retrieve a folded newspaper. "Sure, I read about it this morning. Some reverend who runs a home for . . . uh, ladies of a certain profession . . . took a knife to one of them."

Thinking we could not be talking about the same story, I reached for the paper, but he held it back. "It's pretty gruesome. You might not want to read it."

"I found her body, Mr. Hirschfeld. I think I can stand the sight of newsprint."

Just then Mrs. Rutherford demanded they begin the song again. Hastily handing off the paper, Leo started playing, leaving me to read . . .

WOMAN BRUTALLY SLAIN

A young woman was found murdered in an alleyway
on the Lower East Side in what police describe as a

particularly vicious and inhumane killing. Sadie Ellis, 18, was slashed in a manner so indiscriminate that the exact cause of her death was difficult to distinguish. Professional men paled at the sight and one officer was sick.

Suspicion initially fell on a young man of Miss Ellis's acquaintance, a Joseph McInerny. But Mr. McInerny has been incarcerated at City Prison for the past three weeks. And when told of Miss Ellis's demise, Mr. McInerny wept and cried, "What has he done to her? What has he done?"

I had to read that paragraph three times. Mr. McInerny's wails I took as embellishment—who on earth was "he"—but even the *Herald* wouldn't put a man in jail unless he was really there. Which meant . . .

I kept reading.

Miss Ellis had been living at the Gorman Refuge, which houses young women who have left a life of shame. The refuge is run by one Reverend Tewin Prescott. The refuge is notorious in the neighborhood, which is now home to many respectable families. It was once a house of ill repute, and there are those who believe its purpose has not changed. The Reverend Prescott used to serve at Emmanuel Church but was asked to leave in the '90s when it was decided that his interest in women of the street exceeded the bounds of what is seemly. Beyond that it is not known what was between Miss Ellis and the Reverend Prescott.

Twisting the paper, I looked at the front page. No byline, but this was not Michael Behan's writing style, and by his own account, he wasn't writing about crime anymore. No, I knew who had smeared this muck. The growling disheveled man who was there last night. Probably with considerable help from Mrs. Clementine Pickett.

I whispered, "Mr. Hirschfeld, may I borrow this?"

Head bowed, he murmured, "Miss Prescott, right now, you have the look of a woman who could lay me out cold and step daintily over my entrails. Sure, take the paper. You can have my shirt, if you want it. Trousers, socks, underwear—the shoes I'd like to keep, and leave me my teeth. But other than that, Miss Prescott, you go ahead."

Then he turned his head ever so slightly. "One condition, though. You let me take you dancing tomorrow night."

6

The moment rehearsals concluded and the ladies retired to the Orientale for afternoon tea, I headed straight to Herald Square. I had once enjoyed a tour of the *Herald's* offices when I accompanied William's young cousin Mabel on her visit. So I had some idea of where the reporters were kept. But there was a guard in the lobby. I could hardly ask to see the grubby man with the red face and yellow hair, and I didn't want to involve Michael Behan. The solution was to state an interest in placing an ad for employment—and look rather pathetic while doing so. That got me past the watchman in the lobby, and from there, memory took me to the newsroom.

In some ways, it was a factory like any other: chaotic, noisy, without decoration, only the things necessary to produce work—clocks, calendars, and other measurements of time—and the work itself. The room was crowded with long tables and chairs set at no particular spot; many were occupied by reporters, writing at ferocious speed, but some men seemed to like composing their stories while pacing, fists fixed to their hip, darting down every so often to scribble or type. No one seemed to have a desk of his own, or even want one. Chair, surface, typewriter—that was sufficient. A few men did no work at all, snoozing with their hats over their faces for peace.

It was a place without women. The few reporters of that persuasion were not allowed in here. And since I wasn't supposed to be here, it seemed I didn't exist. No one spoke to me or even looked at me. For a while, I stood stymied by their self-preoccupation.

Eventually, one man sensed something amiss. A few glanced at me, then at one another. Finally, a balding dark-haired man in a nearby chair said, "Are you looking for the switchboard, miss?"

"No, I'm looking—" I had started without thinking how I would finish. Holding up the newspaper, I said, "I'm looking for the man who—"

Then I saw him. He was one of the sleepers, but his blond hair poked out from under the brim of his hat, and his pudgy hands rested atop his belly. I had come with the notion of rational appeal: surely he could see, and so forth. Rational thought evaporated at the sight of him placid and sprawling.

"Him," I finished, pointing the paper as I advanced. "I'm looking for him."

An angry woman was cause for mirth in this world: laughter, shouted warnings ("She's coming for you, Harry!" "Looks mad, Harry, better run."), and frenzied bets on the extent of the injuries. The noise woke the reporter, who tumbled out of the chair to a roar of amusement. I saw a snap of recognition when he looked in my direction. He began to scuttle backward like a spider in retreat but found himself trapped in a snarl of chairs. Some of the men tried to block my path, more for fun than loyalty, and I heard a stray "Now, miss, calm down . . ." But I had a rolled-up paper in my hand, and I meant to use it before Harry could get on his feet.

I was within swatting distance when something took hold of my middle and lifted me off the floor. Instinctively, I swung my elbow, then heard a curse as I struck home. The next lift was more assertive, and I found myself hustled out into the hallway and deposited onto a bench. Michael Behan stood in front of me, wincing as he rubbed his side. I thought to apologize, decided against it, and moved to get up.

He moved—with some pain—to stop me. "Wait."

"No."

I started back toward the door, and he called, "Do you want to be his next story?"

I hesitated.

"Do you want it said that Mrs. William Tyler employs a harridan who assaults people at their place of business and whose uncle runs a brothel?"

"It's not—"

"Do you?"

"No."

"Then calm down."

He was right. I knew he was right. I sat back down and put my hands flat on the bench and stared hard at the wall opposite. When I trusted my voice, I said, "What's his name?"

"Harry Knowles."

There was a lack of loathing in Behan's voice, and I asked, "Is he a friend of yours?"

"He's a philosopher drunk on his way to being a kidney drunk. But he has his good days."

I strangled the paper again. "Well, this wasn't one of them."

"Did he write anything that's untrue? Anything that's a lie?"

"Of course he did. My uncle was the one man who ever tried to help Sadie Ellis. And he doesn't run a brothel."

"The article only said other people think he might."

"Clementine Pickett—of course that's what she'd say. Fine, I'll *talk* to Mr. Knowles."

I made to stand, but he put a hand up. "You accused Mc-Inerny, right?"

"Yes. He'd hurt Sadie before. Threatened to kill her. And she was going out to meet him . . ."

"You also implied your uncle was home that night."

"He came back *minutes* after we got there."

"But you see how this could sound?"

As if I had accused another man and lied about where my uncle was because I thought my uncle guilty. I saw it. But I didn't like it.

Seeing that he had made his point, Behan relented. "You think someone's got it in for your uncle?"

"Mrs. Pickett and her Purity Brigade. They spend their days standing outside the refuge, harassing anyone who goes in or out. She wants the refuge out of the neighborhood, so it's very much in her interest to accuse my uncle of murder."

"And she's got a brigade. What do you have?"

"The truth," I said. "The dull, boring truth."

Behan crossed his arms. "Fine. Tell me the dull, boring truth of where your uncle was last night."

I pulled at my fingers. "I don't know. He won't tell me. And he wouldn't tell the police."

Behan clucked unhappily. "The police don't look kindly on people who tell them to mind their own business when there's a dead body in the street. He must have been somewhere. Yours isn't a neighborhood where an older gentleman just decides to take a stroll at night."

"Most older gentlemen, no."

I hesitated. To share this part of my uncle's story meant gambling that I had the loyalty of the Michael Behan who was not a reporter—and that there was such a person.

"This isn't for Harry Knowles," I said. "Or you."

"Understood."

"My uncle used to serve at Emmanuel Presbyterian. But he was asked to leave, as the article said. The reason he was asked to leave was that he wandered. At night. He went to places and talked to women some might think unsuitable for a clergyman. When the church officials challenged him, he said he could hardly expect these women to come to church, and so the church must go to them."

"Fair enough."

"But then they said, In that case, let another clergyman come with you. They said they were worried about his safety, but really, I think they just wanted to make sure he wasn't . . . that he was doing what he said he was."

"How did he answer?"

"He said no. Quite violently. He talked about his work with these women in terms that were, so I've heard, disturbing. Disturbing enough for Emmanuel, at any rate. So they threw him out."

"I see."

Michael Behan enjoyed language; his verbal restraint was disheartening. Feeling defensive, I said, "He was a much younger man then, more headstrong, more . . . At any rate, it's been years since he went out like that. Women either come to the refuge of their own accord or they're sent by a forward-thinking policeman. He doesn't need to . . ."

Aware I was babbling, I threw up my hands. "He was at a colleague's, I'm sure of it. And he won't give their name because he's a private man and he hates being questioned. Hates it. He doesn't want to trouble his friends by sending the police to their homes.

Which is understandable. I don't know why we're even discussing it. It's ridiculous. My uncle would never . . ."

I had talked so much, I was no longer sure which acts I was dismissing as beyond my uncle's capacity. I finished by saying, "You must know he would never harm anyone."

Was I wrong or did he hesitate before agreeing? "I know it because you tell me so, and I'm inclined to believe you. If I weren't so inclined, I'd wonder about a man who lives alone with twenty or so women who don't pay him rent. I'd wonder what that does to him. I'd wonder if any man is really that decent. I'm sorry."

I wanted to be angry, but Michael Behan was only telling me how *Herald* readers might see it. Those little wonderings, the ripples of distrust that come when we encounter someone who does things we simply would not do. Out of self-regard, we sniff out the self-interest: *He's not really so pious. It's all a sham. Pride. Arrogance. Or worse.*

Perhaps to cheer me up, he tapped my elbow and said, "That's an impressive weapon. I think you did damage."

"Not really?"

He looked down at his ribs. "Bruise at least. I'll have to come up with some story for this one. Jumped by hoodlums, pounded by political bosses, something a little more dignified."

"Well, you should have let me hit him."

"Whacking an inebriate on his already-aching head, that's a fine way to persuade the press to be on your side."

Be on my side. The words resonated, and I realized perhaps that was what I had hoped for from Michael Behan. Silly, since he wasn't even writing about crime anymore.

Now he said, "Explain something. You said Sadie Ellis was sneaking out to meet McInerny."

"Yes."

"But McInerny's locked up."

"She may not have known that. They lived not far from the refuge; she was probably going to their rooms . . ."

As I said it, I saw my error. Berthe had told me Sadie had been leaving the refuge for weeks. But Joe McInerny had been in jail most of that time.

Where on earth had she been going?

Still thinking out loud, Behan said, "So poor Sadie thought she was going off to meet her sweetheart, but she runs into a knife before she gets there . . ."

No, I thought slowly, Sadie was going off to meet someone else. But I didn't want to share that. Not if Michael Behan thought Harry Knowles had his good days.

"What about the other women?" he asked. "Any of them ever run into a difficult customer?"

"You think Sadie turned a man down and he did that to her?"

"Been known to happen."

I shook my head. "I saw Sadie. After. Whoever killed her, it wasn't just about ending her life. He wanted to hurt her. Mark her. He . . ."

He did it slow. You know why? Because he enjoyed it. That deep, southern voice that made everyone else sound rushed and sloppy. That dark split skin, red and white at the bone . . .

"He enjoyed it," I said bluntly.

"Then I'd ask the other ladies if they know a man like that. Unless, of course, you do, which I sincerely hope you do not."

Wanting to end the conversation before it became obvious I wasn't sharing all my thoughts, I stood up. "Well, the Lower East Side is a crowded place. I should start looking for this man if I'm going to find him."

"And if I pointed out that bringing yourself to the attention of a man who does this sort of thing to women might be . . . misguided?"

"No, I wouldn't listen. But I thank you for the thought, Mr. Behan."

★ ★ ★

On my way back to the refuge, I pondered the matter of brains. How we give them shelter under our skulls. Do our best to fill them with knowledge, protect them from blows. When they are bored, we seek distraction. When they are tired, we allow them rest, if possible. In return, they should concentrate on the things we wish to think about and ignore those we don't want to.

And yet my brain returned again and again to the same question: Why had Sadie left the refuge?

Joe McInerny had been in jail for weeks. Once, twice, she could have made a mistake. Sooner or later, though, a neighbor would have given her the news. I believed Sadie was fond of Joe, despite everything he did to her. But she was also practical, in her own way. She wouldn't waste her time on a man who'd be no use to her for months, even years. She had no money to go dancing, and no friends or family to give her any—aside from Carrie Biel, who would have returned her to the refuge straightaway. Of course, she could have earned it . . .

But the truth kept insisting on itself: Sadie had gone to meet a man. And that man was not Joe. I felt sure someone would have told her about the arrest. Joe and Sadie were unpopular in their building due to their fights and the business they were in. One might have expected Sadie to return weeping once she found out, but according to Berthe, Sadie had been in a good mood. Mischievous and self-centered as ever. Yes, she'd been sulking about the other women avoiding her, but the arrest of her man would have been an obvious chance to regain their attention. If she hadn't used it, it meant she had moved on.

Who was Sadie meeting? And was he the same man who had

killed her? She would have had little opportunity to meet men outside the refuge. It would have had to be . . .

My thoughts were interrupted as I turned the corner and saw the Purity Brigade. Their numbers had swelled since Sadie's murder. There was Orville Pickett, Mrs. Hilquit, and Miss Cobb, and several new arrivals I didn't recognize. One of them held a copy of the *Herald* bunched in his fist. Instinctively, I looked across the street to see the Duchess and her court. Instead of their usual antics, they stood with their arms crossed, keeping careful watch on the brigade. The Duchess, I noticed, kept one hand to her thigh, where she was reputed to keep a spring-loaded flick knife she called Ladyship's Will.

At the back of the crowd was Bill Danvers, his hair slicked close to his scalp, scrawny neck rising from his snow-white collar. Even as he prayed, his fox eyes stayed sharp on the refuge door. Coming the day after Sadie's murder, this was an outrage of decency by anyone's standards, and striding up to Orville Pickett, I said as much.

Pointing to the refuge, Orville shouted, "There's the outrage, Miss Prescott! Right there. That young woman died because of what goes on in that house and we all know it."

Bill Danvers bellowed, "You tell her, Orville!" And the crowd, eager for conflict, shouted encouragement, with the kind of feeling that feeds on its own righteousness when its appetite is really for bloodshed. That they should treat Sadie's death like a point scored in their favor infuriated me.

My voice rising, I said, "That house is the only place Sadie Ellis was safe from the sort of man who got his hands on her last night. And you know that, Mr. Pickett. Somewhere in your heart, I think you know it."

A shout from the back. "And who was that man, Miss Prescott? You ask yourself that?"

"It wasn't my uncle."

Mentioning my uncle had been a mistake. The crowd reacted like a bull to red, shouting, badgering. Orville demanded, "How many men had she talked to recently? Just one that I can think of."

The crowd roared its approval. I countered with "Well, she talked to you, Mr. Pickett."

Orville had not anticipated that response, and he went pale. Pressing my advantage, I shouted, "Or perhaps she talked to you, Mr. Abrams. Or maybe Bill Danvers. See, Mr. Pickett? I can shout names, too. Mud is cheap, it costs nothing to throw, anyone can do it."

"Now she's accusing me!" Danvers cried. "First McInerny, now me!"

That was all the group needed to make me the villain. I heard accusations that I was a fool, a liar, an accomplice, and worse. Because of me, an innocent man was accused. Because of me, the women trusted my uncle. Because of me, they went with him. A hand reached out and shoved me. Another grabbed at my coat. Panicked, I swung my arm to be free, felt pain as someone wrenched my hair. Twisting to get loose, I saw Bill Danvers grinning, his fist raised.

Fresh howls told me the Duchess and her ladies had joined the fray. Men were knocked sideways, women shoved into the gutter. Frantic, I looked for the Duchess, terrified that Ladyship's Will might assert itself. Shouting, "Stop it! Stop!" Orville cleared a space by placing his large self between me and the crowd. Shocked by the sudden turn to violence, I hurried off in the wrong direction, not toward the refuge but farther down the street. After a few moments, I became aware that someone was following me.

"Miss Prescott . . . Miss Prescott . . ."

The calls were ragged, the breath short, the tone . . . pleading. I slowed, turned around to see Orville Pickett bent from the waist, gulping air.

"I'm . . . sorry," he panted.

"I suppose you see yourself as Christ saving the woman taken in adultery."

From his bent position, he waved a finger. "I don't take your side, Miss Prescott. I just didn't want to see you hurt because of your own rashness."

"*My* rashness—" I clenched my teeth through several responses. "Mr. Pickett, I know you and your mother feel you have a mission, but you need to send these people home. The bottles, the rocks, now this." I gestured to my hair, which had been pulled from its coiled plaits. "Send them home before it gets worse."

"All benefit from hearing the word of the Lord," he said stubbornly.

Having parroted his mother like a good son and a weak man, he turned to rejoin his group. I called, "If you have any decency, you'll say a prayer for Sadie's soul."

"I have already remembered her in my prayers," he said, and took his place next to Mrs. Hilquit and Bill Danvers.

Berthe was waiting for me at the door, broom in hand, Sal and Ruth behind her. My uncle had said that no one was to engage with the Picketts, but clearly, they had been ready to break that rule. "We were going to come get you," said Berthe. "Then the fat fool pulled you out."

"Where is my uncle?"

"Upstairs. Doing the accounts."

Going to his office, I knocked, then opened the door without waiting to be invited. My hair was still down, my coat sleeve torn at the shoulder, and my skirt was spattered with mud kicked up in the scuffle.

My uncle removed his spectacles. "Who . . . ?"

"Have you seen the *Herald*?" I demanded.

"I have not."

"Joe McInerny is in jail. He has been for weeks." My uncle did not react. "That means he didn't kill Sadie."

"Yes, I understood that."

"The article mentioned the refuge. It mentioned you specifically."

"Jane . . ."

"People listen to Mrs. Pickett."

"That's unfortunate for them."

"She's talking to the newspapers. She's talking to the police, who have no suspect for Sadie's killer." I left the words "except you" unspoken.

"What will you do?" I asked finally.

"I'm not aware that I have to do anything," he said.

"Tell the police where you were the night Sadie was killed."

"I will not do that." Over my objections, he said, "I do not have to give an account of myself in order to satisfy gossips and fantasists. Who will not believe me in any case."

For a long moment, we stood in silence. I thought, *At least tell me where you were that night. At least then, I'll know it's a thing that can be told.*

My uncle went back to the accounts. But I had other questions. "If Joe McInerny was in jail, where was Sadie going at night? Why sneak out if not to meet him?"

"You expect me to have the answer."

"Do you?"

Slapping his hand on the desk, my uncle said, "You want me to respond to false accusations against myself with false accusations against another man. Do I understand you correctly?"

My head still aching, I thought, *I wish you to accuse Bill*

Danvers. I wish you to tell the police he is dangerous. I wish you to do something.

My uncle said, "I will speak to someone about this afternoon's incident."

Incident. Such a tidy word. And even I knew there were too many people involved for guilt to settle directly onto Bill Danvers. The Picketts might well claim the Duchess or one of her number had pulled my hair. They certainly weren't going to admit any wrongdoing by a member of their group.

I tried to think of someone else who might have seen Bill Danvers in a different light at a different time—maybe when he was that "difficult customer" Michael Behan had spoken of. I had. Sadie had . . .

He did it slow.

"Do you remember Otelia Brooks?"

Surprised at the seeming shift in the conversation, my uncle said, "Of course."

"You remember when she came to us. Her face." He guessed my meaning and shook his head. "You don't think it's curious?"

"It was years ago."

"She told me about the man who did it. He told her he wanted to hurt her." My uncle winced. "What if it was the same man?"

"What if it was?"

Then we could prove that man was not you. My hands became fists in the effort not to shout. "Do you know where Miss Brooks is now?"

"I do not."

"Did she say nothing of her plans? Even if she went back South, that could—"

"She said nothing to me, and even if she had, I wouldn't tell you. Jane, these women come to us in trust. They leave to rebuild their lives, and when they do, they want never to hear from us again."

"That's not true. Some of the women—"

"Some of the women return, yes, but that is their choice, and I would never ask it of them. As far as I am concerned, I lose all knowledge of a woman's existence once she walks out those doors. If I see her under other circumstances, I do not acknowledge her, and I do not expect her to acknowledge me."

"Why on earth not?"

"What would you have me say? 'Ah, yes, Mrs. So-and-so, I know you, of course.' And the people in her new life will not wonder, How does he know her? Think, for one moment, Jane."

"I *am* thinking," I said. "I am thinking what may happen if we do not find someone who can vouch for your character—"

"There are many people who can vouch for that poor creature."

"But none of them who might have met the man who killed Sadie. Why do you not see that?"

"Because I see other things," he said. "Such as Miss Brooks's right to her new life, undisturbed by us."

Here it was, at last, a show of genuine anger. At me. I dropped my gaze to the floor, took a long breath. The man had all but saved my life. Really, I had no right to ask more than that. Trust, affection, respect—those were a little girl's hopes. They made as much sense in my uncle's world as Tootsie Rolls and dollhouses.

★ ★ ★

I had just gotten into my nightclothes when Sal called upstairs to say someone was on the phone for me. I sighed, thinking it must be Louise, anxious about tomorrow's rehearsal. She would be apologetic. I would have to reassure her, a task I did not feel up to. But I couldn't ask Sal to make my excuses. So I pulled on my robe and trudged downstairs. Picking up the phone, I said, "Yes?"

I was answered with an epithet. One word, quick, brutal, a

backhanded slap. It was a man's voice, rough, angry, and—yes, drunk. He said it again, grunting.

He liked the word, I thought. He'd shouted it at one of the women two weeks ago.

I heard commotion in the background. Voices. Shouts of laughter. He was inside, surrounded by people. Oddly, that made me feel safer. Aware of Sal watching me, I said, "I'm sorry, Mr. Danvers, there's a lot of noise, I didn't quite hear you."

He chuckled. I felt the chill wariness that follows a misstep.

". . . come after me . . ."

He was rasping, mumbling, and it was hard to match the voice to my memory of Bill Danvers's manner of speaking. Fear had taken hold, and clarity wouldn't come.

". . . come after you."

For a searing instant, I knew, *knew*, he was in the house. Then reality reasserted itself as I took in the faded wallpaper, the worn hallway carpet, the sconce light, Sal, a shawl wrapped round her shoulders, clutched to her throat as she listened. He was not here. But he was close.

Swallowing in order to breathe, I said, "Thank you, I'll let Officer Nolan know you said that."

Laughter. Free and easy before dwindling to sighs. "Oh," he said. "Thank you."

He hung up.

I made Sal check the locks on the door. Then I checked them, pulling hard to feel the door hold fast. Then we went to the back entrance and to the cellar to make sure every entrance was secure.

"Windows," I said, trying to sound matter-of-fact. "We should check all the windows."

Sal went to make sure the windows were shut and locked. The windows on the first floor had bars over them. Not so on the upper floors. Where the classrooms were. Where the women slept.

My legs were suddenly very light. Almost hollow. I sat down heavily on the stairs. I emptied my mind. Held my hands so they would not shake. I told myself to be sensible. This was no real shock. I had known Sadie's killer was still out there. I even had a fair idea who he might be.

And he knew it. And he knew where I was.

7

The next morning Berthe and I agreed: the women should stay inside. If they had to go out, they should go in pairs. Rather than being chastened by yesterday's madness, the Purity Brigade had grown; as many as twenty people now stood outside the refuge. And it was no longer just the devout. Men out of work, mistreated women, boys hoping for the chance to jeer and throw things; the restless and aggrieved had gathered under Mrs. Pickett's banner. Destroying the refuge would not get them a job or convince their husbands to quit drinking, but they would have at least made *something* happen. Through the locked door, you could feel their agitation, the hunger for another confrontation. As proof of their renewed commitment, Clementine Pickett herself stood at the head of the group.

The women were restless, too. Under siege, the refuge felt cramped, overcrowded. There was no place to be alone, no place to breathe. Thinking of the shouting, whirling happiness of the cotillion just two nights ago, I wanted to throw a rock through the window myself.

Looking out the window, I saw that Mr. Danvers was not present. Perhaps he was tired, hungover, after his late-night calls.

Could Sadie have been meeting with Bill Danvers? I remembered her complaint about how he stared at her. *I said, Mr. Danvers, you need to bring me flowers or something, you come here so much.* He had told her to go to hell—or so she said. Sadie was bold; it might have appealed to her to tease a man whose condemnation was tinged with lust. It was easy to imagine that game going horribly wrong.

Sadie, I thought, liked secrets, but she liked people to know she had them. If she had a new suitor, there was a good chance she had bragged to someone. But who? I thought of Maja Woycek, a Polish woman who was the softest touch at the refuge. Not only was she easily moved—she had wept when a hawk tore a nest of newly hatched pigeons to pieces on the fire escape—but her limited English ensured she did more listening than talking. (It was her opinion that English was a ridiculous language that made no grammatical sense.)

I found Maja in the yard, scrubbing sheets against a washboard with brisk, determined strokes. When she saw me, she waved the suds from her hands and wiped them on her apron.

"Good morning, Miss Woycek."

"Good morning, Miss Prescott." Her pronunciation was precise, careful. "How are you?"

"I am sad," I said, then realized I was echoing her cadences. "I'm sad about Sadie." Maja shook her head. "You and she talked a lot. May I ask what about?"

Maja wrung out the wet sheet. "Oh, it is all that man. What he did to her, what he make her do. I say, yes, good, you are done with him. Sometimes she says, Yes, done. Then . . ."

Not done. "Was Joe the only man she talked about?"

"To me? Yes. Only Joe. That is why I tell her, I don't want to hear any more. I want to help. Joe is not . . . help."

He certainly wasn't. Unfortunately, Joe was also not a killer. At least not Sadie's killer.

In between classes, I managed to catch a few other women, all of whom echoed Maja's story. "She was like a little kid," complained Doris Barton as she rethreaded the bobbin on a sewing machine. "Wouldn't do a lick of work, but oh, she was getting out of here, had better places to be, finer people to know."

"Did she say who they were, these finer people?"

"They weren't anybody, they were in her head. King of England, I don't know. I stopped listening after a while. Ruth might know."

I found Ruth Renehan upstairs, frowning over sums. Tapping her pencil as she calculated, she quickly wrote down an answer. Then just as quickly scratched it out. Falling back in her chair, she sighed, "I'll never understand percents."

I smiled to think of Otelia Brooks's reaction. In my place, she would answer, *If a man told you he was taking ninety percent of your earnings and giving you ten, you'd know you were being cheated, wouldn't you? Then you understand percents. Keep at it.*

Taking the seat next to her, I said, "Doris tells me you were friendly with Sadie those last few weeks."

"I wouldn't call it friendly. But I knew she was close to getting thrown out, and so I told her straight she had to give up on McInerny and start thinking about her own life or she wouldn't have one."

"And she said?"

"She got cute and said, Well, how do you know it's Joe I'm seeing? And I said, Who else would it be, you don't talk about anything else. She said, Maybe that's what I want everyone to think. Maybe it'd shock you all if you knew who it really was."

"Did she mean you knew him?" Ruth looked puzzled. "Well, how else would you be shocked?"

"I just thought she was trying to make out he was someone important."

Would Bill Danvers shock the women of the refuge? Absolutely. I could think of someone else even more shocking, but I put that thought from my mind.

"He had money." Ruth snapped her fingers. "Enough to take her out. I remember because she said for once she'd have a decent meal, not the slop Berthe puts on the table. I should have known that couldn't be Joe. He'd never spend money on her."

So Sadie's new friend was willing to pay for the pleasure of her company. That didn't sound like Bill Danvers. But then it occurred to me I didn't know much about the man. For example, what he did for a living . . .

Reminded of livings and the need to make them, I glanced at the clock and saw I was late. Answering Ruth's curious look, I said, "I have to be at Rutherford's. It's something for Mrs. Tyler."

"Weren't you supposed to be on holiday?"

"I was, wasn't I?"

★ ★ ★

An hour later, I arrived at Rutherford's department store to find the Crystal Palace packed with women. Not just the ladies of Mrs. Rutherford's circle; none of the newcomers could afford to shop at Rutherford's. Some wore the practical outfit of the working girl: shirtwaist and dark skirt. Others wore cotton day dresses with a bit of trim or lace that hinted at some income, but not much. They were all terribly excited, gazing up at the ceiling, wandering the hall as if they could not believe they were truly here. A few of them had gathered around the piano; Mr. Hirschfeld was playing Joplin and looking rather excited himself.

The American Beauties had arrived.

As I looked wonderingly at the crowd, Louise came over and said, "Mr. Rutherford said to tell you they all need costumes."

"Oh, dear God."

"Emily is here, too."

Yes, I had seen her, leaning on the piano, inquiring as to the function of its keys. "And the black ones, Mr. Hirschfeld, what do *they* do?"

"She promised me she was going back to Vassar," said Louise. "But it seems she had tea with the Rutherfords, and now she's keen to try out for the contest. My mother-in-law will be furious."

"Does Mrs. Tyler care so much about education?" Mr. Hirschfeld, I noticed, was now assessing the span of Emily's hand, finding much to admire.

"No, but she cares very much that Emily is kept in a women's college behind stone walls. Especially after last summer . . ."

Before I could ask what had happened last summer, Mrs. Rutherford came up and said irritably, "My goodness, Louise, is your woman here at last? She's late."

Between domestic staff and employer, there is a tacit understanding that the staff has no existence beyond the employer's needs. To suggest otherwise is . . . vulgar. It is for them to show a benevolent interest in our family; it is for us to burden them with only the briefest pleasantry. Yes, my mother *is* feeling better, thank you, Mrs. Waterman. My brother did get that job; how kind of you to ask. What they do not ask about, we do not speak of. They pay for our services and attention; they have the right to command them. But for some employers, it goes beyond that. The very idea of an independent life, separate from them, is threatening. To point out that I was on vacation, needed to attend to a family matter, or had a friend who had been murdered would be extreme provocation to someone like Mrs. Rutherford. As would pointing out that I was a person to be spoken to in her own right, not simply Louise's "woman." I would not have minded giving such provocation, but I didn't want to embarrass Louise.

"Jane is on holiday, Dolly," Louise retorted. "It's very kind of her to give us her time." Her voice cracked under the strain of such a bold statement.

"I'm happy to do it, Mrs. Tyler," I said, leaving the words "for you" unsaid. "I am concerned about how we're to dress the new cast members, though. Perhaps I could speak with one of the saleswomen. Or someone in the stockroom."

Dolly Rutherford gave me a smile a Doberman pinscher might give a throat. "My husband is right over there; you might ask him."

Her husband was indeed right over there. And Emily Tyler, having moved on from Mr. Hirschfeld, was beside him. For once, Mr. Rutherford's face did not show rage or weary disapproval; he looked almost . . . happy. He gestured expansively to Emily, as if outlining some vision. For her part, she laughed, then gave his shoulder a playful shove with the tips of her fingers.

Louise and I exchanged glances. Then I headed over to Emily and Mr. Rutherford—pointedly ignoring Mr. Hirschfeld's smile as I did so.

As I approached, the two were in animated conversation about the contest. Should Emily try for next year, or would it be good fun to sneak her in at the last moment? Emily was demurely insisting she couldn't possibly crash, but Mr. Rutherford seemed enchanted by the element of surprise. Also, he seemed to find this year's contestants lacking. "Look at that one," he said, flinging a hand toward my favorite, Celeste Dwyer. "Hair like straw. And that one"—a dismissive wave at Eleanor Gosnell—"the grace of a stevedore." Emily let out a shocked but encouraging giggle.

I drew near, and Mr. Rutherford pressed Emily's hand and headed in the opposite direction. Once again, I was going to have to chase after him if I wanted answers. I called out, "Mr. Rutherford." But he only wiggled his fingers in the air and said, "Measure them all, measure them all . . ."

So I began with Emily, murmuring as I held the measuring tape around her waist, "What are you doing here, Miss Tyler?"

"Having fun."

"Is there no fun to be had in Poughkeepsie?"

"No," she said. "There is not."

I wanted to say there wasn't really much fun to be had with a middle-aged married man either, no matter what kind of crown he promised. But there were ten other girls who needed my attention. For nearly two hours, I measured and avoided questions I had no answers for. What would the costumes be like? How much time would each have onstage? Who was coming to the pageant? I felt so rushed it was even hard to be excited when I met Hattie Phipps, the telephone operator, who was lovely beyond imagining and made me rethink my bet on poor Celeste Dwyer.

I was not the only one who failed to be excited by the Beauties' presence. Dolly Rutherford was even more snappish than ever. I wondered how pleasurable it would be, being married to a man who spent his days gazing at other women. Now that he was married, William adored only Louise. Other men—I glanced at the piano—were more like Mr. Hirschfeld.

When I was done measuring, I looked around for George Rutherford. Not seeing him, I asked his wife where he was and received a very curt direction to his office.

Catching my eye, Leo grinned and nodded at the doors as if to say, Go on. I pretended not to see him. He could go on, too, as far as I was concerned. He could grin at Emily Tyler and explain his stupid little keys. No doubt his mother would be happy to sell Emily some underwear. No doubt Mr. Hirschfeld would be happy to advise.

George Rutherford's office was clear on the other side of the top floor and was guarded by a secretary who sat just outside. When I arrived, she gave me a very grim look and told me Mr. Rutherford could not be disturbed.

"Mrs. Rutherford said specifically that I should speak to him."

This did not have the desired effect on the secretary. Then, through the door, I heard, "Let her in, Miss Ambrose."

There was a moment's hesitation. Should I open the door? Should Miss Ambrose? Mr. Rutherford? Who granted access to the great man? Or should I simply take it? I preferred not to be screamed at if it was avoidable. Finally, I turned the knob and opened the door to find the raging tornado of the other day seated calmly behind his desk.

It was a surprisingly small office for a man with a strong sense of spectacle. A large, cluttered mahogany desk with a leather chair for Mr. Rutherford and two chairs for . . . the word "supplicants" came to mind. Along one wall, there were filing cases; along the other, sheets of paper with architectural plans, cuttings from magazines, and sketches. In the corner sat a ponderous safe; the cash for the store's business was probably kept there, stacks upon stacks of money spent by grateful, hopeful women.

"I'm very sorry to interrupt, Mr. Rutherford."

"Why? Didn't my wife tell you to speak with me?"

"She did."

"Well, there you have it. Mrs. Rutherford said you should speak with me and I should speak with you, and here we are speaking. You see? The woman is all-powerful. Sit."

He gestured to the empty space before his desk, and I sat.

"Now, why did my wife ask you to speak with me?"

"It's the additions to the pageant. The American Beauties. How do you want them presented?"

He considered. I found myself holding my breath in prayer that his vision wouldn't be too elaborate. Burlap bags would not be an unwelcome suggestion.

"They should all . . . look the same," he said.

One look. I exhaled.

"Nothing elaborate. A sort of blank canvas until the end. When she is . . . revealed." He waved a hand in the air, a gesture of self-conscious showmanship. "Some sort of smock," he said. "Simple. White."

Then he scribbled something on a pad of paper and handed me the sheet. "See my head saleswoman on the third floor. She'll fix you up with something suitable."

"Thank you, Mr. Rutherford."

"No," he said. "Thank *you*."

For a moment his gaze held. For a brief, disoriented instant, I had the strange certainty that he found me pretty. *You*, he seemed to say, *it's you*. He would insist I enter the Miss Rutherford's contest—although I had never felt desirous or deserving of such a thing. But it was heady to be examined so closely. No wonder the ladies of New York fought for his attentions, even if you were at risk of hearing you lacked grace or that your hair was straw.

I also felt what Emily must have only a few hours ago. Remembering Sadie's dream of her mystery gentleman and how cruelly that had turned out, I asked, "Will Miss Tyler be joining the pageant?"

"Certainly."

"So eleven smocks." He nodded, wanting me gone. "Only—I know her mother, Mrs. Florence Tyler, wants her back at school."

"And so do I. Miss Tyler is a Vassar girl. All those scholarly young ladies will see her and think, She shops at Rutherford's, so must I shop at Rutherford's."

He smiled briefly, as if to let me in on the secret that he was, after all, a salesman from Ohio and that the rest of it was all a bit of an act. Hurrah for pageantry and poetry; but the goal was merchandise bought and sold.

Then, as I turned to go, I heard, "Your . . . hair."

"I beg your pardon?"

He shook his head. He had not been able to help himself; he noticed such things without thinking. But I could not buy his clothes, and so should not have his attention. What would it be like, I wondered as I made my way back to the Crystal Palace, to walk into Rutherford's and simply spend? To try on and cast off as many versions of yourself as you liked? Dresses, hats, shoes. Your hair done this way or that. Would it materialize in the mirror, that best you? That ideal version of yourself, what you were truly meant to look like? What if you never got the chance to see that self?

Then I shook my head. Yes, Jane, your true self lies in a Paquin hat. If only you could let money fly from your fingers, then you might fulfill your purpose on earth. If only George Rutherford would tell you what you should look like, you'd be worth looking at. Vacation, it seemed, was making me spoiled and self-indulgent.

I returned to the hall to find Mrs. Rutherford and Louise rehearsing the scene in which Mrs. Lincoln urged her husband to write the Emancipation Proclamation; in this version, the words seemed to spring from Mrs. Lincoln's own imagination. Louise's only line as Lincoln was to pronounce her "idears mighty fine."

"Poor old Lincoln," said Leo. "First Booth, now this. How was Mr. R?"

I jotted notes about the costumes on a pad. "Very pleasant,

as a matter of fact. I'm to see the head saleswoman on the third floor."

"Are you?" He slid off the piano bench. "Well, let me come along and introduce you properly."

"To whom?"

"My mother, of course."

* * *

Some men might have been hesitant to step into the lingerie department, but not Leo Hirschfeld. And from the cries of "Hello, Leo!" it was clear it was far from the first time he'd been there. Singling out a brunette inexpertly folding a negligee, he said, "Myrtle, is my mother here?"

"By the fitting rooms." Then, crossing her arms on the counter, she said, "You know, I've had such a craving lately for pastrami."

Leo grinned. "You know, that's funny, I have, too." He did not, however, break his stride, leaving Myrtle to give me a singularly filthy look.

As we approached the fitting rooms, I realized that while Leo might exaggerate about many things, he was telling the truth when he told me that no one sold underwear like his mother. Elegant, poised, with long tapered fingers and not a single dark hair out of place, she might have been a customer were it not for the purple Rutherford's smock she was obliged to wear. If I looked carefully, I could see the faintest suggestion of lines at her eyes and mouth. But otherwise, she might have passed for a woman in her late twenties. She made her way around the floor, dispatching orders to junior girls, compliments to clients who had chosen wisely, and thoughtful corrections to those who had strayed.

"Oh, Mrs. Kanfer, I apologize, we've brought you entirely the wrong item." This to a woman who bulged from an optimistically sized corset.

"But this is my size, it's always been," breathed the stout Mrs. Kanfer.

That patent falsehood was met with a wide, warm smile. "Of course, but we've brought you the wrong fit—that's why it feels so constraining. Madolyn." An eloquent finger brought the salesgirl running. In a low voice, Mrs. Hirschfeld said, "Bring the 40; don't call it a 40." Then, to the client, she said soothingly, "You see, when blessed with a gorgeous bosom such as yours, Mrs. Kanfer, the run-of-the-mill garment won't suit. They're cut for the average woman, not the gloriously endowed such as yourself. I envy you your proportions. Mr. Kanfer is a fortunate man. Alas—" She indicated her own slender frame. "My husband must be satisfied with my conversation."

I imagined myself adept at the art of the constructive compliment: praise that persuaded the person being dressed to risk notice, discard unrealistic ambitions, or acknowledge that she had areas in need of artful ornamentation. But Mrs. Hirschfeld was a master. A debutante who was all sharp points and weak chin was fascinating. A rotund lady with a belligerent aspect was regal, while a shy middle-aged woman was committing a crime—an absolute crime!—by hiding her splendors. Like her son, she spoke and moved at speed, but unlike him, she seemed completely sincere. Even I began to see possibilities in the women I had not seen before. In the space of one half hour, Mrs. Hirschfeld made Mr. Rutherford richer by hundreds of dollars and improved the mood of every woman in the room.

I must have looked the picture of dumb adoration, because Leo said, "Yes, that's my mother. Here, I'll introduce you."

The maternal smile that greeted him was loving, but she pulled his hair rather than embrace him and asked, "Why is Mrs. Rutherford missing her accompanist?" Then, turning to me, she said, "Hello, dear. I am Leo's mother, Mrs. Hirschfeld."

I confessed to being Jane Prescott.

"Miss Prescott is doing the costumes for the pageant," Leo explained. "She's in need of cheap—"

"There's nothing cheap here, darling. Reasonably priced for the discerning woman; never cheap."

"Reasonably priced—also known as free—nightgowns for the American Beauties. Mr. Rutherford told her such a thing might be available."

"I see. And you generously offered to carry the nightgowns for Miss Prescott because they're so heavy and she's such a fragile little thing."

"No, I wanted to see you."

Mollified, Mrs. Hirschfeld looked at me. "Do you work in the theater?"

"I work for Mrs. William Tyler."

"Oh? A client told me they saw her last month at Mrs. Howell's, looking very handsome. She's—" She lowered her hand at a straight angle down the front.

"Slim, yes."

"That can be a challenge."

"Less so now that the fashion favors a more streamlined silhouette. And posture helps."

"But only goes so far. Have you heard of something called the bra? Leo, dear, go make yourself useful to Mrs. Rutherford."

"I'm here to carry smocks," Leo reminded her.

"No, you're here to play piano." A wave of the hand. "Upstairs."

Leo went, flashing a smile at Myrtle. She affected not to notice. I tried to do the same.

Mrs. Hirschfeld clapped her hands. "Now, the bra. The first I heard of it was from a friend of Miss Polly Jacob. One evening, Miss Jacob found the corset too visible on a dress she wanted to wear. So she connected two pieces of cloth with string, and voilà.

It just slips over the back and shoulders, lifts and separates. And, I would imagine, could even enhance. Which could be useful to a graceful lady of slender build."

I tried to envision such a thing. "It goes under the corset? On top?"

"There is no corset," whispered Mrs. Hirschfeld.

"No corset." She nodded. "Just—"

"Two little pieces of cloth and some string."

My hand went to my whaleboned midsection as I tried to imagine walking around with nothing between my belly button and my shirtwaist except . . . well, nothing. My first thought was *Indecent*. The second was *Oh, to breathe* . . . And how fast could you get dressed, if you didn't have to lace and snap and layer?

"I told Mr. Rutherford, They'll be in every store one day; you might as well be one of the first. Come, let's see what we have in nightgowns."

We found the perfect nightgown. But there were not enough of them in the store; they would have to be ordered from the warehouse. Mrs. Hirschfeld promised me that it could be her head on the platter if they weren't here in two days or Mr. Rutherford wasn't satisfied.

As I headed back up to the sixth floor, I caught sight of a pale yellow head of hair and paused, thinking it familiar. When the girl behind the counter turned and I saw the freckles, I said without thinking, "Carrie Biel! What on earth are you doing here?"

"I work here!" She held up a suggestive item that seemed mostly ribbon and frill. "Can I interest mademoiselle in something for the bedroom?"

As we laughed, I remembered how remarkable Carrie's brightness had always seemed to me. She could not have had a worse beginning in life, and yet she was undiminished. With her blond hair and blue eyes, she might have been ravishing, were it not for the abundance of freckles that made her look six years old.

"How is your uncle?" She rolled her eyes. "How's *Sadie*?"

I stopped laughing.

"What?"

I told her quickly in matter-of-fact terms. Carrie listened, eyes staring. Then her mouth started to tremble and she raised a shaking hand to her face. I took hold of her, my shoulder giving her a place to hide her tears. She cried hard for a minute or two. Then she stood upright, straightened her blouse. As she wiped her tears with the back of her sleeve, I saw she still had her old rope bracelet on her wrist. Her mother always told her it was the one thing her father left them when he went back to sea, and Carrie never took it off.

"Now, how do you get away with that at Rutherford's?" I teased.

"Keep my hand behind the counter when the boss is around." Then she exhaled in misery. "I thought I'd saved her."

"You did. There are just more . . ." The word "demons" came to mind, but more darkness was not what Carrie needed right now. "We still have her things at the refuge. Maybe you'd want to collect them."

She hesitated. "I don't want them going in the garbage. Only I work late tonight . . ."

"That's all right. I'm sure the other women would love it. It would be wonderful for them to hear about your job. And my uncle will be especially pleased to see you."

I had spoken the truth; my uncle had always been fond of Carrie and would be pleased. But I saw a tightness in Carrie's expression, doubt or fear. Unease at returning to her past? The look was gone before I could decide.

"I'd like that," she said.

We left each other with smiles and promises to talk more tonight. But returning to the Crystal Palace, I found it hard to shake
off the memory of Carrie's weeping. She had tried to save Sadie;
we had all tried to save Sadie. Even Sadie, in her way, had tried.
There were demons in the world, though, and Sadie had been
unlucky. Or foolish, I thought, thinking of Bill Danvers mouthing prayers while his eyes lingered. Easier to run across demons
when they pretended to be angels.

Mrs. Rutherford was trying to work the new girls into the chorus. Many of them had been placed at the back, with the older,
more sedate ladies up front. Emily, I noticed, stood on tiptoe, insisting on being seen.

I found Louise drooping on a small gilt chair. Her dark Lincoln sleeves flowed over her hands. Reaching for the pins in my
pocket, I said, "Let me shorten those for you, Mrs. Tyler."

Lifting her arm, she said, "I'll write to William tonight. Perhaps he can come home for a few days." She dropped her gaze,
as if worried she would be accused of unjustified self-interest in
that area.

"I'm sure he'd welcome the excuse," I told her.

"Well, and he could talk to Emily. Make her see she should go
back to school."

"I don't know that Miss Tyler is destined to be a scholar," I
said.

"No, but she's not destined to be the wife of a jockey either."

Seeing my astonishment, Louise elaborated. The summer she
and William had become engaged, Emily had been in Saratoga
Springs, where she had developed a passion for the racecourse.
(*We thought she just liked the horses*, said Louise.) While a girl-
ish love for ponies might indeed have inspired her first visit, it
was a jockey named Snapper Wilkes who inspired several more.
But when Emily had tried to join her diminutive inamorato on a

train headed to Florida, William had caught them at the station and brought Emily home. Soon thereafter, she was dispatched to the halls of academia in Poughkeepsie, far from the city and all racecourses.

I said, "I suppose when her mother went to Boston, she saw her chance."

Louise nodded. "But she'll have to go back. We can't have her just running loose."

Removing Louise's now-pinned coat, I returned to my sewing spot by the piano. Mr. Hirschfeld was doggedly pounding out "When Johnny Comes Marching Home." I looked up at Emily, who was still standing on tiptoe. On every hurrah, she soared upward, cheering louder than anyone else. Despite her antics with Mr. Hirschfeld, it was hard not to smile. High-spirited, defiant, impossible, she put me in mind of Sadie. Breathing in sharply, I rubbed my eyes to catch tears before they fell.

"Psst."

I blinked, saw Mr. Hirschfeld.

"Tell me where you'll be. I'll pick you up around seven."

"Why would I do that?"

"We're going dancing. Remember? I asked you during the Operetta of the Strangled Cats."

"I can't go dancing with you, Mr. Hirschfeld."

He glanced down. "I see two feet. A right and a left."

"Truly, I'm not in the mood."

"I know." The song ended, and he swung around to face me. "That's why you have to come. Your friend died. You didn't. You can be sad for her and then you can enjoy life because you still have it. Come dancing with me."

His voice was serious, and although he had moved no closer to me, I felt . . . affected. It suddenly seemed very important that I go dancing with Leo Hirschfeld.

"Where?"

"The Acme Café. That's near where you live, right?"

It was, and I knew it well. The Acme was owned by Chick Tricker, who had taken over a third of the Eastman gang when his old boss, Big Jack Zelig, was killed last year, probably on orders from Tricker himself. The club was a second home to some of the most dangerous gang members and Tammany's greasiest politicians, as well as some of the best bands in the city. Over the past decade, gangs had realized they could turn a profit by capitalizing on their notoriety. The well-heeled citizens of the city would pay handsomely for the chance to indulge in the behaviors deplored by their newspapers—gambling, prostitution, drink, drugs, and dance—if they could do so in the company of New York's most colorful gangsters. And Tricker certainly was colorful, having made his name in the war over a young lady known as Ida the Goose. The Eastmans had stolen Ida from the Gophers, igniting a turf battle over the rights to her affections and earnings. One of Tricker's clubs had been the scene of the final shoot-out of that war; five Trickers had been killed.

The Eastmans made most of their money in thievery, gun sales, hijacking, and contract work; if you needed a relative, a rival businessman, or a unionist intimidated or killed, the Eastmans were only too happy to help. They had gotten their name partly because they controlled the brothels of the Lower East Side. My uncle would not approve of my going to any establishment run by Chick Tricker.

On the other hand, the dance floor was said to be vast, there was a rumor that Johnson's Brass Band played the Acme sometimes, and my uncle did not have to know everything.

"We'd never get in," I said in a token resistance.

"They better let me in," said Leo Hirschfeld. "My shift starts at eight."

8

Over the past few years, New York had become "the City of Dreadful Dance." A physical activity so closely linked to courtship, dance was strictly regulated, kept to ballrooms for the well-off and to municipal dances—often supervised by clergy—for the lower classes. Parts were kept at a proper distance, the music was decorous and suitable, and any movement that even hinted at the next stages of intimacy . . . well, there were none.

But New Yorkers young and old had started dancing in clubs and restaurants across the city. Establishments that had once entertained their diners with floor shows and singing waiters saw another use for the boards: dance. Women from all walks of life were now going out—unescorted!—and moving in new ways. They were trotting, slinking, and dipping. Couples no longer held each other at arm's length; they pressed close above and below the waist.

As I waited for Leo Hirschfeld to pick me up at the refuge that evening, I thought that what none of the thundering critics understood was that the new dances didn't *feel* scandalous.

Dancing was like . . . a good walk through the park. Energizing. Healthy. A way to banish nerves. Yes, I had mostly danced with girls. Still, I didn't see what the panic was about.

Before dinner, I told my uncle, "A young man will be calling for me this evening. Also, Carrie Biel will be coming by around nine to collect Sadie's things."

I piled one revelation on top of the other, so that if my uncle did not wish to address the issue of the young man, he didn't have to.

For a long moment, he looked at me, then said, "It will be nice to see Miss Biel again."

Of course, I couldn't be sure that Leo Hirschfeld would call. Leo Hirschfeld seemed a man of the moment; whoever and whatever was in front of him merited his complete and almost too intense attention. Who and what was not ate their pastrami sandwiches alone. He had asked me hours ago, more than enough time to forget.

But he had not forgotten. A few minutes after the hour, the bell rang and I was out the door. The Acme was not far, and it was a warm evening, so we walked. Conversation with Leo was a tennis match—no, Ping-Pong. Back and forth, back and forth, punchy, speedy, percussive, with a great slam of a joke at the end that left everyone weak and laughing. Once you had the feel of it, it was easy to keep up. He was looking quite spiffy in a short dark coat and a flat cap. Sometimes he walked alongside me; other times, he walked backward to face me.

"How do you become a singing waiter?" I asked him. "And *why* do you become a singing waiter?"

"If you're the youngest of six kids and you want to eat, you have to get your mother's attention. Also, my uncle publishes sheet music. One time when I was nine, he came to dinner and I decided I would show off for the big-time agent. After everyone took their fingers out of their ears, my uncle said, Kid, you don't sing good, but you have no sense of shame. I'm putting you to work."

"As what?"

"A plugger. People can't buy a song they never heard, right? That's where the plugger comes in. After school, I'd stand on a corner in Times Square, plant myself on the floor of Macy's, the line outside Washington Park—anywhere there was a crowd—and start singing whatever song my uncle needed to move. Usually it was love songs. People thought it was funny, this skinny little kid singing his lungs out over a broken heart. I could do Italian." He gestured to his dark springy hair. "So I started getting songs like 'My Mama's Spaghetti' and 'In Old Napoli.' For Irish, I went to saloons, and all the drunks would start crying and throwing pennies. One time, he even sent me up in a hot-air balloon over Coney Island with a megaphone."

"What does your father think of your career?"

"My father and career," he mused. "Well, Father has the distinction of being the worst tailor in all of New York. I'm not lying, the title belongs to him alone. Things on this earth—" He waved his hands to indicate a delicate connection. "Me and my brothers, he can never keep us straight: 'Irv . . . Dave . . . Artie.' 'Leo, Pop. It's Leo.' 'Oh, the little one.' 'That's right, Pop.'"

I was wondering what it would be like to be a part of a family so large you got lost in it when Leo said, "Oh, here we are."

And here we were: right in front of the tenement known as the Acme Café. By the door, there were twenty or so images of women in rather coy states of undress; all these, it was implied, awaited within, and for an odd moment, I thought of the American Beauties. The club, Leo informed me, had a hundred ways in and out, because "you never know who's going to have to make a

hasty exit." We went in through the kitchen and through a circu-
itous route of dodgy stairs to the dance hall.

Deliberately tawdry, the Acme Café's décor reassured tourists
that they were entering a lair of authentic depravity. Red burlap
flecked with gold covered the walls, cigar smoke fogged the air,
and the light from overhanging cones was dim. The furniture was
teak, inlaid with ivory, to give a flavor of the Orient. An emaci-
ated man worked sullenly behind the bar; never acknowledging
the order, he nonetheless kept a steady stream of spirits, beer,
and champagne flowing. (For the less affluent or more desperate, there might be a mix of water and camphor or a hot punch
made up of rum, whisky, benzene, and scraps of cocaine.) Last
year, Leo told me, Tricker had provided the attraction of a "genuine" opium fiend: Hophead Lil, an elderly Chinese woman who
worked in a chop suey house down the block during the day.
Wrapped in a kimono, she posed with a pipe, so exhausted after a
long day feeding people she was able to convince visitors she was
in the grip of Morpheus. Suitably horrified, they dropped money
into a small bowl on the floor, which she split thirty-seventy with
Mr. Tricker.

Since Leo had to work, I would be sitting by myself for parts
of the evening. Putting me in an inconspicuous corner where I
could see but not be seen, he sat me at a small table rescued from
the storeroom.

"Remember, if anybody asks, you're waiting to speak to the
manager about a job. Unless it's someone who looks like the manager, in which case, your friend just went to fix her hair and she'll
be right back." Then, promising to return, he went to work. Before the band came onto the stage, the waiters were expected to
entertain guests as they dined. Leo's uncle was right: he was never
going to have a career at the opera. But he threw himself into
every song with a gusto that charmed his audience and earned

good tips. When he snuck back with a plate of hash, he deposited a handful of loose change on the table.

"Seems to me you're a bigger success as a singer than songwriter. Maybe you should change careers."

"Actors work like dogs, get paid less, and kicked harder. Once 'Pickle Barrel Rag' hits big, that's the last time anyone sees Leo Hirschfeld perform. How's the hash? I think it's real horse tonight."

I tried it. "It's good."

"Yeah? May I?" Leaning in, he kissed me. "You're right, that is good. Be back soon."

I murmured, "Yes, be back," as if it were the expected pleasantry. Sitting up, I settled my hands in my lap. But I was not breathing efficiently, and I could think of nothing but that life could be very unexpected. Leaning on the table, I put a hand over my lips, as if I were rather bored by it all. But my eyes were still on Leo as he launched into "Melinda's Wedding Day," and the thought Yes, *that is good* drifted through my mind.

I did recover myself, and for a while I enjoyed the spectacle, setting aside the reality that I was surrounded by men with guns who sold some people and killed others for profit. I had been seated with the unstylish tourists, boys down from Harvard daring one another to drink this or swing off that, and a table of monosyllabic gentlemen who wanted privacy for their game of stuss. But I could see the stage and the ring of tables around the dance floor just fine.

This was where the well dressed and well connected sat. I thought I spied a junior member of the Vanderbilt family and a gentleman in tails whose mustache looked distinctly imperial, although I couldn't decide whether Austrian or English. There was the elegant Mrs. Frosby-Beers, who was said to be carrying on affairs with two senators of opposing parties and at least one member of

Wilson's cabinet. Sitting near her was a quiet, bespectacled man who was paring his fingernails with a knife. This was Lolly Blum, who ran Monk Eastman's pet shop on Broome. And there was the dandified young assemblyman, James Walker, laughing his head off at something a delectable young woman had whispered into his ear.

The Harvard boys made a game of trying to get my attention by pitching peanut shells at my table. I said I favored Yale men, and when they jeered, I pointed to the burliest thug within view and said that was my beau there, and he was majoring in the art of snapping bones. They sat quiet after that. Meanwhile, I followed the progress of an ostentatiously good-looking fellow who approached any table occupied solely by women—except mine. From his gestures and the women's reactions, it was clear he was making elaborate efforts at charm. He always singled out one of the older women to dance with. After a few tables, I noticed that it wasn't only age; quantity of jewelry was also a factor.

The waiters having served and entertained the guests, the band came onstage. It was a group of six, too small for Johnson's Brass Band, I saw with disappointment. One sat at the piano, another at the drums, the others arranged themselves on chairs or stood alongside. There was a clarinetist, a trombone player, a trumpet player, and a bass. As they struck up the first notes, people surged onto the dance floor. In the hubbub, I felt Leo grab my hand and pull me into the crowd, much to the outrage of the Harvard boys. At first it was hard to find room, but skilled, energetic dancing will create its own space, and it wasn't long before we could hop, trot, waddle, and scratch with abandon to the song "I Want to Love You While the Music's Playing."

"Won't your boss mind?" I asked him.

"My pal Stumpy's looking after my tables, and the club doesn't mind us showing young ladies a good time as long as people keep buying drinks."

The band finished "I Want to Love You," and, holding up a finger, Leo ran to the bar, then crept onstage, where he handed a drink to each musician—two for the piano player—before hurrying back to the floor. The band drank, then struck up the first notes of a tune that I knew but couldn't quite place. The crowd loved it, though, with more people surging onto the dance floor in a tidal wave of energy and excitement.

Falling in beside me, Leo shouted, "'Pickle Barrel Rag'!"

"It's good!"

"I know!"

It was also, I thought, just slightly reminiscent of Joplin's "Maple Leaf Rag." But you heard that song so often, maybe it was easy to get mixed up. The song ended to a raucous burst of applause. The next melody was slower, more insinuating. Sliding his hand around my waist, Leo brought us closer. "It's the tango, the latest thing from down south."

In the earlier dances, we had either known the steps or communicated through hands and footwork. Here, all the communication was done below the waist, the turn of hips and the nudge of thigh. I registered his hand at the small of my back, and it occurred to me I might object. But I didn't.

"You have to look at me. The tango is all in the eyes." He widened his own comically.

"Oh, is that where it is?"

Thankfully, there were several turns where we separated at arm's length before returning to the embrace. Which I decided was not so shocking, once you got used to it.

As we glided, arms extended, I spotted the handsome man I had noticed earlier. He was gently maneuvering a blushing, weak-chinned girl around the floor. I asked Leo who he was.

"Oh, that's Frank. Likes to be known as Eduardo. Why? Oh, you're wondering why he didn't ask you to dance."

"I wasn't."

Leo grinned. "Frank's a tango pirate. The richer, older ladies who come here want an experience, only they don't have the first idea how. Frank provides the 'experience.'"

"For which he gets paid."

"That's right. Hard worker, Frank."

Frank was not the only hard worker in the club. There were several young ladies accompanied by neither friends nor beaux. They made their way around the tables, speaking brightly to any man who seemed receptive to their company. Some of them only had to put in a minute's flirtation to earn their seat at the table. Flattery, artful posing, and a well-placed hand earned them a drink. After that, some of them took their gentlemen onto the dance floor; others simply went downstairs.

One man was very clearly not there to enjoy himself. He sat at the table in the corner, surrounded by men but speaking with none of them. He had a cheap hard shine about him. It was in the sleek otter look of his hair, the polish of his shoes, the brass of his buttons. He watched the laughing, dancing crowd through narrowed eyes, and I thought he rather despised them. At one point, a lady who had spun too much or drunk too much stumbled into his vicinity. She was immediately intercepted and returned to her partner.

"Who's that?" I asked Leo.

"That's the boss. Don't ask to be introduced."

"Why? Doesn't he like women?"

"Sure, the way the banker likes stock. Stop staring. It's not smart."

He was right. I knew he was right. And yet I found myself looking back at the infamous Chick Tricker. Over the course of the next few dances, I saw a few men approach. Some were allowed to sit down; others were blocked. Then I saw a familiar figure make

his way to the table. He held his hat tightly, crumpling the brim
in one hand as he scraped at his mustache with the fingers of the
other. To my surprise, he was allowed to approach. But not to sit.
Whatever Bill Danvers had to say would be whispered directly to
the one man who needed to hear it.

So this was what Bill Danvers did for a living. The newly
devout Christian worked for Chick Tricker. A lot of people did,
one way or another. Leo did. But there were others who robbed
drunks, guarded scab workers, poisoned horses, and shot people.
Mr. Tricker had many business interests and a lot of work to give. I
had the distinct feeling Bill Danvers did not wait tables.

I watched as he made his way to the other end of the club.
At first, he seemed in no hurry, but then he drew up short and
charged around several tables until he caught the arm of a very
young dark-haired girl. She had been on her way to a gentleman's
table and did not appreciate the delay. But when she pulled free,
Danvers grabbed her by the neck and shoved her into the darkness beyond the front tables. After a few agonizing minutes, she
emerged, a hand to her belly, her hair in disarray. No blacked eye
or bloodied lip, but there wouldn't be. Bill Danvers would have
struck where it didn't leave a mark.

Then I saw him come out of the shadows and with a jolt realized that he might see me. My heart began to pound; I lost the
rhythm of the music. Frantic, I began to look for a way off the
dance floor.

"What's wrong?"

"Could we . . . I think I feel a little faint . . . is there a place we
might get some air?"

A fraction of hesitation showed Leo knew perfectly well I
wasn't faint. Still, he said, "The lady wants air, she shall have air. I
have access to a very exclusive part of this establishment. If you'll
permit . . ."

He gestured upstairs, and I nodded. Taking my hand, he led me off the dance floor and away from the malignant rolling eye of Bill Danvers.

The exclusive room, it turned out, was simply the rooftop. But this was very much in fashion, I thought as I caught my breath after the climb. The best clubs in the city often extended the party to the roof, where their more honored guests could relax with a string quartet and free-flowing champagne. All the Acme Café had managed was some Chinese lanterns and an old divan. But at least there was no one else up here, and the night air was fresh with the warmth of early spring. Leo put a large brick in front of the door, and I gazed out at the city rooftops and thought of the painting of the young women washing their hair with the splendor of New York all around them. And that other drawing, the windows at night, men and watching . . .

Leo invited me to sit down, and I did, arranging myself as if we were in a parlor and not on the rooftop of a club with music sounding in the distance. The divan's upholstery had seen better days, but it had been protected from the elements by an oilcloth that lay nearby.

"Why would someone bring a divan up here?" I wondered.

"I don't know. Why would they?" Nudging my foot with his, he said, "You want to tell me why a girl who stood up to George Rutherford got scared off the dance floor by some lowlife?"

So he had noticed Danvers, too. "Does that man work here?"

"I've seen him around. Why? He hurt you?"

"Why would you ask that?"

"Because he's too ugly to be your husband. Tell me what happened."

I opened my mouth, but I found I wanted to be free of the refuge, Pickett's Puritans, and Sadie's murder for one evening. Let it all blow off in the wind and sail over the East River.

"Okay, you won't tell me. Let me ask you another question." He sidled closer on the divan. "Do you believe in love at first sight?"

"No."

"Good, me neither. Do you believe in kissing?"

"Its existence or as an ethical proposition?"

"The former—no, latter. Gosh, you're pretty."

We decided to answer the question a third way: an experiential assessment of its efficacy. Honestly, I hadn't been sure I did believe in kissing; the mashing of mouths could be an awkward way to begin. But Leo Hirschfeld made an excellent case for it.

Every age has its notions of sexual propriety. Only a decade later, people might have been appalled by my prudery. But many in my own era would have been shocked by my behavior. Certainly it went beyond—or beneath—my own expectations. The tango had achieved its purpose. Leo Hirschfeld was a good dancer—and a good kisser. And it is all too easy to recline on a divan. One has the idea that because it is not a bed, events that occur in beds cannot take place there. Maybe that's true of divans in parlors; divans on rooftops, not so.

At some point, I realized my faith in furniture was mistaken. I sat up, dislodging Mr. Hirschfeld. As I repinned my hair and did up buttons, Leo gasped, "Really?"

". . . really."

"You know *Romeo and Juliet? Wilt thou leave me so unsatisfied?*"

"*I do. I will. Henry IV.*"

He sat panting, a hand to his chest. Then he nodded, acknowledging either the aptness of the quote or the wisdom of the halt. "I . . . need to get back to my tables anyway. Don't talk to those Harvard boys. I'm not allowed to hit the customers."

I was about to reassure him that I had no interest in Harvard

boys when we heard the sounds of panic from the street far below. Going to the roof's edge, we looked down to see the Acme
disgorging its gorgeous clientele. People richly and rudely dressed
poured out the front doors, scrambled through side exits, and
clambered over the fence in the backyard. Policemen stood outside, herding the captured into wagons.

"It's a raid," said Leo. "Chick must not have paid the cops on
time. Come on."

Taking my hand, he led me to an adjacent rooftop. Then the
next, and the next, until we found one with a fire escape that
wasn't rusted out or falling away from the brick. Creeping down,
I kept my eyes averted from the windows, although Leo called
greetings and apologies to a few people who were startled to see
us passing by in the middle of the night. We reached the ladder,
and before I could drop, he took hold of my waist and helped me
down. In a moment, we were out on the street again with not a
policeman in sight.

It was after eleven as we headed up the Bowery, and Leo felt
free to put his arm around me and whisper mildly insulting things
about passersby.

"Does this mean you're out of a job?" I asked him.

"Not for long. See, you didn't know it, but tonight, you attended
a ball hosted by the Piano Tuners Benevolent Euchre and Whist
League. Not a dance hall, certainly not a club. That way if things
get rowdy—which they do every night—Chick can say, What
can I do? I rented out the room, things got out of hand. Those
piano tuners are crazy! Nobody believes it, but everyone gets
a cut to look the other way. The licenses alone cover a lot of
bribes. Someone probably upped the price, Chick got stubborn,
and they showed their muscle by calling out the cops. In a few
days, they'll work it out and we'll be serving the Holy Sisters of
St. Clare."

A woman lurched forward to observe that Leo looked man enough for two women. Leo waved her off, but I remembered Danvers and the girl clutching her stomach and asked, "What would a man who hurts women have to say to your boss?"

Putting his hands in his pockets, he shrugged. "Well, you saw at the club, there were . . ."

"Women, yes."

I thought of Sadie's Joe. I assumed she gave him whatever money she earned, a fairly common arrangement. But what if Joe had been giving some of that money to someone else? Lots of shiftless, angry young men found their way into the orbit of men like Chick Tricker, feeling it was worth it to hand over their girls' hard-earned money in exchange for the odd job of robbing a house or beating up people who won playing cards.

Of course, the young woman might object to her money being handed over to a man who'd had nothing to do with the earning of it. But that's what gut punches were for. And if you were Chick Tricker, there was no need to administer these things for yourself; you had men like Bill Danvers to do it.

And what would a Bill Danvers do if one of the women decided she wanted to stop working? Joe had been locked up, so he couldn't keep Sadie in line. Time to send in the experts. And if you were trying to lure a girl back to work, why not start with charm? Take her out. Flatter her. Listen to her complaints about her present situation, agree she could do better. Then if she still balked at coming back, you show her—and others—the penalty.

And what better way to keep an eye on former employees than to stand right outside their rooms, reminding them every day of the risk they were taking by refusing to earn? Had it been Bill Danvers's idea to pretend to be part of Mrs. Pickett's Purity Brigade, or did Chick Tricker come up with that scheme? I suspected Tricker; it seemed too clever for Bill. I thought of the other women still at the refuge. How many of them might have worked, even unknowingly, for Chick Tricker? Had Sadie's murder been both revenge and warning? Perhaps I would ask Carrie if Sadie had ever worked in one of Tricker's clubs.

And Clementine Pickett. Did she have any idea what sort of man stood beside her in her moral crusade?

As a train rumbled overhead, Leo charmed passersby—and perhaps me, a little—by singing, "*She could sew, oh, could she sew, but when she danced . . . I was entranced, my heart it pranced . . .*"

"Prancing heart?"

"You're right, prancing heart is no good."

Then he took my hand. "I like you, Miss Prescott."

I liked him and considered saying so. But it felt right to stay one step ahead of Mr. Hirschfeld, so I just smiled.

Which was enough for Leo, who sang cheerfully, "*There's something about a girl who smiles. . . .* No, wait." He looked up at the train, as if caught by the rhythm of its wheels. "*She smiled at me / On the IRT.*"

He swept me up, gathering speed. "*And now I see, she's the one for me. I was riding high, time flying by, then me oh, my . . .*"

He was about to kiss me again when I saw it. The crowd at the end of the block. People. Where they should not be. Police. And something on the street.

Someone.

Leaving Leo behind, I ran. The crowd parted, letting me see the body.

It was Carrie Biel.

9

It was like freezing to death, I thought. A sight this terrible. So extreme that you simply went numb. Everything slowed to an unnatural degree. It was hard to think, which was probably best. To think you would have to understand. I did not want to understand the horror that had been made of Carrie Biel. How could we do these things—twist one another, slash, destroy? Behind me, I sensed Leo, anxious, unsure what to do. The world felt cold. There was no kindness here, and to believe otherwise was willful delusion.

"You see? What he does to these young women? You must arrest him, arrest him now!"

Mrs. Pickett's voice cut through the fog; the sight of Carrie snapped into sharp focus. She lay sprawled as if dropped, arms out, legs askew. Death had come quickly, in a last spasm of life. Her face was a patchwork of blood and skin. The cuts were the same as Sadie's, random slashes to the forehead and arms. Although the arms, I thought, might have happened in a fight. Carrie would have fought. She would have known what was happening and she would have fought hard.

But I knew there was something I wasn't seeing. *Take away the blood, take away the cuts—they're blinding. See Carrie, imagine her fighting. Look to her arms, her hands.* These lay palm up, fingers slightly curled. The sleeves of her coat had ridden up, and I could see her wrists, pale and vulnerable. I could see . . . not the wrists, it wasn't just the wrists, it was . . .

Her bracelet. The rope bracelet was gone.

Dazed, I looked at the faces around me, found Officer Nolan. "Cover her, please," I said. "Don't let them see what he's made of her."

He directed the other policemen to surround the body, protecting it from public view. There was a moan of disappointment from the twenty or so onlookers—they had roused themselves for a show, and now it was denied. Mrs. Pickett said, "You cannot hide his crimes from our eye." Roused from her bed, she had thrown her coat over her nightgown. Her graying hair was in a plait, and there were mottled pouches under her eyes. The hand that held the neck of her coat closed was spotted and heavily veined. She looked old, I thought. Old and terrifyingly sincere.

"I'm well aware of that," said Officer Nolan wearily. "Do you know this woman, Miss Prescott?"

"Yes, her name is Carrie Biel." I raised my voice so Mrs. Pickett and her associates could hear Carrie's scandalous profession. "She works at Rutherford's department store." To Officer Nolan, I added, "It's my fault she was here."

"How's that?"

"She was a friend of Sadie Ellis. I told her she could come get her things if she wanted them."

"What time did you leave the refuge this evening, Miss Prescott?"

"Around seven."

"Then you wouldn't know if your uncle was at home this evening."

The shift in attack left me jolted. "That was certainly his plan. He was looking forward to seeing Carrie—"

"I'm sure he was." Mrs. Pickett stepped forward. "Why don't you ask your uncle what he and Carrie Biel were speaking of earlier tonight?"

"I imagine it was her new job."

"Oh, yes? On the street? Why did she tell him to get away from her? Why did she tell him to take his hands off her?"

There was a gasp from the crowd. To me, the scene was simply unimaginable; as I struggled to choose between the words "preposterous" and "outrageous," Mrs. Pickett shouted, "It was only a few blocks from here. I heard them. Open your eyes, Miss Prescott. See your uncle for what he truly is."

I disliked hating a woman this much. Her righteousness, her malice, her lack of human feeling parading under the banner of purpose. With more anger than I wanted, I said, "The police might also ask where Bill Danvers was tonight."

I turned back to the patrolman. "Danvers is an associate of Mrs. Pickett's. He is also an associate of Chick Tricker's. He was at the Acme Café tonight. I saw him there. But I didn't see him all evening; I'm afraid I did lose sight of him. Perhaps he left the club. Perhaps he came here. Did you know that, Mrs. Pickett? That the man you've stood beside for weeks works for a gangster, and when women don't do as they're told, he beats them up? Or worse."

I realized I was shouting, and I struggled for composure. Leo put his arm around me. Doing so brought him to the attention of the officer, who asked his name. Leo gave it, and I felt the bristle of animosity in the crowd, not unlike hearing the low growl of a dog before it snaps its teeth.

"What brings you to this neighborhood this evening, Mr. Hirschfeld?"

"I'm escorting the lady home, Officer."

"Night out?"

"At the Acme Café," Leo offered. "Only a hundred people saw me. It could be difficult to find witnesses."

Leo's sarcasm earned him a tight smile. "That's fine, I'll take Miss Prescott's word for it."

I had never been quite so aware of the Christian quality of my last name; Leo didn't miss it either. "Naturally."

"Excuse me?" said the officer.

"I only meant your faith in Miss Prescott's integrity is well founded." Leo was speaking just a little too fast—and it was not out of deference. He was making the officer work.

"You live in this area, Mr. Hirschfeld?"

"I do not."

"Work in this area?"

"I work all over the city, Officer." Now his hands were in his pockets and he rocked slightly on his feet.

"Including this area?"

Leo rattled off his days and places of employment, ending with the Acme on Wednesdays and Fridays. Then he added, "Today's Wednesday, by the way."

Ignoring him, Nolan asked, "You were with Mr. Hirschfeld all evening, Miss Prescott?"

"I was."

"The entire evening?"

The casual precision of the question told me I must be both truthful . . . and careful. Taking hold of Leo's arm, I said, "I don't recall losing sight of him."

It was not, I knew, strictly true. There had been times I was watching other people, unconcerned as to Leo's whereabouts. The café was half a mile away. Technically, a man could leave, commit murder, and return in little more than half an hour. But Leo had no reason in the world to kill Carrie. He could not change his clothes so quickly. And while my understanding of what people were capable of had changed in the last half hour, I just couldn't believe him capable of this kind of brutality.

Bill Danvers, on the other hand—I had no knowledge of his whereabouts after nine thirty. Or, for that matter, before then. He had come to the club to speak with Chick Tricker; what news was so important that it allowed him private conversation with such a powerful man? The murder of another wayward working girl connected to the refuge? I took in our surroundings. We were close to where Sadie had been found—once again not far from the refuge. I could see the vast windows of the warehouse, but we were not directly by the slaughterhouse. There was not the same quantity of blood on the pavement; Carrie had been moved. But not hidden. So near the empty warehouse, perhaps the killer did not think it necessary to hide a body in such a deserted area late at night.

There was an ugly rumble, and I was aware of bodies turning, energies rising. My uncle had arrived. He walked slowly, his eyes shifting to take in the gathering. Then they settled on the covered form of Carrie Biel and closed briefly.

"What?" called Mrs. Pickett. "Ashamed to look at your own work?"

Officer Nolan led my uncle a little way down the street. I followed. In a low voice, he said, "Another woman has been murdered. Your niece says she is Carrie Biel."

"Then I would think it is Carrie Biel."

"You knew her?"

My uncle broke away from the policeman, approached Carrie's body. His voice heavy, he said, "Yes, I knew her."

"Knew her?" shrieked Mrs. Pickett. "You assaulted her! Murdered her!"

The crowd surged forward, and the junior policeman put his arms out, holding Mrs. Pickett and her followers at bay. But only just.

"Mrs. Pickett says she saw you on the street this evening," said the officer.

"Well, then that is what she says."

"She says you spoke with Carrie Biel. That there was an argument."

"There was no argument." I thought I heard genuine confusion in my uncle's tone.

"But you spoke with Miss Biel. What about?"

There was a pause. The silence became a weight on my heart. *Tell him*, I thought. *For God's sake, just . . . speak.*

My uncle did speak. "Officer, I should like to take my niece inside."

I was startled to see my uncle reach for me, but Officer Nolan took his arm, saying, "I think it would be better if you came to the station."

"Why? Because I am less difficult than Mrs. Pickett?"

"Because you admit talking with the dead woman earlier. And we need a full accounting of your whereabouts."

Both men had raised their voices, speaking loudly enough to be heard by the crowd, which was demanding my uncle be questioned, arrested, and charged. "This poor woman deserves justice," shouted Mrs. Pickett. "You left him free to roam among us once before, and here you see the outcome. We will not stand it for a second time."

Officer Nolan took this challenge to his authority no better than he had taken my uncle's. Barking at his partner to keep order, he started to lead my uncle down the block. The crowd, feeling vindicated, roared its approval.

Leaving Leo, I hurried around to face Officer Nolan. "Where are you taking him?"

"Cells."

"On what grounds?"

"On the grounds that I'm tired of talking in the street at one in the morning and your uncle might be more willing to talk if we went inside."

"You can't put him in the cells. You've got no reason."

The patrolman nodded sharply at Carrie's covered form. "There's my reason. Come along, Reverend."

And so to jail we went.

★ ★ ★

At the precinct, my uncle was questioned for some time. Then I was allowed to see him. A tired officer held the door open to the room where he was being held. As he did, I realized my first memory of this country was a policeman's face.

Who is this? Do you know this man?

I could remember it clearly, even though I was only three. I was shown an envelope, the one that was pinned to my dress. A man wearing a blue coat pointed to writing in the corner. It was the swooping curly letters I did not yet know how to read. But the question felt important.

He said it again. "Who is this?"

I shook my head, my way of saying I couldn't read the words. Another man in a blue coat said, "Come on, Charlie, she can't read that."

The first man looked at the envelope. "The Reverend Tewin Prescott. Who is that, sweetheart?"

I knew my name was Prescott. Hope must have shown in my face, because the man asked, "A relative? Your father maybe?"

I shook my head immediately; my father was gone, but I had

the strong feeling that if I gave some other man that title, his place would be taken and he would not be able to come back. Names seemed to matter, though, so I said, "I'm Jane."

"Jane Prescott." I nodded, and the policeman looked to his partner. "So, he's family. Have you met this man, Jane? Do you know him?"

Now as I sit opposite my uncle, I remember that night. The questions.

Who is this man? Do I know him?

I said, "Tell me that Berthe will say you were at the refuge all evening. That after you spoke with Carrie, you went back inside and you stayed there."

"I cannot tell you that."

"Then you must tell the police where you went."

"I disagree."

I realized I was headed into an argument over the nature of coercion. So I switched to "If you do not tell the police where you were, and have someone else who can say that your account is true, it will be dangerous."

"And how will it be . . . dangerous?"

"Don't pretend you don't know what I mean."

A raised eyebrow told me I was close to the line of propriety. "I am not pretending. I am asking for your definition of the term."

"It will be dangerous," I said through gritted teeth, "because if you cannot prove you were not in the alley where poor Sadie was killed or that you were at the refuge when Carrie Biel was killed, people will think it possible that you killed them."

"That is an absurd thing to think," he said.

"Of course it is. But people think absurd things all the time. People think electricity is Satan's fire."

"And do you need me to point out that we cannot be ruled by absurdities?"

"It is not being *ruled* to give an account of your whereabouts."

"It is if I do not wish to do so."

"And the consequences of refusing? Can you put those off so easily, too?"

I waited, giving him a chance to think of the refuge without him. Of what it would mean to be charged, maybe convicted, in Sadie's and Carrie's murders. He was not a man to fuss over physical comforts. But he was not young, and it was cold and damp in the jail. The food was no doubt poor. And the company . . . rough.

"Will you be safe here?" I asked.

Exhausted, he said, "It's a jail, Jane."

I gazed at him; he was not the only one to be exhausted. I felt as if my blood had turned to lead.

On a sigh, I said, "Why won't you let me help you?"

"There's no need. They can't hold me here. They've no proof of anything. This is a show to get Mrs. Pickett and her followers off the street."

"And if they want to keep them off the street, does that mean they keep you here?"

"The patrolman acted hastily. He was tired. He'll realize it in the morning and let me go."

"And if he doesn't realize it? Did you see Carrie this evening, uncle?"

"Yes. She came by and collected Miss Ellis's things. I congratulated her on her job, and she left."

"What time did she come?"

"A little after nine, I think."

I had seen Bill Danvers before nine. Certainly enough time for him to kill Carrie and get back to the club.

"And . . . the argument?" I said carefully.

"I remember now, Berthe said she should walk quickly and

avoid trouble. Miss Biel said something to the effect that she'd
already encountered someone troublesome, but she got rid of him
easily enough."

My uncle was not usually so adept at remembering other
people's conversations. But if he was right, Mrs. Pickett had not
overheard Carrie fighting with her killer. At least . . . not when he
killed her. Of course, Bill Danvers could have waited until she
left the refuge.

"If nothing else, Uncle, don't you care about who murdered
Sadie and Carrie?"

"Of course I do," he said sharply.

"Well, if the police and the mob decide they have their man,
how hard do you think they'll be looking for the actual killer?"

"That is out of my hands."

I opened my mouth to argue, to press my uncle to give me
permission to do something. Then I realized he would never do
that.

And I didn't need him to.

I stood. "Stay here, then. Go home if they release you. But
whether you like it or not, I am not going to let you stand accused
of something you didn't do. You often tell me if behavior pleases
or offends you—well, your presence here offends me. That the
man who killed Sadie and Carrie is still free offends me. And if
thy right eye offend thee. . . . You're a clergyman, you know the
rest. Good night, Uncle. I hope you can get some sleep."

★ ★ ★

As I was escorted out of the jail, I wondered what time it was.
Much of the city was asleep, but it was a busy time at police
headquarters, with officers coming off their shifts exhausted and
hollow-eyed as enraged drunks and shouting women were being hustled in. It was not a long walk back to the refuge, but it

wouldn't be a pleasant one. I was wondering if I could call Berthe to come and meet me when I heard Officer Nolan say, "Miss Prescott? Do you have someone to take you home?"

The collar of his uniform was unbuttoned, his gray hair mussed; they kept cots downstairs for patrolmen working the late shift, and I guessed he had been about to retire for the night. I felt a pang of sympathy, then remembered my uncle was now lying on a cot behind bars.

"I'll be fine, Officer. I imagine the streets are crowded, even at this hour."

Buttoning his collar, he called, "Frank? Sign me out, I'm taking the young lady home."

"You don't have to—"

"I don't want you to be the third woman killed on my watch, Miss Prescott."

As I had predicted, the streets were still bustling even at this time of night, and the walk to the refuge from the new police headquarters at Centre Street was a path crowded with people, horses, and their leavings. I held my skirts up and saw that Officer Nolan kept a firm hand on his nightstick. He was not a young man. I wondered if mediocrity or malice from higher up had kept him walking a beat all these years.

"You wouldn't do this if you thought my uncle was guilty," I pointed out. "You'd think the killer was behind bars and all was right with the world."

"Still plenty of trouble on the streets," he said, refusing to be drawn.

"How much do you know about Chick Tricker, Officer Nolan?"

He glanced at me. "Not as much as I'd like. The man's got his friends." From the careful way he spoke, I understood those friends to be his fellow officers.

"But you know he runs several brothels and clubs."

"Did either of the women who were killed work for him?"

"I don't know. But they worked in this neighborhood, so it's not impossible he was taking money from them. Have you ever heard anything about Bill Danvers?"

"The man you mentioned earlier. Can't say that I have."

"He works for Chick Tricker. Tonight at the Acme, I saw him assault a woman."

"You've got no business being in a place like that."

My presence anywhere was hardly the point. But I wanted to stay on Bill Danvers.

"It's in Chick Tricker's interest that the refuge close. If women have nowhere safe to go, they'll be more frightened and more docile. Danvers works for him, even as he pretends to be an ally of Mrs. Pickett's. Isn't that odd behavior?"

"Odd behavior." Officer Nolan gestured to two men across the street, drunkenly circling each other with broken bottles; every so often, one lunged at the other and stumbled.

"I think it's Danvers's job to keep the women in line. Why else would he stand on the street all day with the likes of Clementine Pickett, unless Chick Tricker was paying him to? Doesn't it stand to reason that Sadie and Carrie were killed as a warning: You can quit, but we will find you?"

"Did either woman know Mr. Danvers?"

"Sadie did, but not Carrie."

"Then why didn't anybody hear screams tonight?"

"It's the Lower East Side. People ignore screaming all the time."

"They ignore brawls, couples fighting. Screams for help, screams of terror—that they usually remember. I talked to a lot of people in the area. No one heard a thing. Your man doesn't sound like the type to inspire trust."

I considered. "Maybe he took them somewhere. It looked to

me like Carrie had been moved. There wasn't nearly as much blood as there was with Sadie."

"But Sadie was killed where we found her. And I think it was by someone she thought she had no reason to fear."

"Officer Nolan, my uncle is not young. Sadie and Carrie were healthy young women, not easily overpowered."

"They wouldn't necessarily have to be overpowered, not if approached by a man they trusted. We think . . ."

He hesitated, not wanting to share grisly details with a young woman, then realized the young woman had already seen everything he had seen.

"We think he cut the throats first," he said shortly. "Everything else came afterward."

I said a quiet prayer of thanks that neither woman had suffered too much. But it made me think of another point in my uncle's favor.

"The man who killed them, he would have had blood all over him, wouldn't he?"

"Nearby, you've got tanneries, slaughterhouses, butcher shops. How many times have you passed a man with blood down his front and not thought twice, Miss Prescott?"

"But you saw my uncle's clothes were perfectly clean the night Sadie was killed."

"I also saw he had a bag with him. Not so hard to bring a change of clothes, then dispose of the rest."

"And he changed in the middle of the Bowery with not a single witness?"

"Plenty of dark, secret spots in the city, Miss Prescott. Unfortunately for Carrie Biel and Sadie Ellis."

I couldn't tell if he meant to have an answer for every objection I raised as a matter of professional pride or whether he truly believed my uncle was guilty.

"And are you looking for Sadie's stocking and Carrie's brace-let?"

He looked wary. "Why do you ask?"

"Carrie Biel had a rope bracelet. It was left her by her father, and she never took it off. I saw her with it the day she died, but it was gone when we found her body. It's not the sort of thing any-one would have stolen; it had no value. And surely you noticed one of Sadie's stockings was missing."

He shook his head.

"Well, it was. It was black, darned in two places. Just the sort of thing Danvers would show Chick Tricker to prove he'd done the job."

We were at the refuge. Standing by the front steps, I thought it had grown much colder.

"The day after Sadie was killed, someone called the refuge. He said he knew I was—'coming after him' was the way he put it. And that if I came after him, he'd come after me. Earlier that day, I accused Bill Danvers of talking to Sadie. I think he took it that I was accusing him of her murder."

"Were you?"

"I wasn't then. I am now."

His shoulders slumped. I was making more work for him—in his eyes, for nothing—and I wondered: Did he really care if Sadie and Carrie's killer was caught?

I said, "You must get tired."

"In what way?"

"You catch one criminal, there's always another. Or he gets out. When does Joe McInerny get out?" I knew I sounded child-ish and discouraging. But I felt childish. And discouraged. And scared.

"I like to think of it as one less," he said, his tone apologetic.

"I'm sorry, I must sound brattish and ungrateful. But I can't help feeling somehow the killer's already gotten away with it. Just by doing it. Carrie and Sadie, they can't ever get their . . . selves back. Their faces, they . . . I'm not making any sense. I just feel that's why he did it."

"What do you mean?"

"To make them look like he wanted. Turn them into things. Good night, Officer. Thank you again. I hope I will see my uncle back here tomorrow?" Today, I thought. It was already today.

"I hope so, too, Miss Prescott. You let us handle this."

"He's the only family I have in the world, Officer Nolan. I don't think I can do that."

"Well, there's not much you can do."

Gentle. Patronizing. I smiled politely. But he was wrong. There was something I could do.

I could find Otelia Brooks.

10

I had decided to find Otelia Brooks. But I did not have the first idea of how. One woman in a city of five million. A woman known to only one other person I knew, and he refused to help me. Not to mention, a woman who would probably rather not be found.

She would not have stayed on the Lower East Side, I felt sure of that. Having been attacked, she would probably want to go to a neighborhood where she would not be conspicuous. In the neighborhood where I worked, Otelia Brooks would have been conspicuous. Ten years ago, she might have found work in service; now the fashion was for immigrants—the paler, the more preferred. And while the Tenderloin was home to poor people of all colors, I could not quite see her there. She had too many skills, too large a sense of purpose—her path.

Where had that path taken her?

I had to discount the possibility that she had returned to Mississippi. The trip would have required money, and she had said she brought everything she cared about when she came north. I didn't remember her as a woman who went back, only forward. She had named the cotillion for Southern Baptists, but that may or may not have been her personal faith. Looking in the telephone directory, I found nothing under Brooks.

There were two neighborhoods where I could imagine a skilled seamstress and hairdresser might have set up shop: San Juan Hill in the low Sixties and the top of the Tenderloin in the low Fifties, where poverty was giving way to more middle-class families. I wandered San Juan Hill for a pointless hour—unnerving several people by gazing too long or peeking in salon windows. Then I made my way down to Fifty-Third Street between Sixth and Seventh Avenues, a stretch known as Black Bohemia, where famous musicians, actors, dancers, and writers gathered. I had a perfectly good reason for going; it made sense that Otelia Brooks might have found work as a dresser in a theater. I also had a selfish reason for going. I wanted to see the Marshall Hotel.

Located in two brownstones at 127 and 129 West Fifty-Third, the Marshall Hotel was the gathering place for the fashionable and theatrical who were not allowed in the city's white establishments. Both a hotel and a club, it was said to have the best live shows in the city. Bert Williams and George Walker had played there. The bandleader James Reese Europe stayed there when he was in town. So did the Johnson Brothers. It wasn't *inconceivable*, I thought, that one of them might take a stroll just as I was passing by.

But as I loitered outside, the only man to join me was a man carrying a bucket of water and a broom. Setting the bucket down, he set to sweeping away the refuse of last night's revelers. He did the work with minimal fuss, and I imagined this was just one of a hundred jobs he did at the hotel.

After a moment, I got up the nerve to say, "Excuse me, may I ask you a question?"

"No, I don't know Mr. Williams, and I'll be sure to tell Mrs. Castle you think she's wonderful."

"I'm so sorry. I'm actually looking for a woman called Otelia Brooks."

"Haven't heard of her. Dancer?"

"Maybe a dresser. Hairstylist?"

He shook his head with a smile, experienced in disappointing people. "And I know most people who work around here."

"I'm sure. Thank you anyway."

"My pleasure."

Before leaving I gazed up at the building, imagining what it would be like to listen to Europe's band or see the Castles dance.

Then I heard, "You better get in quick if you want to see it. They're trying to close us down."

"Why?" Many of the city's clubs were vermin-infested firetraps, but not the Marshall. Florenz Ziegfeld went there, for heaven's sake.

"Apparently, we're 'disorderly.'"

Thinking of the many saloons and clubs on the Lower East Side for whom "disorderly" would be high praise, I said, "I'm sure they'll never close it down."

"Well, as long as you're sure."

I turned to go, then impulsively turned back. "You've never met Mr. Joplin, have you?"

"A few times. I hear he's working on an opera."

"Opera?"

"That seems to be most people's reaction. Have a good day, miss."

Armed with the dispiriting awareness that I had wasted time— and that Scott Joplin had turned to opera—I walked to the trolley stop. How did people find people when they could not afford private detectives? I didn't know.

But, I realized, I did know someone who might. And his offices were only a mile away.

When I presented myself at the *Herald*, the gentleman at the front desk said, "Oh, no. I remember you. I'm under orders: you don't get upstairs."

For a moment I was dumbfounded. Then I remembered I had been guilty of a lapse in decorum the last time I was here.

"I promise you, I only want to place an advertisement."

The gentleman gestured to a security guard, who started walking toward me with purpose. Pointing to the phone, I said, "Will you please call Michael Behan and tell him I'm here? Miss Jane Prescott." I put my hands up, said to the security guard, "I'll stay right here."

Given a choice between lethargy and exertion, the guard found the former more attractive and sank back into his chair. A few minutes later, Michael Behan came trotting down the stairs. "Good work, Jim, keeping this madwoman out. I'll show her the door."

I protested as he took my arm, but under his breath, he said, "Don't."

When we were outside, he said, "Harry Knowles took a tumble last night after doing a lengthy interview in Murphy's Saloon. Knocked out two teeth. The *Herald* accepts a certain level of inebriation in its staff, but he's pushing it. So he's implying it happened when you took after him with the rolled newspaper, calling you a menace and a danger to the free press."

"Does that mean I can knock out two more teeth?"

"It does not. Now, what's this about an ad?"

"I need to find a woman named Otelia Brooks."

When I had explained who she was and why I wanted to find her, Behan asked, "And you want to place an ad? Saying what?"

Between dancing and my uncle's arrest, I had had very little sleep and was not thinking clearly. Wanted: One Otelia Brooks. Or anyone with knowledge of her whereabouts. No, it wasn't likely to get much of a response.

This was also Michael Behan's opinion, although he put it gently. Then he said, "Anyway, the *Herald*'s probably not the paper they read."

"What do you mean?"

"Well, just like *Il Progresso* or *Der Amerikaner,* they've got their own papers."

There was something odd about his explanation; *Il Progresso* or *Der Amerikaner* existed for readers who didn't speak English. Otelia Brooks spoke English perfectly well. But then so did the Irish, most of the time, and they had their own papers, too.

"What are their papers?"

"There's one I remember takes ads. Called . . ." He snapped his fingers. ". . . Street name, called it after the place he lives. *Amsterdam News.*"

"All right. Thank you."

That was the end of it, I knew. But I didn't want it to be the end. I wanted to sit down—fall down, actually—on a bench in wretched Herald Square and talk until breath ran out. I wanted to tell Michael Behan about Carrie, how it felt to see her last night. Wanted to ask all the questions I hadn't dared ask myself: What was my uncle hiding? How could Sadie's and Carrie's lives be over, just when they were starting fresh? What kind of animal did this to women?

He broke into my thoughts to say, "I was sorry to hear about the young woman who got killed last night."

I stared at him. "How did you know about that?"

He pulled a newspaper out of his coat pocket. "Early edition."

Taking it, I read:

SECOND WOMAN FOUND SLAIN OUTSIDE REFUGE
REVEREND CALLED IN FOR QUESTIONING
BY POLICE

In the early hours, a scream rang out on the East Side
as the body of a second young woman was discovered
outside the Gorman Refuge. The victim, Carrie Biel,
was a resident of the refuge.

Was, I thought. Not had been. Convenient grammatical error.

Like the previous victim, Miss Biel had been killed
with a slash to the throat. Her face was hideously dis-
figured . . .

I read just enough to know that Harry Knowles had either
seen poor Carrie himself or spoken to someone who had.

Witnesses report seeing Miss Biel in the company of the
Reverend Tewin Prescott earlier that evening. The two
were heard arguing on the street, with Miss Biel repeatedly telling the Reverend Prescott to stop molesting her.
One resident overheard the dead woman say, "Take your
hands off me."
    Feeling in the neighborhood is running high. In an
effort to maintain calm, the authorities brought the con-
troversial clergyman in for questioning late last night.

I crumpled up the paper and threw it on the ground.
"I'm sorry," said Behan.
I thought to say, *You tell Harry Knowles that if he comes within
a mile of me, it won't be just teeth he'll lose.* But threats weren't

going to stop these articles or get my uncle out of jail, and neither
was lolling around on park benches with Michael Behan.

"*Amsterdam News.*"

"*Amsterdam News,*" he confirmed. "Just moved their offices to
Harlem."

★ ★ ★

When my first employer, Mrs. Armslow, became bedridden, her
relatives, hopeful of postmortem bounty, would come to visit her.
One of the chief topics of conversation was the history of their celebrated family, especially its follies. The story of Walter Armslow
was a favorite, often reducing the gathering to helpless laughter
and gasps of "But the cows!" A gentleman farmer by aspiration,
Walter had bought property by the Harlem River and started a
dairy farm. He had the novel approach of choosing livestock by
attractiveness rather than ability to give milk, and his farm pros-
pered accordingly. The cows were charming to look at and came
in handy whenever Walter—a history buff—decided to reenact
Washington's victory and needed docile Redcoats to chase. The
story of Walter charging a herd of bovine British soldiers across
the plains of Harlem, waving a saber and shouting, "For liberty!"
was a cherished family memory, even for those who had never
witnessed it. Sadly, the crash of 1873 had acted on the farm much
as the returning Redcoats had acted on Harlem, demolishing it
entirely. Which, as the Armslows pointed out, was just as well
because once the IRT extended its line, Italians had come, and
Jews—"taking advantage of misfortune the way they always do"—
and Walter certainly could not have stayed through that. Opera
House by Oscar Hammerstein or no Opera House.

But if the neighborhood's boom-and-bust fortunes were woe
to the Armslows, they were an opportunity to Philip Payton Jr.,

who saw desolate landlords unable to lure tenants and so founded the Afro-American Realty Company. Attracted by the chance to live in homes with marble fireplaces and actual closets, people began moving uptown. White newspapers had sorrowfully predicted that Mr. Payton's success would mean the downfall of the neighborhood. Some stores closed rather than serve the new arrivals. John G. Taylor, who had made his fortune in saloons, had launched a Save Your Property campaign, demanding that the elevated be resegregated and that a fence should be built along 136th Street to keep out the "colored invasion." But it hadn't worked, and so far as I could see, Harlem was thriving. As I came off the train, I was surrounded by voices—Jewish, Italian, Spanish, West Indian, and southern. Some familiar, some new, and for a moment I stood, just listening.

It was still a place where mansions on the west butted up against the coal-dust-covered shacks on the east. But attractive six-story apartment buildings now lined pleasingly wide boulevards, their window boxes filled with geranium and tomato plants. Streetcars and horse-drawn carriages sped down to the Riverside Drive Viaduct. In 1911, the Polo Grounds—where no polo had ever been played to my knowledge—had burned down. But they had been rebuilt in time for the Giants to win the pennant, as they always seemed to. Businesses flourished along 135th Street, where signs for Italian tailors and kosher butchers vied with newer dress shops and cafés. Nickelodeons crowded 125th Street. On a single street corner, I saw three men standing on soapboxes, surrounded by crowds. One was talking about slavery, another socialism, the third the French Revolution. As they spoke, other men handed out literature.

When the people moved uptown, their chroniclers followed. As Michael Behan had said, the majority of city newspapers dutifully recorded the births, weddings, and deaths of many of its citizens. But black lives were seldom seen on their pages. *The New York Times* did note the passing of Edward Sharps, negro, who claimed to be 123 years old. The outrages in the South sometimes found their way into the news. The speeches of Booker T. Washington were duly noted. But when Aida Walker, the Queen of the Cakewalk, performed her celebrated interpretation of Salome or sixteen-year-old R. W. Overton of Stuyvesant High School won the long-distance record for model aeroplanes in greater New York—greater New York took no notice.

So newspapers like the *New York Age* and the *Amsterdam News* stepped in, beginning life as six sheets of loose paper. The *News's* office was on 135th Street, just off Fifth Avenue in a humble storefront. The large glass window suggested its former life had been a grocery. There was a counter in the front, and as I walked in, I could see desks and hear typewriters from the back. A young man in a high collar and spectacles greeted me.

"Excuse me, I'd like to place a personal ad."

"I see. Would this be for employment?"

That story hadn't occurred to me; could I pretend to be looking for a job, but only with a woman who matched Otelia's exact description?

Puzzled by my silence, he prompted, "Are you in need of a cook? A housemaid?"

"Oh, no, I am a maid."

"Oh." Now he was simply waiting for me to make sense. Any kind of sense.

"I'm looking for a woman I used to know."

"And what is her name?"

"I knew her as Otelia Brooks. It was several years ago; she may have married by now . . ." He wrote the name on a pad of paper. As he did, I noticed a young woman lingering at the doorway from the back.

"Any other description?" asked the gentleman.

"She had a scar, but I suppose you don't want to put that in the ad." I struggled to describe the impressive person I had known in a few lines. "She was very skilled with hair. And hats. She liked to make hats. That was more of a hobby, though. She was an excellent seamstress."

"Excuse me." The woman stepped up to the counter. She was of medium height with an elegant little head; her hair rose in an enviable pompadour, three inches high, but was tight at the sides and back, a style I had never seen before. She wore simple gold studs, a high-necked white blouse, and a dark suit. The no-nonsense set of her mouth suggested purpose. If she had interrupted, I thought with a twinge of hope, she had a reason.

"Did you say you're looking for Otelia Brooks?"

"I am helping this lady, Miss Dodson." From his tone, I guessed that he was used to being interrupted by the young woman. And he did not care for it.

"I can't see that you are, Mr. Ransom." To me, she said, "The woman you're looking for, she does hair?"

"She was very good at it. I don't know that she—"

"And you say she makes hats?"

"She did. Do you know her?"

"She does not know her," opined Mr. Ransom, sensing lost ad revenue.

"But I know *of* her." Miss Dodson leaned on the counter, her eyes bright. "And I can take you right to her."

"Oh, that would be—"

"There's a condition."

"I haven't seen Miss Brooks in many years. I can't agree to conditions on her behalf."

"Can you agree on your own behalf to introduce me?"

"That I can do." I could at least try, I thought.

"Very well, then. I'll get my coat."

Exasperated, Mr. Ransom called after her, "Miss Dodson, you cannot leave the office whenever you feel like it."

Returning with her coat, she said, "I'm a reporter, Mr. Ransom. I do what the story requires. Maybe the name Otelia Brooks doesn't mean anything to you, but if you were a woman, you'd know better. Come along, Miss . . ."

"Prescott, Jane Prescott."

Before leaving, I bought several copies of the paper to make up for the ad I had not taken. I had the feeling Mr. Ransom had had better days.

Ella Dodson was a small, trim person, and she weaved in and around the midday crowd with speed. Without looking back, she said, "How do you know Miss Brooks?"

That was not something I was prepared to share, and I said so, assuring Miss Dodson that I remembered the woman with great admiration and wished only to renew our acquaintance.

"How do *you* know Miss Brooks? Are you also from the South?"

"No, New York," said Miss Dodson. "And every woman in this neighborhood knows Miss Brooks. Well, they've heard of her. Mostly rumors." She pulled up short to let traffic pass, then started moving again. "I hope to give them the truth, with your assistance, Miss Prescott."

Uneasy, I said, "What sort of rumors?"

"About the hats."

"Hats?"

The first hat, she said, had appeared at the Mercy Street Baptist Church four years ago. Navy blue straw, twisted into a fantastical shape, crowned with a halo of feathers. It had been worn by a Miss Adella Terrell.

"A lady of means?"

"Not at all," said Ella Dodson. "Miss Terrell played the piano at the church. She knew every hymn ever written, but her poor hands were getting a little stiff. She lived with her brother and his wife, and they made her sleep on the sofa, because she didn't have a penny of her own. So when she turned up in that hat, everyone had to know, where did she get it? But she said the person who gave it to her said it was a gift and wanted it kept between them. Then six months later, another hat turned up, this time worn by Miss Mary Ann Deets, who had lost her fiancé to pneumonia and been melancholy ever since. And she got married the very next year."

"Because of the hat," I said skeptically.

"Well, if you'd seen Miss Deets, you'd know that hat didn't hurt. They also say that when she was dying, Mrs. Victoria Earle Matthews of the White Rose Mission got a hat. Now, the White Rose helps women from the South find their way in the city, making sure they don't get mixed up with people who just want to put them on the street. It's a settlement where they teach domestic skills, cooking, laundry."

"It sounds familiar," I said.

"And you just said Miss Brooks is from the South . . ." Had I? Yes, I had when I said "also from the South." Miss Dodson was indeed a reporter. "*And* she worships at Mercy Street Baptist. And Miss Deets's mother knows her."

"Really."

"Really indeed, Miss Prescott. Oh—here we are."

We stood in front of a handsome brownstone building. "Is this where she lives?" I asked.

"I couldn't say. But it's where she works."

Before we went up the stairs to the door, Miss Dodson checked her hair in a small compact mirror and smoothed her jacket, looking unsure for the first time since I had met her. Then, recovering, she hurried up the steps and rang the bell.

As we waited, I said, "If you know where she works, why haven't you interviewed her already?"

"Miss Brooks doesn't talk to just anybody. In fact, Miss Brooks doesn't talk to most people. Some think there is no Miss Brooks, it's just a fancy name they put on the store. Two months ago, I spent good money having my scalp treated. I still couldn't get in to see her. I'm hoping you're my way in."

We entered what would have been the large parlor room. But instead of curtains and lamps, there were small tables, chairs, and basins of water filled from an overhead tap. Smaller sections were created by a series of white curtains that could be pulled around the room to create privacy. If I craned my head, I could see stylists dressed in crisp white uniforms tending to customers draped in capes to keep their clothes safe.

It was a very homey atmosphere. Two women waiting to be served sat companionably on an emerald-green love seat. Towels were kept in a butler's desk that might once have held dining silver and linens. A glass case held products for sale, all the creation of a Madam Walker. Glossine, vegetable shampoo, scalp ointment, hair grower, and something called Tetter Salve. Framed pictures on the wall showed beautifully coiffed, satisfied customers. But I also caught sight of one or two images of families standing on dusty porches in front of farmhouses, the women wearing cotton dresses that hinted at the heat of the South.

Several conversations were taking place at once. A woman having her hair washed was gaily recounting her neighbor's latest embarrassment with her children. Another woman was commiserating with her hairdresser about the general loathsomeness of men; several women were emphatically agreeing that a dress worn by a mutual friend was so ugly, they no longer feared hell.

But heads turned as we entered, and what had been a lively, talkative place went quiet. Feeling conspicuous, I looked to Miss Dodson to lead the way. Which she did, approaching a young woman at a writing desk that served as the reception area.

"Pardon me," she said. "We're here to see Miss Otelia."

The young woman gazed at her as if she had asked to see President Wilson. All very well to ask, but . . . be reasonable.

"Miss Otelia only sees clients by appointment," she explained.

I stepped forward. "Perhaps you would tell her that Miss Jane Prescott is here and would like to see her."

"And Miss Ella Dodson," said Miss Dodson.

The young woman got up and went to the back of the salon. A few minutes later, she came back and announced that we might go into the office. Taking a deep breath, I walked the length of the apartment and into a room where a woman sat at a desk. Beside her, a worktable.

Filled with hats.

11

It was her.

I knew from the scar. And the eyes, which fixed on me for a long moment before she smiled and said, "Little Miss Jane Prescott. Well, let me look."

Without thinking, I turned. She nodded approvingly and said, "I see you wash your neck now."

She had put on a little weight, which suited her. Her face was fuller, the skin radiant and without age. The eyes were bright and clear. The scar had thinned and faded over time, but it did drag down the corner of one eye. She was dressed in a suit of maroon velvet with black braid. She looked every inch the prosperous businesswoman.

She told the young woman to bring us some tea. I said, "I still have the hat you made me."

"*You* have a hat?" Miss Dodson said, offended that I had not shared that information with her.

Otelia Brooks looked pointedly at Miss Dodson. Who held out

her hand and said, "Miss Ella Dodson of the *Amsterdam News*. It's a genuine pleasure to meet you, Miss Brooks."

Otelia Brooks's expression indicated she did not share that pleasure. "What do you do for the *News*, Miss Dodson?"

"I'm a reporter."

"Then you may take your tea outside, Miss Dodson. This is a social call."

"I was hoping you might—"

Otelia Brooks blinked once. Then waited. Her gaze was too strong, even for the intrepid Miss Dodson, who retreated with a sighed "Yes, ma'am."

When she was gone, Miss Brooks indicated I should sit on the couch and arranged herself at her desk. Once we were settled, the warmth returned and she said, "You look *well*."

"You look far better than well." I took in the worktable. "And you're still making hats."

"I am." Her voice softened as a mother's might when looking at her children. On the table there was a block of wood the size of a woman's head, sheaves of dry straw, and a copper kettle with a long spout. Catching my gaze, Otelia explained, "You lay the straw on the block, then you steam it. That way it's soft and you can shape it how you like. Once it dries, you see what you have."

What she had at the moment was like nothing I had seen on any woman's head, rich or poor. Hats in various stages of creation crowded the table. My eye was drawn to one at the end, a black straw, adorned with an expansive bow in orange and gold. Somehow, she had made a wave of water out of the bow; it was not stiff and bunched in the middle but flowed in and around itself, a vision of movement rather than a punctuation of decorum. Out of habit, I assessed it for Louise. It was hard to imagine such a hat in the drawing room of Mrs. Goelet or on the lawn of Mrs. Kluge, although I suspected that the woman who wore it well would be the subject of envious talk for days. "That's astonishing."

"Worthy of the lady who will wear it. Hair pays my bills, and I give thanks for Madam Walker's treatments every day. But the hats . . ."

"I think you called them your path."

"That's right, I did." Dropping her hands into her lap, she signaled that talk of the past was over for now. "And tell me, where's your path taken you? I always thought you might be a teacher."

"I never had the education for that. I work as a lady's maid for Mrs. William Tyler."

"And how is the reverend?"

"He's—" The well-reasoned speech I had planned fell apart in the bright light of Otelia Brooks's success. Maddeningly, my uncle had been right. I couldn't drag this woman into the ugliness of Sadie's and Carrie's murders.

"He's not ill, is he?"

"No. I don't know if you read the newspapers—"

"I do not. I take no interest in other people's business, and I ask that they take no interest in mine."

This was reasonable enough, and for a moment I considered saying I was sorry to have troubled her. But my uncle was still in jail, and Otelia Brooks still the only person I could think of who might have seen Sadie and Carrie's murderer. And so I began. Badly. I stumbled, paused, tripped over words, and finally mumbled, "They were both—"

I drew my finger down my own cheek.

Otelia Brooks had withdrawn. She sat tightly in her chair, head turned, chin resting on her fingers. She had murmured "Oh, Lord," when I told her of Sadie's death, but after that, she had gone silent.

"I'm so sorry to bring this to you," I said.

She absolved me with a slight shake of the head; well, absolved me or attempted to end the discussion. Resettling herself in her seat, she faced me. At the same time, she reached for a piece of straw from the worktable. For a moment she toyed with it, then set it down with a resolute sigh.

"The police think my uncle . . . he knew both of them . . ."

"The police think the reverend did it?"

Relieved by the astonishment in her voice, I nodded. "A woman in the neighborhood says she heard him arguing with Carrie Biel that night. I don't like to call anyone a liar, but this woman has been campaigning for the removal of the refuge, and she's not entirely rational on the subject."

"And she thinks if your uncle is arrested, the refuge is done."

"I think she sincerely believes him to be guilty. Of something. And she's good at working on other people's fears. She's gathered others to stand outside the building and pray. It was bad enough before, but now that they think he's a murderer—"

"It's a mob," she said softly.

We sat silent for a long time. Then I said, "May I ask you something else?"

She nodded.

"Did you ever know a man named Chick Tricker?" She shook her head. "Back then, did you . . . have protection from anyone?"

The past was not a place she wished to go, and I saw her make a conscious decision to venture back there. It was not easy.

Finally, she said, "No. I used to wonder if I had wandered onto some gang's territory and they sent somebody to run me off."

That sounded like work Bill Danvers might do. I felt a prickle of hope. "Can you remember anything of what the man who attacked you looked like?"

Otelia Brooks gazed at her worktable. "I was not in my right mind at the time. I didn't want to see the world straight, and I took things to make sure I didn't. So I can't remember much of how he looked. Things come to me in flashes. But I don't let it stay in my mind for long. He didn't smell, clothes weren't ragged. I remember thinking I'd gotten lucky, that I wouldn't have stink on me afterward."

"Was he dark-haired? Blond?"

She shook her head. "The things I remember of him are feelings of what he did. I think he was tall. I remember him leaning on me, not being able to breathe. And he pulled my hair, hard. Like it was a leash on a dog."

Remembering the burst of pain when Danvers pulled my hair, I said, "Was he thin? Were his teeth crooked?"

"That's really all I can give you, Miss Jane. Unless you want me to start making things up."

"But it wasn't my uncle. You would be able to say that much."

"Say that much to who?"

"The police."

Now it was her turn to laugh. "Miss Jane, me telling the police anything is not going to help your uncle."

"But if you said . . ."

"What? That a man cut me a decade ago, but not this man? At any rate, you can't know it's the same person. That was a long time ago."

I was about to quote what she said to me about the attack, then realized that would be cruel. "The way you described it, I think with these women, it was the same."

"You don't know that."

"I do. I saw them and I know it." My hand bunched in frustration. I knew I should stop, but I had placed too much hope in Otelia Brooks to do that. "Would you at least say it wasn't my uncle? Could you tell the police that he was kind? It will give them a different picture. I'm his niece; they won't believe me."

"Well, I am not his niece." She stood, and I felt a tremor of anger from her. "And that is not a time in my life I wish to think about. Or be known for in any way."

I glanced at the door, thinking of the thriving business that lay beyond. "No, of course not. That was stupid of me. But we can come up with a different story of how you knew my uncle."

"Those other women, the ones who were murdered? They came to the refuge for one reason. The police aren't going to believe any different of me."

"Please." I could offer nothing but this one stupid word, and so I said it again. "Please."

She sat back down. "You were a quick little girl, and you've grown into an intelligent woman. But you're scared and you're trying to find something to hold on to, something that won't let you and your uncle get swept away for no good reason. I'd like to be that for you, but I can't."

"But—"

"If I thought me going to the police would do any good, I'd consider it, I truly would." She took my hands, held them tight as if to impress her words on my flesh. "But it wouldn't. They're not going to listen to me. Believe me. I've been through this before."

There was something in the intensity with which she spoke that prompted me to say, "You never told me what happened to your husband."

"That's right, I didn't."

"Will you now? I don't know anything about him, and I would like to. Even . . . just his name?"

She was silent a long time.

"His name was Norman Brooks." As she spoke, she rubbed her throat as if it ached, but saying his name out loud seemed to loosen something in her. "He wasn't a big man, but he was hand-some." She drew out "handsome," investing that trite word with a wealth of qualities: charm, energy, and, most of all, deep appeal for Otelia Brooks. "He just thought . . . higher than everybody else. That man had ten ideas for every half notion most people have. I said, A man as smart as you shouldn't be stuck here in Mississippi. He said, Oh, you mean I should be stuck with you. Maybe, I said, but I'll have to see."

She stopped smiling. "He wouldn't have come here if I hadn't told him I meant to, with or without him. My family didn't want me to go. I couldn't understand how they wanted to stay. But they had a business, people knew who they were, respected them. My father was going to run for office. Then the federal troops left, and they started rewriting the laws. They said, You have to pay a tax; he said, Fine, I'll pay it. Then they said, You can't own a gun; negroes can't be trusted with them. So he gave up his gun. Then they shot up his store and said he better forget running for office. After that, I told Norman, I'm going. I want you to come with me, but I'll go if you don't. He said, Some women will go where they mean to go. I guess if I want to be with you, I have to go, too."

"So you came to New York."

"So we came to New York. It wasn't bad at first. Don't mis-understand, it wasn't *good*. Norman and I, we got a place in the Thirties. A few little blocks where black people could live, sur-rounded by Irish who thought they had more right to be there than we did. I got a job doing laundry. For Norman it wasn't as easy. Most of the building trades, they want to hire their own, and he wasn't anybody's own. He was good at tinkering. You give him a wire, some nails and wood, he'd make you a radio, he had that kind of mind. Best work he could find was bussing tables. He hated the cold. But he said if I was happy, he was happy. First anniversary, he gave me a blue scarf. I asked him why he'd wasted

our money. He said, You care for someone, you make them beautiful. Show the world what you see."

She fell silent after that. Then, taking up a stretch of ribbon,
she began folding it into a bow. "Do you remember what happened in summer, 1900?"

I shook my head.

"Well, why would you?" She set the bow down. "August. It was
hot. Air heavy, you feel it on you like a weight. Garbage stinking
in the street. You step outside, your head hurts from the glare.
Everyone feels put-upon and mean.

"Where we lived, it wasn't quiet. A lot of saloons, a lot of . . .
well, you know what goes on in the Tenderloin. One night, a
woman comes by one of the saloons, looking for her man. It's late,
she wants him home. He tells her wait, he'll be out in a minute or
two. A policeman—not wearing a uniform, mind you—sees her
standing on the street, thinks she must be doing business. So he
tries to arrest her. The gentleman comes out of the bar, sees a white
man trying to drag his lady friend down the block. He shouts at
him to stop. Policeman takes out his club, hits him over the head."

I winced; there were patrolmen who reacted to any provocation with the use of their nightstick.

"Man gets up off the ground, head bleeding. All he knows is this
man grabbed his girlfriend and clubbed him over the head. Far as
he's concerned, he's been attacked. So he stabs the policeman. Who
dies the next day. At the funeral, the policeman's friends get good
and drunk. They decide they're going to teach some negroes a lesson. And that's what they do. Pretty soon, it's a party, everyone's joining in. People got jumped on the street. Pulled out of saloons and
hotels and beaten. Some of the women in the neighborhood busted
into apartments, carried off anything they wanted. Norman and
I were lucky in that regard; we didn't have anything worth stealing.

"Only we still had to go to work. No one was going to say, Oh, white people breaking heads in the street, it's fine, you stay home. So Norman said to me, I'll meet you after work and we'll take the trolley together. It was okay going; everyone was too hungover to move. In the evening, though, they were ready to go again. Men running through the street, grabbing anybody they could find. Everywhere you looked, people bleeding, holding their heads, legs. Glass all over the streets from broken windows. Carts over-turned and wrecked. I remember being on that trolley, thinking, Just keep moving, keep on moving, we're almost there."

She took a deep breath. "Then the trolley stopped. Man in the next seat yelled, How come we're not moving? I could see why. Ten, twenty men standing on the tracks. They said, Who's riding with you? Anyone who shouldn't be?"

Her mouth disappeared and her jaw shook. In a voice broken with tears, she said, "And that's when they . . . took him.

"Those men jumped onto the car and caught hold of him, screaming, Give him to us, give us the—I was holding on to him, he was holding on to the back of the seat. I was begging the other people on the trolley to help me hold on to him or push the other men off. But they just yelled at the conductor, Keep going, keep going, like it was nothing to do with them. Driver's scared, going too fast. We swerved, stopped short, and Norman lost hold of the seat. The men started dragging him off the back of the trolley. But I still had him, I had his arm, and I remember . . . I remember his eyes . . . he was so scared. Screaming, Keep hold. Hold on. And I did, I tried, I dug my fingers in, and I pulled with my whole body. Then the trolley started to move and I . . . I didn't have him anymore. I let them have him."

She shut her eyes against the memory of what had happened next. When she opened them, she said in a new, hard voice, "And I saw the police, I saw them right down the block, watching. And laughing.

"Afterward, there was an inquiry." The word "inquiry" was drawn out in mockery. "I testified at that . . . inquiry. But they found that there were no facts to support the charge that the police had harmed anyone or neglected their duties in any way. Norman wasn't even listed as a victim of the riots. They said he fell under the trolley in all the fighting.

"I did not take it well," she continued, her tone oddly measured, as if she were reading a report of her own history. "I was afraid to leave my house. Even going to the front door had me shaking. I folded myself up in a corner of our bed, pulled the covers over me, and . . . I don't know, waited to die." Her forehead creased, but then she regained control. "I could not leave my house, and so I lost my job. Then a neighbor suggested I take a drink, make things a little fuzzy. That sounded good, so I took a drink. Then I took another. And it got so I could leave my house. As long as I went to the saloon. It didn't take long for them to throw me out of the apartment. They took our things. Said we owed them for back rent. Took everything I had of his, except that little blue scarf he gave me. I kept it around my neck, hid it."

I looked, thinking she was still hiding it. It was not around her neck.

"Man at the saloon said he knew a place I could stay. He had a friend." She smiled thinly. "I said, I can't pay your friend. He said they'd think of something.

"I kept that scarf until the night I met you. That animal took it from me, ripped it right off my neck. But that's all he took. And he did give me something. When he came at me, I thought, No. You will not take one more thing from me. I'm taking myself back, even if I have to grab that knife out of your hand and cut you to do it."

"Did you?" I asked. "Cut him?"

"I did. After he . . ." She gestured to her eye. "His hand was slippery with blood. So I got hold of the knife and gave him a good swipe across the wrist. Back of it, though. Didn't get the veins. And I should have gone for his throat.

"I had heard about your uncle, seen him out walking. So I knew where to go. I nearly passed out so many times on my way. I kept hearing Norman in my head saying, I didn't come up to that cold place so you could die. I didn't wash other people's dirty dishes so you could die. I let you go so you could live. So live. That's when I realized, he was the one who let me go. Because he knew they'd pull me off along with him. And I didn't have any business throwing away what he sacrificed to save. So I came to you. And from you to the White Rose, which sent me to one of Madam Walker's classes where she trains her sales agents, and here I am."

She inhaled, as if pulling all the memories deep back down inside. "And I hope now you understand why I do not believe the police will listen to a word I say."

The long silence that followed was broken by a tentative knock at the door. Otelia Brooks glanced at the clock, then said, "Come in." She looked at me, and I understood our conversation would stop. Now.

The door opened and a small face peeped in. From behind her, I heard an elderly woman whisper, "Say 'Pardon me, Miss Brooks . . .'"

"Pardon me, Miss Brooks," the child echoed.

Otelia Brooks bent slightly, saying, "Now, who is this coming to see me? Is this a great lady in need of a new hat?"

The child stepped into the room, swaying, hands clasped behind her back. "I don't know."

"Oh, I think it is. And I believe she's brought her grandmother as well." Miss Brooks smiled as the elderly woman followed the child into the room. Her face was remarkably unlined, her eyes long and elegant. I admired the white buttons on the turned-back collar of her dark suit, the intricate lace of her jabot. She gave me a momentary glance before she smiled and greeted me. I was not expected, but not unwelcome.

An enchanting bonnet with a yellow ribbon was for the little girl, who knew it straightaway and had to work very hard to contain her excitement as Otelia Brooks settled it onto her head. The hat with its upturned brim and tenderly tied bow created a halo around her head, at once an image of fragile innocence and a promise of loveliness that made you both mourn and anticipate the day she packed the bonnet away among her childish things.

"You must save that for your daughter," I told her.

"This is Miss Jane Prescott," said Otelia Brooks. "She dresses one of the finest ladies in the city."

The child's mouth opened with gratifying awe. Her grandmother said politely, "Would that be Mrs. Mayme Marshall? Or Mrs. Martha Anderson?"

"I work for Mrs. William Tyler."

"I don't believe I've had the pleasure." Then her gaze fell on her granddaughter and softened. "I like it," she declared. "I think it will do."

"That gives me great pleasure, Mrs. Cross," said Otelia Brooks. "And Miss Cross." Crooking her finger, she motioned the child close. "Now, not a word about who made you this hat. You are a member of a special society now, and I expect you to keep its secrets. Even if you think you recognize another member, you must not suggest you know who made their hat. The very most you may do is nod at them when no one is looking. They will probably nod back, but perhaps not. Can you remember that?"

The little girl nodded. "I'll remember, Miss Brooks."

With exaggerated seriousness, Otelia Brooks said, "And can you remember, Mrs. Cross? And do you so pledge?"

"I so pledge. And I thank you."

When they had gone, I said, "Miss Dodson may notice them as they leave. She is determined to reveal you as the Hat Lady of Harlem."

"And my secretary will show them out the back way for that reason."

"May I ask why you don't take credit for your work?"

"I prefer to make my hats for people I feel deserve them. Or need them. That little girl lost her mother two months ago. And her grandmother is a powerful lady, as you might have gathered. Some in the northern elite have their doubts about southerners. So if I can get Mrs. Cross into my hair salon . . ."

I bowed my head in tribute to her business sense. "My uncle has accounting classes now. He can't bear to be in the room when they are taught, but he does have them, and that's because of you."

She smiled politely, though she knew very well what I would say next.

"If the police don't listen to you, no one need know you were involved. And if they do—"

"If they do, I lose everything I've built over the past decade. Do you think Mrs. Edwina Cross is going to buy her granddaughter's hats from a woman who stood on Minetta Lane drunk and hiking up her skirts? Do you think those ladies want their hair done by that woman?"

No, I thought, and if you were white and sold hats to Mrs. Benchley, I wouldn't have even asked you. And there were no amends I could make for that ignorance except to say I now understood that I couldn't ask her to sacrifice everything she— and Norman Brooks—had worked for.

"I'm sorry I troubled you."

"Don't be sorry. You're fighting for your family. I understand."

"May I ask one last question?"

A sigh of exasperation. "You haven't changed. Go on."

"Why do you call yourself miss?"

"Because I can't give up his name, but I don't feel I deserve the title. Besides, I don't need people asking questions I don't want to answer."

Like all the questions I had asked her today. Trying to acknowledge defeat with some graciousness, I stood to leave.

As I did, Otelia Brooks said, "May I ask you a question?" There was surprise in her voice, as if she had not expected to be curious.

"Of course."

"You ever get the blood out of that carpet?"

Puzzled that she would remember such a thing, I shook my head.

She smiled. "I knew you wouldn't." She imitated my distracted, half-hearted scrubbing motion. "Too interested in everything else going on, so you work it in even deeper."

"I will say that you can barely see it." And yet I had seen it only a few days ago.

"It's there, though. Good thing you're not a housemaid. Stain like that in one of Mrs. Tyler's dresses, you wouldn't let that sit. But the carpet, everybody walks on it, after a while, you stop noticing. Doesn't feel worth the work. Always been that way, can't be too bad."

She took my hand to say good-bye. As she did—I couldn't help it—I blurted, "Doesn't it frighten you, the thought of that man still out there? If he saw you, remembered you . . ."

Withdrawing her hand, she patted a small embroidered handbag on her desk. "I told you how they took my father's gun. But they're not taking this one. No, Miss Jane, I'm not frightened. Not at all."

12

I could not argue with Otelia Brooks's position—much as I tried to on the ride back to the refuge. She was almost certainly right that the police would not take her account as proof my uncle wasn't responsible for Sadie's and Carrie's murders. And in order to salvage his reputation in the court of public opinion, she would have to ruin her own. For several stops, I considered asking her if she would simply come to the neighborhood, cast eyes on Bill Danvers and see if the sight of him would stir any memories. But how could I ask her to revisit that nightmare when she had worked so hard to put it behind her? I couldn't, was the simple and straightforward answer.

Letting my hands drop into my lap as a quiet admission of defeat, I fussed at the edge of my glove. As I did, I saw—still there—a small disfiguration. Many years ago, I'd burned my wrist while ironing one of Mrs. Armslow's nightgowns. I had been making a list in my head and lost track of the distance between the point of the iron and my hand. The result: a pale disk of scar tissue that hadn't faded over time. Wrists, the cook had told me as she put salve on it, heal poorly, being close to the bone.

For several moments, I gazed at my hand until realization settled. She had cut him on the wrist. Which meant there could be a scar. A mark that would support Otelia Brooks's story.

But how to see that scar, that was the question. Bill Danvers was not a man you could lightly take hold of. We were weeks away from the kind of weather where men rolled up their shirtsleeves, and I could hardly ask Orville Pickett if he ever noticed his associate's wrists.

I got off the train. Walking down the street, I pondered a feigned peace offering of a sewed button or mended cuff when I heard a man cry out, "Please don't hit me."

I looked up and saw Harry Knowles. The *Herald* reporter looked no better in daylight, and his presence a few feet away from me was not welcome.

"I warn you, Mr. Knowles, I have several newspapers in my pocket."

"I have a newspaper, too," he said. "Maybe you'd like to read it."

He held it out. I thought to refuse. But better, I thought to know. We were not far from the widow Pickett's house. No doubt she had been spinning more elaborate tales for the reporter. I took the paper.

SHOCKING DETAILS OF LIFE WITH
REPROBATE REVEREND!

Following the arrest of the Reverend Prescott in the murders of Sadie Ellis and Carrie Biel, reports have emerged of strange goings-on at the Gorman Refuge for Women. Many close to the refuge have suggested that

his interest in the women who stay there is not solely hu-
manitarian. At least one woman has told this paper that
the Reverend is odd in his manner and at times acts in
a manner distinctly un-Christian. And then there is the
account of this woman.

"He's strange about women. Sometimes he looks at
me like I'm not wearing nothing. And he doesn't know
what he wants to do to me because of it."

Those were the words of Sadie Ellis, who was murdered not three days ago.

I took this in for a minute, then said, "I thought you got your
stories from the widow Pickett. But it was Sadie, wasn't it?"

He bunched his lips, saying neither yes nor no.

"You were the man she was sneaking out to meet."

"It's a funny word," he said. "Sneaking."

"Leaving the refuge without asking, making sure she wasn't
seen. What would you call it?"

"A grown woman going where she pleased."

"And it pleased her to help you write stories tearing down the
very people who were trying to help her."

"Well, the money pleased her. And the attention. She liked attention. Much the way I like whisky. Even though it doesn't seem
to be good for either of us."

"How long?"

"I guess we met six or seven times. I'd been watching the refuge, hoping I could get hold of one of the girls to talk to me, tell
me what it was like inside. I got a smack in the head from the
gargoyle."

Berthe, I guessed.

"And a few others who said it was a lot of prayer and sewing,
but it was a bed and free meals and they liked it well enough."

Dull, boring truth, I thought, not worth the ink. "Then you found Sadie."

"And then I found Sadie. It was late at night, but when she stepped under the streetlight, I saw the beating she'd taken and said, You're not really going back to him, are you? Just a guess, but she liked the interest, and said, What if I am? I told her I had a dollar for her, plus she could keep her skirts down. She asked what she'd have to do, and I said, Just talk. Keep me company."

His tone had turned wistful. "You liked her."

"Yes, I liked her. She was sharp and selfish and lively. I liked her."

"Even though she lied."

"She didn't lie. Maybe she tailored the truth a bit, but she didn't lie."

"Saying my uncle . . . looked at her?"

"How do you know he didn't? Sure, some of the things she told me were fabrications; she was quite a storyteller. But she told me what her days were like, that the other women were unkind to her—"

"There, right there, that was a lie."

"—and that your uncle was strange and she was afraid of him."

"Which she obviously said because she knew you wanted to hear it. And you wanted to hear it because you knew Clementine Pickett wanted to read it."

"You don't think your uncle is strange?"

"In this world, good men are unusual. Yes, he's strange. It doesn't mean he should be insulted by the likes of Sadie Ellis."

"'The likes of Sadie Ellis,'" he echoed. "She spoke her mind. She did what she pleased. She was earning money and taking charge of her future. You just don't like how she did it, Miss Prescott. You and Mrs. Pickett could have a talk about that sometime. The frustrations of liberty."

I loathed the comparison to Mrs. Pickett, but there was something in what he said. It stuck, uncomfortably, like a bit of apple
between the teeth.

"Who do you think killed them?" I asked. "Honestly."

"Honestly, Miss Prescott? I think it was your uncle."

★ ★ ★

I returned to the refuge to find they had released my uncle without charge—for now. His arrest had had one benefit. The Purity
Brigade considered their work done and had gone home. Clementine Pickett, Orville, Mrs. Hilquit . . . all gone. It was what I
had wanted for weeks. But now Mrs. Pickett's withdrawal in triumph presented only problems. It meant if I wanted to look at Bill
Danvers's wrist, I would have to find him.

★ ★ ★

The next morning, I returned to Rutherford's to hear that the
nightgowns had arrived from the warehouse. As I made my way
to the lingerie department, I realized I hadn't spoken to poor
Leo since leaving him abruptly Wednesday night. When I saw
Mrs. Hirschfeld, I asked how he was.

"Busy," she said with a smile. "I understand he took you dancing."

Catching a note of tension in her voice, I tried to make light
of it. "Yes, I was feeling sad over the death of a friend, and he was
kind enough to try and cheer me up."

We went to her small office to fetch the nightgowns. When
she had piled them into my arms, she asked, "Are you going to see
Leo later?"

Unsure what she meant, I said, "I think he's working today."

"I wonder if you wouldn't mind giving him a message from me?"

"Of course not."

"Tell him Clara came to dinner the other night and was very sad not to see him."

There was a long pause as I waited for her to identify Clara. But she did not seem inclined to do so.

"Of course."

★ ★ ★

The rest of the afternoon, I measured. I sewed. I managed not to stick Emily Tyler with pins when she asked George Rutherford if the smocks "really had to be so plain." I managed smiles and yes-ma'ams for Mrs. Rutherford, reassuring looks for Louise. I laughed at Hattie Phipps's recitation about her life as a telephone operator—*Kandinsky, Nussbaum, and Schlom, how may I direct your call?*—and admired Gertie Walsh's gossip from Rector's. I made it all the way to lunchtime before stalking out of the Crystal Palace, and I might have held my temper even then except that Leo insisted on following me, saying he had connections in the employee dining hall and would I care for leftover knockwurst? At which point I wheeled on him and said that I detested knockwurst and on another subject, who was Clara?

I knew as his habitual smile faded that I had him. Or rather, didn't.

"Clara," he said, "is a very nice girl my mother thinks I'm going to marry."

Then the smile reappeared, as if what his mother thought should be of no concern.

"And what does Clara think?"

He paused, as if trying to recall. "I know she has very strong views on public education. I can't tell you what they are, but I know they're very strong."

"And how is Clara's two-step?"

Taking my hand, he said, "Nowhere near as good as yours."

Two salesgirls passed us in the hallway, clearly intrigued by the situation. Keeping hold of my hand, Leo led me down the stairs and out to the street where the delivery trucks arrived to be unloaded.

Over the shouts of men and thuds of crates, I said, "So you don't only discuss the values of public education. She has other charms."

"Maybe."

"And you have other dance partners."

"Swear to God, I can't remember a single one of them." His hand snuck around my waist. I turned neatly to avoid it. Surprised at the rebuff, he resorted to, "I'm sorry."

He didn't know what he was apologizing for, that was clear. But what was I asking him to apologize for? Dancing with other girls? Sitting on divans with other girls? Maybe that was simply . . . how things were if you weren't Louise Tyler or Charlotte Benchley. William Tyler might have to make his intentions clear before so much as kissing Louise Benchley. Louise Benchley had a lot more to offer—millions more, to be precise—than Jane Prescott. What Jane Prescott had to offer could be had on the dance floor—or the divan. I fiddled with my top button, queasy with both regret and awareness that in some ways I didn't regret it as much as I should.

Clara! The wronged party came to me in a stunning moment of moral clarity. That's who I was angry for, Clara.

"And of course Clara knows about me and all these other women whose names you can't remember."

"We don't talk about everything . . ."

Which meant they talked about some things, a fact that should have been obvious but hurt nonetheless.

"And how does she feel about kissing, either the practice or the ethical proposition?"

There he was silent. And I had my answer. Putting my hands

in my pockets, I started walking. I expected Leo would stay
behind, that I would have a long, miserable walk back to the rehearsal room by myself.

"Jane!"

Catching up to me, he took my arm. His head was very close
to mine, which made me think of kissing, which made me angry,
and I threw him off. For a moment I was either going to smack
him very hard or burst into tears. Then I collected myself, announced that I was not hungry, and went upstairs.

Unfortunately, as I headed down the hall to the Crystal Palace, I was aware that I was sniffing quite a lot. Silly tears kept well-
ing up. Wiping them away, I heard Emily Tyler say, "Jane, what
on earth is the matter?"

"Nothing, Miss Tyler. I'm . . . entirely fine."

"You're not. Your nails are bitten, your eyes are red, and your
nose is running. What's happened? Is it Mr. Hirschfeld?"

Too surprised to come up with a clever deception, I said,
"Why do you say that?"

"Because he likes you, and I rather thought you liked him."

"He does. Me and five thousand other girls."

Emily made a pained face of sympathy. Then I noticed her
eyes were looking rather red as well. "Did something happen?"

"Oh—" Slumping against the wall, she gave it a quick blow
with her fist. "I know you're devoted to Louise, but right now, I
could throw her out a window. Lecturing me about George Rutherford as if I were a complete idiot. 'He's a married man.' 'Dolly's
upset.' As if I meant to run off with him."

She glanced at me. "I suppose you heard about my folly in
Saratoga."

"I did hear you were fond of someone."

"Very fond, as a matter of fact." Hands behind her, she leaned
against the wall, bouncing off it as she spoke. "Snapper Wilkes

was funny and handsome and . . . well, if you'd seen him ride a horse, you'd understand. And he liked me," she added softly. "We'd sit and talk about horses and new songs and where it was nicest in summer, and he acted like I was just about the smartest girl he'd ever met. At least that I had something to say."

Not, I realized, how she must feel at home, with her mother obsessed with her sister's marital prospects and her brother's social standing.

"I hate William for pulling me off that train," she said.

"He only did it because he cares."

"He did it because Mother told him to and they're all afraid of scandal. Scandal—you should have seen me on that platform. Screaming. 'I'll go where I want. It's supposed to be a free country, isn't it?'"

This I knew from Louise. I also knew William's response, which was to start listing things that weren't at all free, like food and clothing and shelter, and to wonder aloud if Mr. Wilkes's salary would stretch to include Emily. Mr. Wilkes had apparently been under the impression that Emily had her own income. When informed otherwise, he had regretfully agreed to part.

But there was no point in pressing the matter with Emily, so I said, "Still—there are better ways of forgetting Snapper Wilkes than flirting with George Rutherford."

"I'm not flirting with him. I'm auditioning. Did you know Miss Rutherford gets a stipend?" I shook my head. "Well, she does. Which means if I win, I'll have my own income and I won't have to go begging to William or Mother."

"And if you don't," I said lightly, "there are other jobs."

Emily smiled. "And other men. Although I don't think you should give up on Mr. Hirschfeld just yet."

That afternoon took us through a very ragged run-through of the full show. I constructed wings out of wire and paper and made some of the nightgowns look worn and shabby. Leo I ignored. Except for those times I looked up to see he was uncharacteristically subdued. No leaping eyebrows or hysterical grins, no matter how many wrong notes were sung—and there were quite a few.

At one point, I heard the first notes of the "Pickle Barrel Rag," played as a mournful dirge. It was an attempt at reconciliation, and I admit it reminded me of the joy of dancing at the Acme, the blare of the trumpet, Chick Tricker sitting at his corner table.

And Bill Danvers.

Bill Danvers, who worked at the Acme.

If I could prove that Bill Danvers made a living by threatening women who tried to leave their employment with Chick Tricker, if I could prove he had left the Acme that night, that he had a scar on his wrist, similar to the one Otelia Brooks gave her attacker . . .

I whispered, "Mr. Hirschfeld, are you working at the Acme tonight?"

"I am."

"I need you to take me there."

Leo looked suspicious. "Is this a trick?"

"It's not a trick. I want to go back and I need you to take me."

"Miss Prescott, nothing would please me more, but I confess that in your present mood, you frighten me. Although I'm still quite enamored. Also, I can't tonight."

"Why? Is tonight reserved for Miss Pastrami?"

The briefest pause in the music. "No. But we singing waiters take turns using the guest table. One night, I get to bring . . . a friend, the next night, Stumpy. Tonight, Mario's bringing his cousin. At least he said she was his cousin; she looked awfully pretty for a cousin . . ."

I wasn't interested in Mario's cousin or Leo's expansive views on pulchritude. "How can I get in, then?"

"Get in where?" Released from rehearsal, Emily Tyler was upon us.

"Miss Prescott wants me to take her dancing at the Acme. Sadly, I am unable to oblige her."

"Well, that's very wrong of you, Mr. Hirschfeld. Jane, I think we should teach Mr. Hirschfeld a lesson."

"What do you mean, Miss Tyler?"

"I mean you and I should go to the Acme tonight. No, don't worry, I'll pay. Poor Mr. Hirschfeld—we'll leave him to sing for his supper, and we'll have a grand old time."

13

That night, as we made our way back to the Acme Café, I took an inventory of my failures in the time William's mother had been away. I had let Louise fall into the hands of Dolly Rutherford. I had not succeeded in returning Emily to Vassar; that alone would not have been so bad, but having her get caught up in something as crassly commercial as the Miss Rutherford's pageant was a different matter. As was flirting with George Rutherford. And now I was escorting her to one of the most notorious dance clubs in the city.

I had also, in a fit of idiocy, allowed Emily to lend me a dress. She had insisted, saying she couldn't go to a club with someone who didn't "look the sort of girl I would be friends with." She had said it flippantly, but I suspected her of matchmaking. It was a beautiful dress, a column of dark purple velvet with a short-sleeved overlay of white silk printed with violets and greenery. A dark purple sash accentuated the waist, and a low-cut neckline accentuated the rest. I felt both outrageously pretty and terrified I would tear the garment.

Leo, of course, couldn't have been happier. As I observed at the outset of the evening, two women probably struck him as the minimal requirement. He answered with his latest effort: "Women everywhere / as far as the eye can see. Yet there's only one girl who's the one for me."

"And her name is Clara," I sang back. "Or Myrtle. Or Edith. Or Josephine . . ."

But no one was happier than Emily, whose spirits were sky-high as she practically pranced down the squalid streets in rose silk slippers—I thanked God it wasn't my job to clean them—to the doors of the Acme, where she was admitted straightaway, the concierge at once recognizing a rich, giddy young thing intent on making a spectacle of herself and spending gobs of money in the process.

It was a very different business going to the Acme in the company of said giddy young thing rather than one of its waiters. Thanks to Emily, we were seated at a table close to the dance floor. Suddenly, all those glittering famous people I had glimpsed from the back of the room were within mere feet of me. No games of stuss or peanut shells up here, just champagne, diamonds, and merriment. And the blast of cornet and trombone, so vibrant it captured your senses; all you wanted to do was move and be part of it.

Sadly, I hadn't come here to dance. I looked to the corner where I had last seen Chick Tricker, but it seemed the club's owner had other business that evening. I was happy not to be under his direct gaze. But it presented a problem. If Bill Danvers was here this evening and there was no boss to draw him into the light, I might not find him in the rabbit's warren of the club. He could be working on another floor or even in another club; Chick Tricker had a few of them.

Leo appeared at the table to take Emily's order for a bottle of champagne. Kneeling at my feet, he put a hand on his heart and began singing in Italian. I resisted the urge to kick him.

Leaning down, I whispered in his ear, "Tell me if you see Bill Danvers."

"That's not very romantic," he whispered back.

"No. It's not."

Leo stood. "What are you going to do if you see this guy?"

"I'm going to look at his wrist," I said, and got a very funny look from Mr. Hirschfeld.

As I watched for Danvers, it occurred to me that if his job was to keep the girls in line, I should watch the girls. There were already several working the floor this evening; it was Friday, and the club was full of people who had just been paid. Then I remembered the dark-haired girl Danvers had assaulted. She might have more information than anyone else about his comings and goings that night. Although she might be too scared to talk to me. And it was going to be hard to find one girl in this excited, noisy crowd.

Then I heard Emily ask, "Who's that enormous man in the corner?"

She pointed out a brawny gentleman standing off to the side in an ill-fitting tuxedo. "That's Frank Walters," I said. "He used to be a boxer. Now he works as a bouncer."

Emily's eyebrows hopped and she turned in her chair, eager to catch sight of any and all tantalizing depravity. It occurred to me that I might utilize her hunger for experience, and I wondered aloud if I might ask her a favor.

"I used to work with a girl who fell on hard times. I have a feeling she might be working here, but . . . against her will, if you understand."

Emily turned again in her seat; I had her full attention. "What does she look like?"

"She's small, dark, about our age. She behaves as if she's here to dance. But she isn't really. She goes around asking gentlemen to buy her a drink. Then if a gentleman shows interest, they have to go somewhere else to . . ."

"Exchange goods," said Emily.

"Exactly. It would have to be somewhere close by, but I don't know where."

Happy to be in the know, Emily gazed at the moving parts of the crowd, trying to find a dark-haired girl she'd never seen before. The band finished their song, and as people returned to their tables, the dance floor cleared. That was when I saw her at a nearby table, leaning on a man who looked barely able to sit upright, let alone stand or do anything else. She had her hand on his shoulder and seemed to be showing extreme concern for the state of his shirt and jacket. Lapels were adjusted, buttons examined, pockets smoothed. Then I watched as she laughed expansively, all the while slipping her hand into the inside of his jacket. The lower pockets, I realized, would have been searched sometime before.

The hand emerged empty; what she sought was either in his seat pocket or too snug to be lifted without notice. The young lady then felt in the mood to dance. Her partner seemed less willing—or able—but she managed to haul him out of his seat and lead him, stumbling, onto the dance floor. I was going to lose sight of her. Telling Emily to keep watch from where she was, I went to find Leo.

He was bringing a tray full of drinks to a table. I followed him and helped him hand them out. Then, swiftly depositing the tray back at the bar, I said, "Dance with me."

"No—although I adore you in that dress and dancing with you happens to be one of my very favorite things."

Taking hold of his hands, I trotted him onto the floor.

"I'll lose my job," he said.

"You were dragged here by an overeager young woman who'd had too much to drink. I'll swear to it."

"Well, if you'll swear . . ."

We began moving in sight of the girl and her client, who now seemed rather overeager himself. She was having trouble keeping him at bay.

"How does it work?" I asked Leo.

"She'll ask him if he wants a more . . . private dance. If he doesn't, he puts a dollar in her stocking. If he does, they go downstairs."

The girl turned her head as if looking for someone. Following her gaze, I saw another gentleman nod. Almost immediately, she started leading her swain off. I guessed a bed had opened up.

I made to follow. Leo said, "Where are you going?"

"I have to talk to that girl."

"That could be a very expensive proposition."

We made our way off the floor, past the tables, and to the far side of the room, which had been left clear for waiters to go to and fro. She would, I thought, take him either outside or downstairs. Bagnios were usually in the cellars. I was right; the girl was leading the man to a stairway at the back of the club. Wherever she was going seemed a likely place for Bill Danvers to be, so I headed that way as well. Then I felt Leo grab my arm.

"Look, I know you want to find this guy. But you can't go down there."

"I see two feet, a left and a right. I think I can."

Pulling myself free, I hurried down the wooden stairs. I could feel Leo start to follow, but someone called his name. He must have hesitated, because they called it again, this time sharply. As I went through the door that led to the cellar, I knew he had stayed behind.

The basement was markedly different from the glitter and gaiety of the dance hall. Cramped and low-ceilinged, it had the feeling of servants' quarters. One low light hung halfway down the long corridor, dimly revealing several curtained booths on either side. The wooden floor was raw timber and rotting from damp. At the end of the hallway, a man slouched on a three-legged stool. Fortunately, he was passed out. I heard the creaking of bedsprings and other sounds of business. If Bill Danvers was down here, I didn't see him.

I stayed half-hidden around the corner. After a few minutes, one of the curtains opened and a gentleman stumbled out buttoning up his pants. As he passed me, he leered—or tried to—confusing me with a girl about to begin her shift.

Then I heard another curtain shoved aside, saw another man take his leave. Here, the young woman was not as shy, coming out with him and giving him a kiss. It was the dark-haired girl. When her customer was well clear of the stairs, I went to the curtain and put a hand through. I heard, "Oh, for—" Then the curtain was yanked aside. But seeing me, the girl tried to pull it shut again.

I said, "I only want—"

She turned on me, fierce, made a slicing gesture across her throat. Then she nodded toward a door cut into the wall on the right. Someone was listening. For a moment I stared at the door; there was something odd about it. Not only its existence—why would a room this small require a door?—but its appearance. Hinges, I realized. There were no hinges. A hook in the center for a robe or coat. But no hinges.

I pointed to her, then myself. Mouthed the word "Talk." She rolled her eyes.

I mimed taking a drink. She glanced at the door, then nodded. Putting her finger to her lips, she led me out of the little room, past the sleeping man, and up the stairs. "You get the bottle," she said. "I'll meet you outside."

I hurried back to the table, where Emily was in animated conversation with Frank the Tango Pirate. The bottle of champagne was still on the table. Saying, "May I borrow this?" I took it and went out to the street.

Friday night on the Bowery was a crowded, raucous affair. I was trying to decide where I could stand so that the girl could find me but we wouldn't be found. I was making my way to the end of the block when I ran right into an old mattress that had been soaked in beer and lain in the hot sun for days—and possibly used as a toilet—until it was a stained, burst mess. As the smell hit my nose, I recoiled—and saw that I had encountered Mr. Harry Knowles emerging from a saloon called the Dump.

The words "You are a disgrace" leapt to mind, but that sounded Clementine Pickett–ish, so I settled on "Mr. Knowles, you should go home. You're in no state to be out."

He had to open his piggy eyes very wide to see who had spoken. When he realized it was me, he staggered and said, "Not . . . afraid. Not a pretty young whore, why should I . . . be afraid?" The eyes narrowed again. "Unless you're going to take another . . . whack at me."

The word "whack," the effort it took to say it, seemed to unsteady him to an intolerable degree, and, lurching to the side, he vomited into the gutter. He was, I noticed, well practiced, taking care to lean against a streetlamp so he could bend at an angle that kept his shirt and shoes clear of the flow. Mostly. I started to ask if he needed a handkerchief, but he raised a finger, requesting silence, then vomited again.

"Yes, thank you," he said when he was upright.

I handed him the piece of cloth. As he wiped his mouth, I said, "My uncle gave me that handkerchief."

"And it's a very pretty thing." He handed it back to me. I folded it carefully, wary of soil. "How old were you?"

"Thirteen. I was leaving home, and I suppose he thought I should have something."

"That place is home to you."

"I suppose so."

"And he's . . . like a father to you."

He had an odd way of asking questions. He did not interrogate as some reporters did; he seemed to ask simply because he was curious.

"My father left me on a dock when I was three. I don't know what fathers are like. My uncle took me in. He didn't have to. But he did. He gave me a safe place to be until I was old enough to go out into the world, and when I went, I was ready. I think many women he works with would say the same. And I'd like you to think about that before you write your next piece."

"Devils don't always show their horns, Miss Prescott."

I looked pointedly at his head. "No, sometimes they wear hats."

He chuckled at that. And when he did, a chill went down my back. That laugh—I had heard it before.

"You called the refuge," I said.

He frowned. "I don't . . ."

"You did. You called a few nights ago. You said if I came after you, you'd come after me."

Even as I said it, I realized confronting a man with his misdeeds could be unwise.

But Harry Knowles looked confused. "I said that?"

"Yes. The day I hit you with the newspaper."

"Oh." He hesitated, then said, "I'm afraid I don't remember that."

"Are you saying you didn't?"

"No. Just that I don't remember. It happens sometimes. When—" He looked back at the bar. "I've woken up in some strange places."

After doing what? I thought uneasily.

"Maybe you should stay out of saloons, Mr. Knowles."

"So people tell me, Miss Prescott. Good night."

He made his way past me, head down, hand to his hat. He was steadier now, but he had to draw up short now and then to avoid another collision, and I wondered: Did he know where he was? Was he even now in that strange state of sleepwalking he had described? Would he remember tomorrow that he had seen me? That we had talked? What I had said about my uncle?

I told myself a man who could barely walk could not hold a young woman down and take her life.

Before I could think more on that subject, I heard "Now what? Did your husband come see me, your brother, your father?"

"I don't have any of those," I said, and offered the dark-haired girl the bottle. Taking it, she made it clear she would have preferred gin, yet drank about half of it in one swallow. She was barely twenty, but there were tired lines around her mouth, a heaviness to her face, a dullness in the eyes, all testament to a dedicated effort to stay as numb as possible.

I asked her name. She said, "You're not here to talk about hellfire, are you?"

"No."

"Then it's Moira."

"I was here the other night. You were arguing with a man. A skinny man with greasy dark hair."

She took another swig from the bottle. "So?"

"It was Bill Danvers, am I right?"

"How do you know Bill Danvers?"

Knowing the bottle wouldn't last through that story, I said, "I know he's a dangerous man."

She snorted. But drank again.

"I know he likes to hurt women."

"Lucky Bill, then. Makes a living from his hobby." She hiccupped slightly, not used to bubbles.

"Why did he hit you?"

"He thought I took the roll."

"Roll?" Then I remembered the pat on the pocket. "The money."

"Right. Men come in here, they come with a lot of cash. The idea is, you get them in the room, hang the coat on the door . . ."

The strange door with no hinges. "It turns, doesn't it?"

She smiled sourly, tapped her head. "I get the gentleman otherwise occupied, Bill reaches around, takes the coat, takes what's in the coat, wraps up the bills with paper so the roll looks fat, and puts it all back in place in time for the gent to take his leave. Most of them are too drunk to know better, and even when they find out their money's missing, they stay quiet because they don't want their wives knowing where they've been."

"How much do you get?"

"Club gets most of it. It's their bed, right? Bill gets a piece, I get . . ." She held up thumb and forefinger a sliver apart. "Only with that guy there wasn't anything to get. Which I told Bill. You saw how he took it."

I didn't ask if she had stolen the money; she had earned it as far as I was concerned. "Is it always Bill on the other side of the door?" I asked.

"Not always. Club doesn't rob everyone. Word would get out,

and there goes your business. Just enough from the tourists to make a little extra and keep the police sweet."

"And was Bill Danvers here all that night?"

She had the sharp ears of someone used to trouble. "Why?"

How much could I trust her? There was every chance she could share the details of my interest in Danvers with Danvers— or even Chick Tricker.

But Bill Danvers already knew I suspected him of murder, so I decided to be honest. "Two friends of mine have been killed, one the night I was here. They both . . . The three of you had things in common. But they were working toward a different life, and I think Bill Danvers might have killed them as a warning to other women who try to leave."

She exhaled, tipped the bottle to find it empty.

"What do you think he would do, Chick Tricker, if you tried to quit?" I asked her.

A shrug. "I'm fine. I don't need to learn how to do laundry."

"Why do you say that?"

"What?"

"That you don't need to learn how to do laundry. I didn't mention the refuge."

"No, but . . . people know. About that place."

"Do they? How did you hear about it?"

"That crazy priest, sure, he takes girls in for their own good." Her voice roiled with sarcasm. "Everyone knows about that place."

"How do you know about it?" I pressed. "Chick Tricker wants the refuge shut down, doesn't he?"

"I don't know. I don't listen to those conversations."

So there were conversations. "Was Bill Danvers here the whole night?"

"I have to get back inside."

I followed her, asked again, "Was he here the whole night?"

"Yeah, the whole night."

"Tell me how you know that."

"He was following me around, going, I know you have my money. His breath stinks. He follows you, you know it."

It was a compelling scenario. But Bill would have been done following Moira before Leo and I went up to the roof. Between divan doings and the chaos of the raid, there would have been more than enough time for him to get to the refuge. Had that been the subject of his conversation with Chick Tricker? Was he making plans to kill Carrie—or was he reporting that he had already done the job? Tricker had several properties around there; any one of them could have served as the necessary dark place where everyone looked the other way. Carrie could have lain there until someone dumped her in the alley later at night when the coast was clearer.

The band was playing, and I had to talk into Moira's ear. "Don't believe what they tell you about the refuge. Or my uncle. He can help you. The building is on Bowery and Third . . ."

All of a sudden Moira gasped in pain as Bill Danvers grabbed her by the shoulder and twisted. Panicked, I thought to shout for help, then realized no one would hear me above the music.

Shoving Moira hard against the wall, Bill said, "Third and Bowery? You don't want to go there, Moira. Girls are dying there. You don't want to be next. You've got more sense than that, I know you have."

"Sure," she whispered. The blow had knocked both the wind and the boldness out of her. Nevertheless, Bill Danvers showed her his fist.

Reaching for a chair, I said, "Stop it. Or I'll tell Mrs. Pickett that you're not the reformed character she thinks you are."

"Go on," he said, eyes on Moira. "My work's done there anyway."

"What work was that, Mr. Danvers? Throwing rocks or something worse?"

There was something in his hand; I could tell from the way his arm was bent and his shoulder tensed. The knife was out.

He said, "Now, this, Moira, is a woman without sense. She doesn't think how this is a very crowded place. A lot of drunken people. Floor slippery with beer, broken glass. Doesn't think that if she fell, she could cut herself. Cut her throat. Did someone cut it for her? Or was she careless? Showed no sense?"

I was judging whether to aim for the throat with the chair leg or just swing and run when there was a crack, a spray of champagne, and, yes, broken glass. Bill Danvers lurched forward and fell onto the floor. Leo stood triumphantly behind him. Next to him, holding the remains of a bottle, stood Emily Tyler.

Crouching, I examined Bill Danvers's wrists. No scar. Not even a trace of one.

"Oh, my Lord," said Emily breathlessly. "That was sublime."

★ ★ ★

It was late by the time I returned to the refuge, so I used the kitchen entrance to avoid waking Berthe, who had a keen ear for the click and creak of the front door. But when I went around to the side, I saw there was a light on. And I could smell coffee. Berthe unable to sleep for worry, I thought.

But it was not Berthe who stood at the stove, coaxing our old coffeepot along. It was my oldest friend. Even in selling tickets, I thought, Anna's dedication to the cause was steadfast.

Putting up my hand, I said, "I'm sorry, I can't think about tickets right now."

"What are you talking about?"

"The pageant. Your—"

Exasperated, Anna turned off the stove. "I'm here because I heard what happened to your uncle. I'm here for you."

"Oh," I said. And burst into tears.

When coffee had been poured and bread toasted, I regaled Anna with the whole miserable story, including this night's events, which had all but proven Bill Danvers's innocence in Sadie's and Carrie's murders. Kneading my eyes with the heels of my hands, I said, "The worst of it is, he's lying to me."

"I don't think of your uncle as a liar," said Anna.

"Not lying, but he's not being truthful. He won't tell me where he was on the night Sadie was killed or the night Carrie died."

A shadow crossed Anna's face. "He likes his privacy." Then, with a small smile, she said, "So, what took you to the Acme?"

Grateful for the change in subject, I said, "A . . . friend."

"Is he good-looking, this friend?"

I described Leo Hirschfeld, both his good qualities and the ones less so. Anna listened, then said, "He sounds very charming. But I don't like the dishonesty." She peered at me. "You don't look heartbroken."

I pressed my feelings, the way one might a bruise. No, I was not heartbroken. Or humiliated. The doomsayers were right: dancing with a man was different. And it could lead to . . . divans. But I had been right, too, and so had Otelia Brooks. The body needed to move, even in ways deemed improper. Dancing—and divans—could be healthy. Energizing.

And I wasn't sure in this case if either one was much more than that.

"Disappointed?" I said finally. "He's a very good dancer."

"So dance with him."

"It's that simple."

She took my hand across the table. "Well, some things should be."

"Thank you," I said.

"You're welcome."

14

"*With a crack of* the whip and a wave of her chair / She said to that lion, now you stop right there . . ."

Leo had written a new song. Inspired by last night's events, it was called "Lady Lion Tamer" and was already much admired, at least by the bored American Beauties waiting to have their wings applied. In high spirits, Leo finished with a ripple of notes ending with a buoyant *bum bum* on the low keys, and the ladies burst into applause.

I was not in high spirits. We were six hours away from curtain, and it did not seem improbable that the cast would collapse in shambles with the first wrong note, missed line, or costume mishap. All this would be witnessed by the press and a glittering collection of the wealthy, sensation seeking, and influential in the arts, who would then spread the word of the Rutherfords' humiliation throughout the city. The champagne and oysters might keep them at bay for a few minutes. The six-course dinner at which the Beauties were artfully shared out among the guests would hold them a little longer. But by midnight, everyone would know: Dolly Rutherford's "Stirring Scenes of the Emancipation" had been an utter flop. Not even the coronation of Miss Rutherford's would nudge that news out of people's minds. Witnesses to the epic embarrassment would be the most sought-after guests for weeks, encouraged to share the mortifying details again and again.

Leo's assurance that all shows were shambles on opening night did nothing to calm my nerves. The paper-and-wire wings had only been completed that morning, and now they had to be fixed onto eleven smocks. Those same eleven smocks also needed hemming, as Mr. Rutherford had insisted that when the girls were lined up in a row, the nightgowns should align evenly. I knelt on the floor, letting Emily's smock down and fighting off a headache. There was crowding and chatter all around me. Nearby, Mrs. Lonsdale and Mrs. Tallworthy were having a spirited conversation about the merits of the Savoy versus Brown's. Mrs. Lonsdale was a great one for gesticulation, and with every fling of her hand she stepped backward and onto my skirt. Her aim was excellent; no matter where I moved my skirt, she landed on it. Since about three steps ago, she no longer felt it necessary to apologize, feeling that if she had done it so often, it was simply the way of the world.

My temper was not improved by exhaustion. We had returned from the Acme very late. I had stayed up later talking with Anna, and woken at seven this morning to remember the dispiriting truth that Bill Danvers was not the man who attacked Otelia Brooks.

Nor was he the man who killed Carrie Biel. After Emily knocked Danvers unconscious, Leo had asked his colleagues at the club if anyone could account for him the night of Carrie's murder. Moira had been telling the truth when she said he was following her for much of that evening. That is, until bouncer Frank Walters decided he was becoming a nuisance and hit him with one of his legendary left hooks. After that, the waiters had carried him down to the cellar and locked him in for fun.

I looked to the stage, where Mr. Rutherford was directing the final moment of the pageant, when the entire cast would part and the winner would emerge from the back of the stage. We were fortunate that day to have the ebullient Mr. Rutherford. Everything had gone from squalid to spectacular, from dismal to dazzling. Every lady was lovely, the singing sublime, and the pageant itself a singular triumph that would have the city buzzing for weeks. Nay, months. Nay, years.

I looked up as squeals of excitement greeted the arrival of handsomely framed portraits of the previous Miss Rutherford's. Their faces glided past me as the workmen carried them to the front: all the young women, hair sleek and full, expressions radiant and hopeful. Beneath each picture was a plaque with the year and name. Miss Rutherford's 1903 to 1913. The frame for 1913 was empty but for a sign: WHO WILL IT BE?

Immediately, I lost all my Beauties as they raced to examine their predecessors. Approaching Mrs. Hirschfeld, who had come with the pictures, I asked her, "Do you have a favorite?"

"You know, I can't say that I do. The Miss Rutherford's have always struck me as a tad—" An eloquent ripple of the fingers stood in for the word "dull."

"Certainly there's a type," I said, looking at the faces.

"Oh, the rules are quite strict. We measure them, you know. Not just the height and waist span. Girls of five feet four and no more than a hundred and twenty-five pounds. Space between the eyes, *shape* of the eyes." She gave me a meaningful look. "Nose must be straight and not too prominent; mouth must be well formed, not vulgar. The skin shade—anything swarthier than a magnolia, unacceptable."

Emily was well above five-four; again, I worried Mr. Rutherford was raising her hopes for reasons other than belief in her talent.

"Well, thank goodness I never entered," I joked.

Taking me seriously, she looked me up and down. "You're about the right measurements. Lovely nose, long lashes. But the eyes are much too sharp for a Miss Rutherford's. And that hair has a bit of a curl to it. Oh, don't be self-conscious; men must find it enchanting." She looked over at her son. "Leo certainly seems to."

Perhaps to get away from that awkward subject, we went to watch the arrangement of laurels around the portraits. Arms neatly crossed at her middle, Mrs. Hirschfeld made her way up the line. At one picture, she paused and let out a small, sad sound.

"What happened to . . ." I looked at the name. "Lottie Burckholdt?"

"Poor Lottie. I liked Lottie. She was a late addition, the eleventh girl. She came to us in a year resplendent with knock knees, thin bosoms, and pocked skin; she was a little bucked in the teeth, but had a life to her and simply gorgeous hair. Mr. Rutherford had his doubts, but I said she could smile mouth closed, and no one would see anything but that hair anyway. She's healthy, I said; people want to see a girl with some spirit."

And humor, I thought, looking at Lottie. Like the rest, she had her eyes trained on heaven, but you could sense the barely repressed guffaw.

"Didn't she marry her millionaire?" I asked, referring to the Rutherford's legend.

"She met a dockworker who left her dead by the river with her teeth knocked out."

"Oh, dear." I wondered how Rutherford's had kept that sad tale out of the papers. It was hardly a fitting end for an American Beauty.

Then I heard Leo say, "Hello, Mother."

"Leo, darling. Your tails are downstairs waiting for you. What are you doing away from the piano?"

"I am taking Miss Prescott to lunch at the canteen."

Aware of Mrs. Hirschfeld—and Clara—I said truthfully, "I don't think I have time, Mr. Hirschfeld."

"For Rutherford's world-famous meatloaf? Consumed in the company of Leo Hirschfeld? You have time."

Pointedly taking my hand, he promised his mother to bring her a slice and led me—not too unwillingly—away from smocks and wings.

The employee canteen at Rutherford's was well equipped with long tables and benches where workers could eat food brought from home or the day's offerings, which were, as Leo had promised, meatloaf and gravy, potatoes and sprouts on the side. I hadn't brought anything from the refuge, and my stomach gurgled. Leo, of course, charmed his way into a double helping of potatoes and extra gravy.

When we sat down, Leo said, "I wanted to tell you, Danvers is done. Turns out he was shaking the girls down for a cut of everything they stole. I guess Tricker figures that's *his* job."

Bill Danvers with no employment could be an angrier Bill Danvers with more time on his hands, but at least he wouldn't be paid to harass the women of the refuge. And perhaps Moira's life would be easier. On the other hand, Sadie and Carrie's killer was still on the street and unknown.

For a little while, we ate without talking. I was about to ask if Leo thought this evening's performance would be dismal or outright disastrous when he said in a rush, "Look, what you said— Myrtle, Edith, Josephine—that's not true. I don't do that."

I waited for him to define what exactly he did do.

"Yes, I will split a pastrami sandwich with a girl from time to time if Clara has class, and she always has class. . . . But it's only a sandwich."

Remembering the divan, I doubted that. "I think marriage means you eat at home."

That sparked a rare show of irritation. "I'm not getting married to Clara. I'm not getting married to anyone. For one thing, I work too much. And for another, I'm not like most people. I don't . . ." He held out his arm to indicate a straight line he apparently couldn't follow. "I hear something, it takes over my brain, it's all I can think about. I can't turn it off. Sometimes I'm up till three in the morning, working. Who needs a husband like that? My neighbors already hate me."

Self-serving—but I remembered the first day I met him, that sense that he absorbed all the sound around him and turned it into song. It would be hard to turn that off.

"And if I meet a girl I like, I . . . get obsessed with her, too. I know, I'm sorry, I shouldn't have asked you dancing. But you looked so sad and so pretty."

I knew. He was not at all sorry he had asked me dancing, and he knew very well the word "pretty" was ringing in my ears, a frustrating distraction to the reality, which was that Leo Hirschfeld liked women far too much to restrict himself to just one. We were the elevated train, the ladies arguing, the laughter at the club . . . passing, random sounds to be turned into melodic fantasy. He would never love any girl as much as the ideal he sang to. Or the time he spent spinning the world's sound into music.

He took up my hands. "I *like* you. I don't want to not know you after tonight."

"I like you, too." I set his hand down. "But the next time you want to go dancing, ask Clara."

"Clara doesn't like loud bands." He leaned his chin on his hand, gave me his big brown eyes. "You see my terrible dilemma?"

I was about to describe several far more terrible dilemmas that could befall him when I saw Orville Pickett come through the cafeteria door. He greeted one or two men at the end of the table and sat down next to them. Then he began to eat a sandwich, prepared no doubt by his mother.

"That's Orville Pickett," I told Leo.

Leo said, "Oh," in a tone that indicated that was Orville's misfortune.

Hunching down so Orville wouldn't see me, I said, "Only Rutherford's employees eat here, is that right?"

Leo indicated himself and me. "Or people working in the store. But he's eating with the warehouse guys, so he probably works there. So what?"

"He lives in my neighborhood. He knew Sadie Ellis. She even . . . flirted a bit with him. Since Carrie Biel worked at Rutherford's, it means he knew both women who were killed."

Leo looked doubtful. "It's a big store. Doesn't mean he knew her."

This was true. Who would know if Carrie and Orville had ever met? I thought of the last time I'd seen Carrie. Laughing behind the counter as she folded up that scrap of a negligee.

"Where are you going?" Leo asked as I stood up.

"I have to talk to your mother."

Thankfully, Mrs. Hirschfeld was still in the Crystal Palace. In fact, she was just putting the last wings on Gertie Walsh's smock when I returned. She smiled, and I had the briefest thought she might have changed her mind about me. But I put that aside and asked if I might speak with her in private.

Going to the far end of the hall, I said, "Do you remember Carrie Biel?"

"The poor girl who was murdered? Of course."

"And do you happen to know an Orville Pickett?"

I didn't want to give her any hints, so I waited while she consulted her prodigious memory. "Works in the warehouse. Unloads
the trucks."

"Yes, exactly. What I need to know is, did Orville Pickett know
Carrie Biel?"

She frowned. "I wouldn't—oh, now that I think of it, yes. He
would show up on the floor from time to time. No business being
there, and I spoke to him very sharply. Once I even mentioned it
to Mr. Rutherford."

I thanked her and turned to go. Then something occurred to
me. "Mrs. Hirschfeld? When you say he works in the warehouse,
what does that mean?"

"Rutherford's prides itself on its vast selection, but we can't
keep everything at the store. So we have a warehouse. When
we needed the extra nightgowns, you remember I called the
warehouse?" I nodded. "Every day we do inventory and restock.
Mr. Pickett is one of the men who drives the goods over here
and unloads them to the storeroom. That's how he saw Carrie.
She was a good strong girl, and I would send her down to collect
things."

"And where is the warehouse?"

"Downtown. Near the Bowery, I think."

Not too far from the refuge, I was willing to bet. I looked at
poor Lottie Burckholdt's portrait. Miss Rutherford's 1910.

"How long has Mr. Pickett worked here?"

She thought. "The store congratulates employees on every
five-year anniversary with the company. I seem to remember seeing his name on a recent list. Five years, I think."

"Thank you, Mrs. Hirschfeld."

* * *

In the few hours before the audience arrived, I went through my duties mechanically, even as my brain reviewed the dull little facts I had just learned and their terrifying meaning.

Orville Pickett worked at Rutherford's.

He knew Carrie Biel. And Sadie.

And Lottie Burckholdt.

All three women were dead.

And Orville Pickett had most likely killed them.

Officer Nolan said it was possible that the women either knew the man who attacked them or felt safe enough around him that they were willing to go with him. And Orville Pickett had always seemed safe, a sort of overgrown toddler still tied to his mother's apron strings.

Although one woman had heard screams that night. Mrs. Pickett, who had said a man accosted Carrie and that man was my uncle.

But she had lied. Because the man who had accosted Carrie had to be her own son. It was the only way that scenario made sense. What had Carrie said? *Leave me alone? Take your hands off me?* In the back of my mind, I had always wondered if the story sounded so false because I couldn't believe my uncle at this stage of life would approach a young woman like that. Now I knew: he never had. To protect her son, Mrs. Pickett had simply replaced him with my uncle.

And now that I thought of it, she had never said outright that she had seen my uncle. *Heard*—that was what she had said. And *knew*. Even as she falsely accused someone of murder, she was sharp enough to leave room for error should the truth ever be revealed. What a horror she was. And what a horror she had created.

What was it like, I wondered, growing up with a mother so enraged by the physical allure of women? Who went on and on about illicit acts and the lives destroyed by them? She didn't ever blame the men who bought the women's services, I realized. No, it was always the women who drew men in, ruining their lives. And, of course, the men who helped them do it, like my uncle. No wonder Orville Pickett had never been seen with a girl; his mother would have branded any woman a harlot just for looking at him.

What would that do to you? How angry must you feel? Sadie's harmless tease, showing a bit of her leg? And Carrie—thoughtful, cheerful Carrie, who would be kind to anyone. He had seen her at the store. Would he have been outraged to see her visiting the refuge? The girl he liked, just another of "those" women, selling herself to men with money when she wouldn't even give him the time of day!

Orville Pickett had grabbed Carrie on her way to the refuge. He had waited until she came out. And then he had killed her.

Several times that afternoon, I glanced at the entrance to the Crystal Palace, terrified that Orville would come through the doors. Leo reassured me that Rutherford's kept a strict time clock; Orville would be expected back at the warehouse after lunch.

"What are you going to do?" he asked.

This was a very good question. I could go to Officer Nolan with Mrs. Hirschfeld's account of Orville pestering Carrie, the fact that he had known both women, that he had access to an empty warehouse where he could have killed Carrie and a truck he could have used to transport her body. But that wouldn't be enough. There would be no bloody clothes; Mrs. Pickett herself might have hidden or destroyed them. And surely Orville would have cleaned the truck, if he had used it to move poor Carrie.

But not everyone was an expert cleaner, I thought, and he would have been in a rush. The police had never checked the trucks or even the warehouse because they hadn't known where to look. The evidence could still be there.

However, Mrs. Pickett would howl, and as I had said so many times to my uncle, people listened to her. She would insist I was only accusing her son to save my uncle. Faced with two women with opposing stories and the prospect of bringing scandal on a wealthy, influential businessman, the police might just shrug.

Unless the wealthy, influential businessman insisted.

I wondered how much George Rutherford knew about the people who worked for him. No one could accuse him of being distant; everything at Rutherford's bore his fingerprints. But would he be familiar with the men who worked in the warehouse? Would he, frankly, care? I thought back to when he had sent me to Mrs. Hirschfeld; he had not given her name. She was only "his woman" on the third floor. Just as I was Louise's woman, in the eyes of Mrs. Rutherford.

On the other hand, if a man in his employ were a danger to the women he relied on for his wealth, that might be a very different story.

Getting his attention was another matter. At the moment, he was an unstoppable whirlwind, shouting directions to the Beauties as he made adjustments to the curtains, moved staging this way and that, and even corrected the tempo of Leo's playing. But there was one person who might command it above all else. Approaching Mrs. Rutherford, I begged her pardon and asked if Mr. Rutherford might have a spare moment.

"He might, but you don't. That girl's wings need fixing."

She pointed to Gertrude Walsh, who was standing by Miss Rutherford 1911, inviting comparisons.

"I only wanted him to see some adjustments I made to Mrs. Tyler's hat. I added an elastic so it would stay on, but I wanted his opinion—"

"Oh, yes, you all want his opinion, don't you?"

Her tone was pleasant, the implication anything but. "Ma'am?"

"Whenever he's around." She fluttered her hands. "'Mr. Ruth-erford, Mr. Rutherford. Look at me, Mr. Rutherford.' Please see to that girl." She pointed. "Now."

As I made my way over to Gertrude, I passed within earshot of Emily, who was gossiping with Mrs. Unger. Seeing me, she said, "Oh, now there's my sister-in-law's maid. Do you know her uncle runs a refuge for women who have been . . . well . . ." She low-ered her voice, and I could just hear the word "prostitutes." "Isn't that tremendously admirable? I think it's admirable."

I was so startled to hear mention of my uncle in Emily's rapid-fire chatter, I stopped dead in my tracks, forgetting for the mo-ment my need to speak with George Rutherford. "Miss Tyler, might I speak with you?"

A brief shadow of guilt came over Emily's face, and I thought she must have looked just like this as a child when caught with her hand in the jam jar. Even with her face covered in preserves, she would have smiled brightly as if she hadn't a care in the world— just as she did now.

"Of course, Jane."

Emily allowed me to lead her into the outer hallway, where I said in a low voice, "Please don't tell people about my uncle's refuge. His work is admirable, but it could be very embarrassing to Mrs. Tyler."

"I haven't told *so* many people."

"No, I'm sure not . . ."

"I mean, I told Mr. Hirschfeld, but I can't think who he'd tell. Oh, and I did tell two other people, but I didn't think you'd mind. I thought, He's awfully rich and gets so much attention, maybe he'll give some money. You once said your uncle wanted to open a nursery wing, and I thought, How wonderful if he could do that, keep mothers and their babies together. Because he was talking about his own mother, and I thought, That's so sweet—"

Utterly confused, I said, "Who was talking about it, Miss Tyler?"

She bit her lip.

"Who did you tell?"

"Mr. Rutherford. I was telling him about it that day we all met at the Armory. Mrs. Rutherford took me out for tea at the Orientale—you remember. Mr. Rutherford came down from his office and joined us. And he was so interested. Liked the idea ever so much and said he'd go look at the refuge as soon as he could to see all the good work being done there. I told him, You absolutely should, Mr. Rutherford. Go straightaway and you'll see. The Reverend Prescott changes these women's lives, he . . . transforms them. He said he couldn't think of a finer mission to dedicate yourself to."

The news that Emily Tyler had spoken with the Rutherfords about my uncle's mission was confusing. This simple piece of information created a fog in my mind; I could neither say it was fine or not fine. And yet because you must always tell people you answer to that they have done nothing wrong, I managed to say, "That was very thoughtful of you, Miss Tyler."

Relieved, Emily said, "I meant well, but I do see what you mean about Louise. I won't mention it again. Nobody listens to a word I say anyway—"

"There you are!"

The door to the grand hall had opened to reveal Dolly Rutherford, an eye-rolling Gertrude Walsh behind her.

"Miss Walsh has been waiting. I look around and you are nowhere to be found. I don't suppose I need to remind you that the pageant is in an hour?"

I felt my face stretch in a smile that was more teeth than

appeasement. A hundred responses crowded my thoughts, some of them glancing off the knowledge Emily had just given me, others sprouting suddenly, nurtured in the rich soil of my intense dislike of Dolly Rutherford.

Emily said, "It's my fault, Mrs. Rutherford. I wasn't happy about my hair, and I dragged Jane out here to show her in private."

"Well," said Dolly Rutherford, denied the opportunity for further outrage, "come in now and attend to Miss Walsh."

As we went back inside the Crystal Palace, Gertrude Walsh pulled a face at me and whispered, "I didn't complain. I think they're just fine." It was true that her shoulders were a little low, with the result that the wings kept batting her on the head whenever she turned. The trick would be to place them high enough to be visible but low enough to spare her ears.

Taking out the earlier stitches, I said, "I know you didn't, Miss Walsh. Still, we do have to fix—"

"Ah, the woman who fixes things."

My hand stilled above the silk and wire, my mind suddenly blank. Still, the voice box seemed in working order, as I managed, "Mr. Rutherford."

I kept my eyes on Gertrude Walsh's back. That was safe. I knew I could not thread my needle again; my hand was shaking too badly. I could feel Mr. Rutherford as he made his way around Miss Walsh, judging the effect. Judging my work. Judging . . .

He was tall. I remember him leaning on me, not being able to breathe.

I instructed myself to breathe.

Told myself I was being ridiculous. This was George Rutherford. A man who walked among women every day, adjusting their hats, changing their color patterns, decreeing . . .

Why would my hand not stop shaking?

Breathe, I told myself. Breathe. Sew . . .

Gertrude Walsh cried out. I had stuck her. The blood bloomed and spread on the white collar of the nightgown.

I clapped a hand to my mouth. "I'm so sorry, Miss Walsh."

There would be rage now. Screaming. A storm would break loose. I braced myself. Heard George Rutherford say, "Oh, now, it isn't bad at all, a tiny scratch . . ."

My stomach eased. I felt a hand on my shoulder. "It could happen to anyone. Here."

A handkerchief was offered. A fine silk handkerchief, the initials GR stitched in purple. I shook my head, intending to say we should never use anything so nice to fix my mistake. I had a scrap of old cloth in my pocket; that would do.

Then I saw it.

The scar on George Rutherford's hand.

15

"*Jane?*"

A knock on the door.

"I'm fine, Mrs. Tyler." I lifted my head from the cool porcelain of the toilet. "I'll be out shortly."

From under the stall door I could see Louise's feet move away, then return.

"I'm worried you're sick."

"Something I ate at lunch. I'm so sorry. I need a few minutes."

There was a long pause. "Miss Walsh said she's not at all mad. She understands it was a mistake."

"That's kind of her, thank you."

"And I want you to know, I had some very sharp words with Dolly Rutherford."

In spite of my terror, I smiled. "You didn't have to do that, Mrs. Tyler."

"Oh, I did. And I want you to know, George Rutherford agreed with me entirely."

This reminder of his existence, not fifty yards away, caused my stomach to heave again. Such an odd reaction, I thought, detached. After seeing the scar, I had fled to the powder room and vomited. As if my body simply couldn't absorb the knowledge that George Rutherford had butchered Sadie and Carrie and who knew how many other women. And that his hand had been on my shoulder minutes ago.

My first conscious thought had been *Run*. As were my second, third, and tenth. I had to remove my body from the orbit of George Rutherford. I would leave the bathroom, race down the stairs, out of the building, and . . .

Then I thought of Louise. And Emily. Gertie Walsh, who had been kind about her wings. The beautiful Hattie Phipps, who made everyone laugh with her wondrously varied repertoire of *Kandinsky, Nussbaum, and Schlom, how may I direct your call?*

"Jane? I'm worried."

I raised myself up, sat on my knees. "Don't be, Mrs. Tyler."

"No?"

"No."

It had to be today, I realized. Tomorrow I would have no more reason to be here. It had to be today. Now. While George Rutherford was distracted with the crowning of Miss Rutherford's.

Because the police would not come without evidence. Otelia Brooks was right; her scar would not be enough. Even her testimony, supposing I was heartless enough to make her be in the same room as George Rutherford again, wouldn't be enough. Emily's report that she had told George Rutherford about the refuge would not be enough. Even though he had attacked Sadie that very evening.

But he had taken things. Sadie's stocking, Carrie's bracelet. And I felt sure he had kept them. They were somewhere, and not in his home. The home would be Mrs. Rutherford's domain. Not safe. No, they would be in a place where he was all-powerful. Here, at the store that bore his name.

The office, that strange closed-off room. The heavy iron safe in the corner . . .

"Go back to the hall, please, Mrs. Tyler. I'll be perfectly fine."

★ ★ ★

The doors opened at six. From backstage, I could feel the wave of energy as two hundred excited New Yorkers poured into the Crystal Palace. Dressed in white tie, George Rutherford was there to greet them all. I peeked out from behind the curtain, watching as he shook hands, praised appearances, and promised a memorable evening for all. Only the fact that we were surrounded by a crowd allowed me to breathe within a hundred feet of him.

Several of the women behind the curtain were frantic with nerves. Louise's lips moved in silence as she ran through the Proclamation again and again. Dolly Rutherford—the only one who seemed calm—instructed Mrs. Fortesque in the proper way to breathe; Mrs. Fortesque insisted no air was getting in and she was about to faint. Mrs. Lonsdale and Mrs. Tallworthy's debate on hotels continued unabated, despite frequent shushings from the other ladies.

At the other end of the stage, dressed all in white, stood the American Beauties. Unlike their wealthier castmates, they were silent. The next hour would bring a new life to one and dashed hopes to the rest. For them, this was serious business, and they were all much too burdened to talk. In their simple smocks, they looked like lovely little ghosts. Or, I thought, young girls prepared for their graves. Even Emily looked wide-eyed and subdued. Like Lottie Burckholdt, she was a late addition. The eleventh girl. The one few would remember ever existed.

Feeling a quick kiss on the back of my head, I turned to see Leo resplendent in his tails. He spread his arms as if to say, *Behold!*

"You look very handsome, Mr. Hirschfeld."

He peered at me. "You look terrible. Which is wrong for a beautiful girl."

"Well, you'll just have to look at another girl."

"What if I don't want to?"

"Mr. Hirschfeld," hissed Mrs. Rutherford. "Get back to the piano. We are about to begin."

I heard the pounding of footsteps as Mr. Rutherford ascended to the stage. "Ladies and gentlemen, welcome to what I hope will be a very special evening. A spectacular conceived and brought to life through the vision and effort of my dear wife—"

The applause broke out before her name was uttered.

"—Dolly Rutherford. Tonight, we honor the great mission of the War Between the States, our commitment to liberty, and those who fell in its cause. Without further ado, I give you 'Stirring Scenes of the Emancipation.'"

The American Beauties had already gathered onstage, stooped and anonymous as they worked in the field, represented by painted wooden rows of earth. As the curtain opened, Mrs. Van Dormer stepped onto the stage as Harriet Tubman. Perhaps it was my roiling terror, but the first scene had a nightmarish quality now; the vision of Mrs. Van Dormer in kerchief and face paint felt like grotesque mockery. In a high, quavering voice she called the Beauties to come with her to see Father Abraham. This was Louise's cue to enter. She gulped, and for a terrible moment I thought she would not make it.

Hurrying to her side, I whispered, "Be brave, Mr. President. Remember, 'That on the first day of January, in the year of our

Lord one thousand eight hundred and sixty-three . . . All persons held as slaves shall be then, thenceforward, and forever free.'"

And with a deep inhale, Louise marched out, hat straight, and delivered her lines in a clear, stirring voice. The audience burst into applause, and for a moment I was distracted by enormous pride and the wish William could be here to see how well she'd done.

The following scene took us to the Lincolns' bedroom. When Dolly Rutherford stepped out, there was another wild round of clapping. As Mrs. Lincoln exhorted her husband to take up the cause of emancipation, I waited for my chance to escape. Mr. Lincoln having agreed to listen to his wife's advice, several of the ladies marched on as Union troops, singing "Hold On, Abraham."

Next, each of the American Beauties emerged to recite one of the amendments, causing a hubbub as people realized the contestants had been included in the pageant. They had taken off the kerchiefs they wore in the first scene but had not donned their wings. (They wore no face paint, as their faces were, after all, the point.) When Emily stepped forward, the murmur became doubtful. There were only ten American Beauties; who was this eleventh girl? Nonetheless, Emily's youth and eagerness were irresistible, and she received a hearty ovation. As she hurried backstage, she whispered in my ear, "It's going to be me, I know it!"

There were problems. One of the wooden rifles got caught in the curtains, and there was laughter as Mrs. Byrd pulled it free. The chorus lost its way during one verse of "All Quiet Along the Potomac Tonight," but Leo sang loudly enough to put them right. And Mrs. Lonsdale and Mrs. Tallworthy managed to continue their conversation about hotels, which was perhaps out of place for Union soldiers under fire. The pistol did not go off as planned, obliging Mrs. Fortesque to shout *bang* before Louise could slump forward. Unfortunately, Dolly Rutherford had already cried, "Oh, my husband has been shot," so Louise had to sit up briefly before collapsing again. At which point the hat did roll off her head.

But the applause at the end of the "Battle Hymn of the Republic" was rapturous. Perhaps because the audience knew the most exciting part of the evening was yet to come: the crowning of Miss Rutherford's.

Which I would miss. I had other things to do while Mr. Rutherford was enjoying his moment of triumph.

Creeping from behind the curtain on the far right-hand side of the stage, I passed Leo, who was playing through the ovation. Seeing me, he whispered, "Where are you going?"

Feeling the need to be quick, I didn't bother to lie about my destination. "Mr. Rutherford's office. He needs something for the crowning."

Leo looked puzzled. But the ladies were taking their places for the finale, so he went back to playing. Although I saw him look back at me as I hurried up the side of the hall and out the door.

The store was now quite empty. Still, I didn't run but walked quickly, on the off chance I met anyone. Then again, if questioned, I had only to say that Mr. Rutherford wanted something and they would understand my haste. So many people were afraid of him, I thought, and they didn't even know what he was.

I approached the door to Rutherford's office, placing my fingers lightly on the wood. It swung wide enough for me to see the room was empty. I went in, heart landing heavily against my ribs.

The covered windows demanded my attention. I remember wondering why a man so well-off chose as his seat of power a room with no view. A place he could not see out? And no one could see in? Now I knew.

Steadying myself on one of the chairs, I looked at the safe. It was a squat, dark, ugly thing, crouching in the corner. The door was shut. I had hoped by some miracle he might have left it open. But if what I thought was true, this safe was never left open. The lock spun rarely—although twice this past week—and only late at night, the great iron door creaking open, the contents pulled out, examined, added to . . .

I should pull the handle, I thought, even as I thought the precise opposite. But having dared come, I felt I had to touch it, see if it yielded at all. It would not, of course. And I would feel very foolish. I reached out a hand.

"What are you doing here?"

I tore my hand from the safe's handle, hiding it behind my back like a child. There, filling the doorway, was George Rutherford. Sweat on his brow and the agitated rise and fall of his chest indicated he, too, had moved swiftly. He wore a black tailcoat and white tie, but there was nothing of the gentleman in his aspect; the veneer of human was badly cracked. He placed his hands on either side of the door, all but saying No escape.

"It's a complete outrage."

"Yes," I said, edging back toward the desk. "Yes, I'm sorry. Mrs. Rutherford asked me—"

"No, she didn't."

How had he known? I wondered. Had he asked where I was? My lie to Leo. Leo would have wanted to assure the fearsome Mr. R that I was on an errand for him.

Before, focused on his slender elegance, I had not fully understood how tall he was, how wide the span of his arms. The last time I saw him here, he had been sitting down, hunched over. Now he smiled. Or showed his teeth, letting me know he understood all of this. His hands came loose from the doorjamb. His hands.

He took a step. I stepped back, aware of the desk less than a foot behind me. And the wall, no windows. I would wait until he was close enough to me, away from the door. I would duck past him, run . . .

"Is Miss Rutherford's crowned?" I tried.

"Oh, yes, she's been chosen."

"Who?" I would keep him talking, keep him in mind of the hundreds of people nearby. This was no dark alley late at night in a neighborhood used to violence. This was Rutherford's. Where women were welcomed, celebrated, I thought in a wild joke.

"I'm afraid your Miss Tyler didn't win. But there will be other honors."

Yes, I thought. Like Lottie Burckholdt, the eleventh girl who wasn't supposed to win. But Mrs. Hirschfeld insisted, and the field was poor that year. How many others? The ones who didn't win and were quickly forgotten. When they died, who would have asked, *Wasn't she once an American Beauty?*

"I should get back."

He took another step toward me.

"Mrs. Tyler will wonder where I am." I let a note of warning into my voice, even as I began to feel behind me for a pen, letter opener . . .

"Oh, dear," said George Rutherford. "Oh, dear."

I darted sideways. He caught my hair, pulled down. An explosion of pain at the base of my skull. Bright lights bloomed before my eyes. Through them, I could just see the crisp whiteness of George Rutherford's cuff, the dull glow of jasper in his button link, the scar on his wrist.

Worse than the pain: knowledge that there was no pretending. I had shown fear. He had shown brutality. I knew what he was now, and he knew it. There was no way out of this room. Scream, I thought. I should . . .

He clamped a hand over my mouth and gave my hair another sharp pull, refusing to let go even when I clawed at his wrists.

"You come in here. In"—another hard tug, and I felt my stomach lurch—"here, where you don't"—this time I cried out—"belong."

Shoving me back against the desk, he put himself between me and the door. "You think you can go anywhere you want these days, don't you? Home is not good enough for you. You want to be out in the streets, throwing a man's money around, showing yourself off. There's no place sacred left. No place a man might call his own, be at peace. While you shut us out anytime you feel like it—mustn't look. Even after you've pushed your way in, demanded our attention . . ."

Something in the accusation *pushed your way in* reminded me of that night, the voice on the telephone. *Come after me . . .*

Then, in a softer voice, he said, "I suppose I shouldn't be angry. Of course you want us to look. What would you be otherwise? You're only what we make of you. The female face, it's blank, like any canvas. It needs the artist."

He peered at my face, suddenly concerned. "I'm afraid I don't see much in you. The hair, perhaps. That, I can see. But it will take a lot of work to get you looking like anything."

Briefly, I thought, he had seen us as colleagues. Employer and assistant, which was at least better than artist and subject. I would try that, get him talking about his work. "Is it frustrating? That people don't get to admire your . . . best work?"

"Some do. I've seen them."

The warehouse, I thought. Those huge windows. Afterward, he had watched as people crowded around the bodies, eager to get a glimpse. He had been that close the whole time.

Sadie, I thought, might never have known who he was. On her way to meet Harry Knowles, she might have been struck from behind, dragged into the alley. Or else been charmed by his money, his flattery.

Carrie was smart and ambitious. The chance to walk with the

owner of Rutherford's would have been appealing to her, especially if he promised her a ride late at night. And she was considerate. If George Rutherford said—and I was sure he had—*Oh, dear, I've left something at the warehouse, would you mind if we stop to get it?* Carrie would have said *Of course*. She would have been helpful, amenable.

I had killed Carrie. The moment I told her to come to the refuge.

I remembered her bare wrist. Sadie's ankle. Dizzy from terror and ragged breathing, I said, "The women . . . give you something in return. Don't they? You don't work for free?"

"I don't ask what they can't afford. Some of the women I am most creative with have very little."

Yes, I thought. A wealthy woman, well known, with many friends, you could never take the kind of creative liberties you took with Sadie and Carrie.

"But I ask for a small token. I don't get to see my work for very long, you see, and the tokens help me remember. Vanity, yes. But still, very precious to me. I keep them safe."

His hand trembled, as if it had been held back too long. The door, I had to get to the door. But he was in between like a snarling rabid dog, teeth shining, froth whipping from his jaws, and I had nothing to beat him back. He had to be put down, I thought. Put down. The words thundered in my head—useless. He had no knife, I told myself. But the hands, red and hard knuckled, thick cruel fingers around the throat. How many had he killed? I couldn't think he would hesitate over me.

I reached behind me, groped along the desk's surface. And that's when it all happened. He was on me, overwhelming, any trace of human burned away. Roaring, he grabbed my hair, yanking my head back as he slammed my hand onto the desk, pinning it. Pain obliterated any fear I might have felt, and I kicked and screamed, landing my fist against the side of his head and his neck. He snatched both hands, used his weight to keep my legs still. I arched, trying to throw him off, and felt choking panic as his hands fastened hard on my neck, nails digging in.

I struggled for consciousness, knowing the moment I let go it would be the end. My uncle came to mind. And that lamp, brass with a smoked-glass bowl. I was going to end with the sight of that lamp; it would be the last thing I saw. Determined to hold on to myself as I left this life, I shut my eyes, put my mind on Uncle, on dancing, fingers curled through Leo's, Anna's swift, hard embrace, Michael Behan's half smile, Otelia Brooks fixing her hat on that child's head . . .

Something in that memory put breath back in my lungs and I attacked Rutherford's red and sweating face with my fingers. I clawed at his eyes, his neck. I would forget his size, forget his strength and rage to kill—my will counted, too. I needed to live. I was going to live . . .

I don't know what I understood first, the thunderclap of the gunshot or the sudden crushing weight of George Rutherford as he fell, first on top of me, then slowly sliding sideways to the floor. I was gulping air and crying all at once, shaking so hard my knees buckled. But I would not fall anywhere near George Rutherford and managed to stay upright just long enough to stagger forward and be caught by Otelia Brooks.

16

My eyes were red. Bloodred. In the hospital, I looked in the mirror and saw an illustration from a fairy tale. The witch, obviously. Although when I turned my head and saw the mottled purple blotches on my throat, the crescent dents of fingernails, I thought, No, this is a different point in the fairy tale. That part of "Bluebeard" or even "Beauty and the Beast" we don't hear. Even if we know very well what happens.

They told me I was lucky. I nodded to show I knew it was true.

A detective gave me a pad of paper. I wrote, *Miss Brooks?*

Miss Brooks had been arrested.

I tried to speak, choked on needles. I splayed my fingers at my throat, waved at my eyes.

"She shot him, Miss Prescott."

One vehement nod: *Good.*

"There will be a fair trial, I assure you."

I threw up my hand, a gesture I had borrowed from Anna. Now I knew why she did it so often; it was an excellent expression

of fury at sheer stupidity. Grabbing the pad, I scribbled, *No trial.*
INNOCENT.

I started to write that George Rutherford had murdered at
least three women, but the detectives were barely looking at the
pad. So I threw it at them. Then, realizing I had thrown away my
one means of communication, I started to cry.

Louise hurried to my bed and demanded, "What have you
said to her?" And when they did not answer immediately, "I think
you should leave. Now."

They did. Through my bloodshot eyes, I looked up at
Mrs. Louise Tyler, who had just ordered two policemen out of the
room. I thought to tell her that Mr. Lincoln's courage and leader-
ship had rubbed off on her a little. But then I fell asleep.

I couldn't remember much of what happened directly after
Otelia Brooks shot George Rutherford. I had been dizzy from
shock and lack of air. I think the first screams came from Dolly
Rutherford. Quickly, the little space filled up; I was aware of legs
all around me, voices far above my head. At some point, I must
have stopped being aware, because when I could see again,
Otelia Brooks was gone and I was in a hospital bed.

They held up fingers. Asked me to name the president. Then,
satisfied my brain was not damaged, they sent me home. Which,
Louise insisted, was the Tyler residence. Lying in my bed at the
top of their house, I took in my little writing desk and chair. The
pale blue rug on the floor. My washbowl and washcloth. Books.
The elegant coat I had worn to the Armory Show over the back of
a chair. The sun coming through my window and the sounds of
the city. And thought, Yes, home.

Louise brought me a fresh ice pack; I had a feeling she was enjoying her nursing duties. Holding it to my neck, I wrote, *Mrs. Tyler,*
I am so sorry.

"Jane, why on earth should you be sorry?"

Scandal.

"I hardly think it's your scandal if a brute tries to strangle you."

I asked for newspapers. Reluctantly, Louise gave them to me.

The stories were ugly—and since no one knew George Rutherford was a murderer, flagrantly untrue. People were told that he had been killed while defending me from an attack by an unhinged woman. No motive for the attack was given. Nor was there any mention of my injuries. An illustration helped those who could not read: George Rutherford, hands raised helplessly as Otelia Brooks shot him down. Another woman, meant to be me, cowered behind Mr. Rutherford.

I was unable to use the telephone, but Louise was eager to help. Calling people on my behalf, she said, was far more interesting than lunch with her mother or stammering through yet another French lesson.

So I gave her a list. The first was Officer Nolan.

Then I wrote, *Miss Ella Dodson, Amsterdam News. Reporter.*

I hesitated a moment, then added, *Michael Behan at the Herald.*

Louise smiled. "Very well." She took the notes. "By the way, I should mention, Mr. Hirschfeld has called the house several times. He seems quite frantic to see you."

Officer Nolan arrived, officious and ill at ease in such an elegant house. He seemed positively relieved to be shown into my room. Although his grip on his hat tightened at the sight of my throat.

"I was sorry to hear of your . . ."

I nodded: *Thank you.* Then I wrote down the names Sadie Ellis and Carrie Biel and showed him the pad.

"Miss Prescott, don't you worry about that now . . ."

George Rutherford killed them. He told me so.

He blinked, then tugged at his collar. "Well, he can't speak from the grave, Miss Prescott. Other than that, we've only got your word that he said it."

I wrote, *Can prove he attacked Otelia Brooks 10 years ago in same way. Scar on his wrist. Look for it.*

"I can't." He shook his head. "They'll be wanting to bury him."

Stop burial. I underlined it.

I told him about Lottie Burckholdt, even if it was unlikely they would look into her death again. I said he should interview the other women who worked at Rutherford's and see if other American Beauties had met similar unfortunate fates.

"George Rutherford is . . . was . . . a wealthy, respected man, Miss Prescott."

I pointed to my throat. He shifted in his chair, clearly wishing himself elsewhere.

"His widow says you, ah . . . that you might have . . . She was under the impression you led him on."

"Led him on?" I mouthed the words in shock.

"She says you wanted a chance to be an American Beauty, that you were promising him . . ." His shoulders jumped. "She says you were asking where he was that day, wanting to talk to him."

Dolly Rutherford, I thought numbly. How much did she know? Suspect? How many women had died because she chose to look the other way? Then I thought, no, I could not blame Mrs. Rutherford for her husband's monstrousness. His crimes were his alone.

Then I wrote, *There's a safe in his office. Open it.*

"I don't see how we can . . ."

Frustrated, I wrote, *SADIE ELLIS. CARRIE BIEL. OTHERS. OPEN IT.*

I scribbled, *He keeps things there.*

★ ★ ★

It was hard not to smile at the sight of Leo—or sound, rather. I heard him as he came up the stairs, talking a mile a minute to poor Louise, who could only interject an "Oh, really?" or "My!" every so often. He opened the door himself, saying over his shoulder, "'But on Fridays' . . . it's my new song, Mrs. Tyler. I'll play it for you later, you'll love it, I assure you."

Then, shutting the door, he said, "Hello." He looked eager, healthy, and optimistic—everything I didn't feel.

Pulling up a seat next to the bed, he said, "Hey, did I ever tell you how I'm crazy for a girl who can gouge a man's eyes out?"

I wanted to make a droll face but couldn't. There were still times when my body felt the crushing weight of George Rutherford, and I found it hard to breathe.

Leo poured me a glass of water. "He's dead," he said flatly. "My mother saw him and she said he's dead. Mother Hirschfeld never lies." He handed me the glass. "I hear her son takes after her."

"O . . . mits," I mouthed.

"Only with girls smart enough to catch him." He rubbed my hand. "I can't believe I told Rutherford you'd gone to his office. I keep thinking . . ."

He had also told Otelia Brooks where I was, so I smiled and shook my head. Then I waved my hands in the air to show how lively I felt.

"Good," he said. "I want you to get better. And when you're better, I'm going to take you to dinner at Delmonico's."

I wrote, *Never lies?*

"And we're going to go dancing in Union Square and they're going to play my song. 'But on Fridays.' I wrote it for you." I shook my head. "No, really, I did."

He sang, "A maid's life is endless toil / sewing hems and cleaning soil. / She sweeps, she braids, / but on Fridays, these maids . . . Oh, these maids." He swung my hands. "They dance. Oh, yes, they dance. / With no thought of work or dirt / or anything but romance . . ."

I laughed.

"There you go. Uncle Hesh even took the cigar out of his mouth when I played it. So it's dinner, dancing, and we'll see what happens next." He took my hand again, smiling in a way that made me feel as if next could last a lifetime.

Of course, I knew what would happen, and I knew it would not last a lifetime. But I smiled anyway.

* * *

Michael Behan did not smile. He did not make jokes or promise dinner at Delmonico's. He settled himself on my small desk chair, gently turned my head, and described George Rutherford in terms I won't repeat.

Then he said, "I'm sorry. You don't need me showing off my vocabulary at a time like this."

"Do . . . need . . . your vocabulary."

"Don't talk." He slid the pad over to me. "Strain your . . ."

Vocal chords, I wrote. *Opera career over.*

I showed him the newspapers howling for Otelia Brooks's blood. Then told him what George Rutherford kept in his safe.

You need to write different story. George Rutherford murderer. Otelia Brooks heroine. Saved me. Saved others. Make people see that. Make jury see that.

"I can't call him a murderer until they open that safe."

Impatient, I waved at my throat. Then wrote, *Remember when you thought I killed Norrie Newsome?*

"Ah, yes, I do."

You promised to defend me in the papers. You said you would make me sound like . . . I frowned, unable to remember . . . *woman from Bible who killed man* . . .

He smiled. "St. Agnes. Even a Lutheran would know that."

Otelia = St. Agnes.

"Looks a bit different," he said quietly.

I smacked the paper. Then I turned the page, circled the words DEATH NOTICES, and wrote my name underneath. Then I underlined *Otelia = St. Agnes* and croaked, "She *is*."

He put a hand up. "Don't strain . . ."

Either he forgot the word or something else came to mind. His hand drifted, and I felt a light touch at my throat. Nothing very much, just the back of his fingers; then it was over and he said, "Your voice. Don't strain your voice, you'll need it for the trial. And I'll want a quote."

Then he picked up the newspaper and stood up. "I haven't been on crime for a while. I'll have to ask my editor."

And his wife. He had stopped writing about crime so he could be home more. I was endangering the Behan family future.

Under *Otelia = St. Agnes*, I wrote, THANK YOU.

★ ★ ★

Ella Dodson arrived the next morning, settling herself in the chair and smiling a thank-you to the offer of tea. Her eyes widened slightly at the sight of my throat, but I waved to assure her I would be okay. Then I wrote, *Otelia Brooks.*

"They arrested her, I know," she said.

I pointed to her, wrote in the air with my finger. *You write.*

"I intend to."

I wrote the details of what had happened that day, beginning with my realization that George Rutherford knew about the refuge. At one point, I worried I had not explained the importance of that moment and wrote, *You'll have to tell readers—*

Ella Dodson put a hand over mine, stilling it. "You tell me what you know. Then let me tell the story."

★ ★ ★

"Jane."

The voice came from above my head. I wasn't sure if it was real or a dream. If a dream, I preferred to stay with my eyes closed, the pillow warm and comforting around my head.

"Jane?"

Once I knew the voice, I opened my eyes, but remained unsure whether I was dreaming or not. My uncle had come to the police station, but . . . he looked wrong. Older. And it was day, not night. And I was no longer three years old, but an adult.

Struggling to sit up, I said, "Uncle."

"Mrs. Tyler said you were not to talk."

His voice was nervous, hesitant. He sat in my chair close to the bed; his legs had always been short, and it made him seem small.

"I didn't know where you'd gone," he said.

"I'm sorry. I didn't think."

"Mr. Pickett informed us. Apparently it was in the papers. He . . . assumed you would be with us. He wished to know whether you were all right. Are you? All right?"

His hands were at his stomach, fingers tangled. He twisted his ring finger quite cruelly, and I said, "Yes, I'm fine." I stopped his hand. "Truly."

"I have been to see Miss Brooks. To thank her. She explained . . . what Mr. Rutherford was. That not everyone knows yet, what he was. Did you know, when you went to his office?"

"I suspected. That's why I went. I thought there might be proof he killed Carrie and Sadie."

"Jane . . ." He sounded distressed, disapproving.

"Was I supposed to let him get away with it? Let them charge you with murder? Close the refuge?"

"There were other ways."

"There was *not* another way." I had spoken too harshly, and my throat hurt. But I said it again. "There was not another way. The only thing to do now is to make sure Otelia Brooks doesn't pay for that fact."

As I spoke, I was aware of an echo. Someone had said these things before. Or used that tone before. Determined. Stubborn. Unswayable. Infuriatingly so, in fact.

My uncle was smiling. He had heard the echo, too.

"Yes," he said. "That is right." And then, for the first time since our first meeting all those years ago, he took my hand and said again, "That is right."

Then I said, "I want you to tell me."

He was puzzled by the change in subject. After a moment he said, "Ah."

"Privacy is one thing," I said. "This is a secret, and I don't think we should have secrets between us. We are family. In our way."

"And what is a secret other than something one party wishes to keep private and another wants to know against their wishes?" When I didn't reply, he sighed. "Yes, I saw a woman, and yes, I went into her place of business. And that woman and that business would be seen as illegal and unsavory by most."

Well, I had asked to know, and if my face went red and I found my gaze fixed on the coverlet, I had only myself to blame. "I don't see why you didn't just tell the police that. No doubt it's what they assumed."

"Because Miss Bullotte asked me not to."

He said the name casually, assuming knowledge on my part. I was about to say, *Who on earth is Miss Bullotte?*

Then I remembered. "You were with the Duchess?"

My uncle looked curious. "Why do you call her that?"

"She calls herself that, and that is hardly the point. I—"

There were too many questions in my mind, and all of them were impossible.

In a rare act of sensitivity, my uncle said, "My friendship with Miss Bullotte goes back some years. We both have a care for the women in this neighborhood who work in a certain trade. She admires the work we do at the refuge and has even contributed funds. She herself has no moral qualms about her employment, but she does understand that it is not for every woman, and not every woman has her as an employer. That is one of the reasons she came out to defend the refuge against Mrs. Pickett. She was extremely distressed when you were attacked by their group."

That attack had occurred the day before Carrie was murdered. "Was that why you went to see her the second time?"

"To thank her, yes. Also to say I felt it would be safer if she did not continue her presence. Provocation was not what the situation needed."

"And the first time? The night Sadie was killed?"

"I enjoy her company," my uncle said simply.

I considered for a moment, then said, "Well, yes. She seems an exceptional woman."

"I'm sorry I was not more forthcoming with you. But it has always been Miss Bullotte's view that a public announcement of our friendship would serve neither of us well. Also, that it is no one's business."

I nodded, even as I thought, It should be my business. On my next day off, I would pay a call on Miss Bullotte to thank her. Or

I might suggest she come to supper at the refuge. After all, if there was this friendship, we ought to get to know each other.

Then I realized my uncle probably had no more desire for me to be acquainted with Miss Bullotte than I had for him to be acquainted with Leo. That had been my business.

"Just don't tell me I owe Clementine Pickett an apology."

He smiled. "I would never tell you that."

★ ★ ★

On the excuse that he was needed at home, William returned from Washington, determined, he said, never to go near the place again. Louise was overjoyed to have him back and so the Tyler house was a happy place. Still, there was pain. Nightmares, in which George Rutherford was not dead and Otelia Brooks had not come. Once, trapped in sleep, I found myself back in his office, the walls and ceiling closing in, his fingers hard on my throat and every second, less air. I was dimly aware of twisting, trying to call out. And then a different hand, gentle on my head, a reminder that no, no, that was over now, all over. Just a dream.

Two days after my uncle's visit, I visited Otelia Brooks at Blackwell's Island Penitentiary. The sight of her in drab prison garb, her hair pulled back and bunched behind her head, hurt my heart. That I wasn't rotting in the ground was due to her. That she was in this place was due to me.

"We're going to get you released" was the first thing I said when we were seated on rough stools at the end of a long table where prisoners met with visitors.

"I know you'll try."

Her voice was not unkind, but it was a tone you might use with a child. And like a child, I repeated myself, saying, "We *are*."

In the silence that followed, I thought to ask, "How on earth did you know where I was?"

She sighed, clasped her hands in her lap. "After you came to see me, I felt badly. You asked for help, I didn't give it. I asked my-self what would have happened if you hadn't opened the door to me that night. And even though I knew the police weren't going to listen to me, I felt I had to try. At least see this man you thought might be the man who did it.

"So I called the home of Mrs. Tyler, and the housekeeper told me you were all at Rutherford's for some pageant. I came over there. They didn't want to let me in. Store closed. But I told the man at the entrance I was there for Mrs. Tyler, so he let me up. In the lobby I saw that painting of . . . that man." Her head jerked in an odd way. "And that's when I remembered.

"I made it upstairs to the hall." A rise of the eyebrows made it clear what she thought of that scene. "Needless to say, I wasn't welcome. I told them I was looking for Mrs. Tyler, but they either didn't believe me or just wanted me out. I said, Well, if I can't see her, may I speak to the woman who works for her? That was when a young man came up to me and asked if he could help."

Leo, I thought.

"He said you'd gone off to Mr. Rutherford's office. And I knew that was not somewhere you should be, so I asked him where it was. And you know the rest."

For a moment I considered what would have happened if Otelia Brooks had not changed her mind, if she had been a step slower, or walked through the lobby on a route that did not take her by the Rutherford portrait. Then I took a deep breath. Because I still could.

"There's a safe in his office," I told her. "I've told the police about it. Sadie's stocking was missing. So was Carrie Biel's bracelet. I feel sure he kept them, along with your scarf. If the police find them, it will be proof of what he was."

"We'll see."

"And I'll testify if there's a trial, but there won't be a trial, I'm sure. They'll have opened the safe by then."

She smiled tightly, nodded. But she was not convinced.

"Oh, and I want you to speak with Miss Dodson. The young woman who came with me that day? And a Mr. Behan; he writes for the *Herald*."

"Miss Jane, I want you to listen to me for a moment. Stop talking."

I had one more thing I meant to tell her, an important thing. But then I realized she had asked me to stop talking. So I stopped.

"I didn't do it for you. This is not your fault."

"Of course it is. If I hadn't come to see you, if I hadn't gone to see George Rutherford, you would not have been in a position where you had to shoot him."

"You put me in that position, yes. But I didn't have to shoot him."

"I wouldn't be alive if you hadn't."

"Yes, but I shot him for my own reasons." She let me take that in, then said, "So I will speak with Miss Dodson and Mr. Behan. And I appreciate your willingness to speak for me. But I think you and I both know there will be a trial, and we know how that trial will end. And when it ends, I want you to remember that I shot that . . ."

Her raised hand went stiff as she thought of George Rutherford.

". . . for my own purposes. I think our time is up, Miss Jane."

★ ★ ★

As promised, Michael Behan wrote a stirring tale of virtue delivered from the despoiler's foul hand. I retained my role as St. Agnes, the virginal and pure maid, and Otelia Brooks was cast as the avenging angel who had preserved my chastity.

"She saved my *life*," I pointed out to him.

"For my readers, your chastity's more important."

As he could not yet accuse George Rutherford of actual murder, only a callous disregard for my need to breathe, he invited his
readers to wonder what sort of man would devote so much time to
dressing—or was it undressing?—women. Eloquently, he sneered
at a man who would enrich himself at the cost of his fellow man's
impoverishment; why, how many husbands were on the verge of
ruin because their wives could not stay out of the shops? At the
same time, he sympathized with women who could not afford to
shop at Rutherford's, suggesting that what happened to me might
happen to any genteel yet poor girl who stepped foot in that palace of vanity and avarice. How noble, how inspiring—the spectacle of one of the city's working women coming to the aid of
another! He called upon future jurors to recall their finer natures,
their wives to remind their husbands of their duty to protect and
defend ladies from the likes of George Rutherford. For a tale that
skated lightly over the facts of the matter—which were far worse—
it was a compelling narrative.

Ella Dodson stuck more closely to the truth, regaling her
readers with the triumphs of a woman who had overcome tragedy to start her own respected business and now faced new
tragedy because she had saved a woman from the hands of a
monster. Like Michael Behan, she could not reveal the full extent of Rutherford's crimes, but her message that certain people
were allowed to get away with assault and others punished when
they fought back was not lost on readers. Otelia Brooks might
have chosen to keep to herself, but her customers and neighbors
were ready to come to her defense, especially the intimidating
and influential Mrs. Edwina Cross, whom I had met at the salon with her granddaughter. Ministers spoke on Otelia Brooks's
behalf in churches. Civic leaders demanded to meet with city

officials, and people stood vigil outside the prison where she was held.

And yet the safe remained unopened. Dolly Rutherford was adamant: nothing of her slain husband's should be touched. She was in mourning and quite unable to admit police into the place where her husband's life had ended at the hands of a madwoman. There was considerable sympathy for her. Many Rutherford's customers remembered George Rutherford as a wonderful man. Incapable of cruelty to women. Why, said Mrs. Tisch, were it not for George Rutherford, she might have worn chartreuse to the Eaglemonts' regatta picnic—and *that* would have been a genuine tragedy. Mrs. Worplesdon said whatever social success she had, she owed fully to Mr. Rutherford, who had put her in a Poiret dress the night she met Mr. Worplesdon. The impact of the dress was such that he had proposed, wed, and perished in the space of a year, leaving her with a massive fortune. What dress could do more?

There were other voices, however. Two former American Beauties recalled his habit of entering the dressing room without knocking. One observed that Mr. Rutherford was not always as delicate as he might have been about the sanctity of the female form. Arms were yanked, backsides crudely inspected, features harshly judged. But unspoken or understood in what was not said was that Mr. Rutherford was, after all, a man. Really, an artist in his own way. And women, some women, would offer what they could . . .

That, according to Dolly Rutherford, was what I had been doing in his office that day. Offering. Persistently. So persistently that Mr. Rutherford had no choice but to physically throw me out of his office. Of course, very few people believed that story, although they were tactful enough not to say so. The truth of the matter was obviously that I had made myself available and then threatened to tell his wife. What man wouldn't want to strangle a girl who did that?

In that version of events, Otelia Brooks was my accomplice, arriving to catch us in the act and increase the pressure.

And so the safe remained unopened.

★ ★ ★

On a day in early April, they set the date for Otelia Brooks's trial. And I asked to see Harry Knowles.

"Are you sober?" was the first thing I asked when we met in the park outside the *Herald*.

"Mostly."

"I'm here to thank you." If possible, the piggy eyes narrowed behind the fringe of dirty blond hair. "You made your readers care about Sadie and Carrie. That's something few people were willing to do in their lifetimes."

"And?"

"Because your readers care about Sadie and Carrie, they care about who killed them. Do you? Really care about who killed them?"

His eyes were almost shut; it occurred to me the sun's glare might be a trial to a man whose brains were swimming in alcohol. "Behan says you think it was George Rutherford."

"Because George Rutherford said it was George Rutherford. There's a safe in his office. He took things from Sadie and Carrie, a stocking and a bracelet, and I think he kept them in there. But Dolly Rutherford won't let the police open the safe. I need you to ask why not."

"Hard to attack a widow . . ."

"She's a rich woman who looked the other way while her husband assaulted other women. Maybe she didn't know what he was. But she has no right to stop us from finding out. Not if it means Otelia Brooks goes to the chair."

"Behan's already got the story that Rutherford was a cad. I don't see what my story is."

"Rutherford the killer. You're good at making people angry, Mr. Knowles. Ask your readers to demand they open the safe. Tell them to stay out of Rutherford's until they do. Open the safe, that's the headline." Then, as he got up to leave, I said, "By the way, that phone call to the refuge?"

He turned. I could see the thought that he had made threats in a drunken stupor haunted him.

"It wasn't you, Mr. Knowles. That call came the day I met George Rutherford. I needed to get an answer from him about costumes and he wouldn't listen, so finally, I just stood in his way. He hated women being where he felt they shouldn't. I imagine he felt I was 'coming after him,' so he threatened to come after me."

After a long pause, Harry Knowles said, "Thank you. For telling me that."

Michael Behan was right. Harry Knowles had his good days. And on those good days in the spring of 1913, he called forth the righteous in defense of Sadie Ellis, Carrie Biel, Lottie Burckholdt, and—although they didn't know it—Otelia Brooks. For days, OPEN THE SAFE! blared forth in bold black ink on the front page of the *Herald*. What was Rutherford's hiding? Who would demand justice for the innocent and the slain? He got Officer Nolan to express regret that the police were being hampered in their pursuit of the truth. Surely, such a man as George Rutherford had nothing to hide. Far better to clear his name of all suspicion. I had no way of knowing, but something told me that Mrs. Hilquit and others of Mrs. Pickett's brigade switched their Wednesday afternoons from street prayer to letter writing.

And in the end, they opened the safe. I had a bad day waiting to hear the results. What if Dolly Rutherford somehow got inside and removed evidence? What if there had been no evidence to remove? Time and again, I brought to mind the memory of Sadie's calf, splattered with blood—only visible because her black stocking was gone.

They found Sadie's stocking. And Carrie's bracelet. And several other items that would never be returned to the families of the unknown women who had died at George Rutherford's hands. Among them was the old blue scarf Norman Brooks had given to Otelia, which I said should be returned to her as soon as the investigation was concluded. After the safe was opened, the police had grounds to search the Rutherford warehouse. They found a small basement room, barely larger than a closet; it was padlocked shut. Inside was what the papers quickly dubbed "a true chamber of horrors."

Gripped by the revelations about George Rutherford, the public forgot his killer. Otelia Brooks was found guilty of owning a firearm without a license—but nothing more. Harry Knowles celebrated his victory privately at the Dump, but both Ella Dodson and Michael Behan were at the prison when she was released. They had entered a sort of competition as to who could cover the Otelia Brooks story to greater effect. To that end, they had brought their newspapers and exchanged copies, reading as we waited.

"What's this?" Behan pointed at the page.

Miss Dodson looked. "I believe it's the word 'white,' Mr. Behan."

"Why on earth would you write that? Officer Dennis Nolan, white." He pulled a face at me. I declined comment.

Ella Dodson gazed at her copy of the *Herald*. "Don't you read your own newspaper, Mr. Behan?"

"On occasion," he said with the politest sarcasm he could muster.

"Then you'll notice that we are referred to as negro. Maisie Phelps, negro. Charles Napier, negro. Delia Sands, negro."

"Yes, but that's so people will know . . ."

"Know."

"Well, otherwise, they'd just assume . . ."

I saw by Mr. Behan's expression that he was trying to find the right words to say what he meant, and failing, and had begun to realize a lack of right words might indicate a wrong position.

"It's odd, is all."

"Odd."

"You like to repeat things, don't you, Miss Dodson?"

"I'm helping you hear yourself, Mr. Behan."

Before he could answer, Ella Dodson spotted Otelia Brooks as she emerged from a side door of the prison.

Officer Nolan, who had received great credit for his handling of the case, stepped forward to introduce himself. "I'm very glad it ended well."

He expected a smile. He did not get it. Miss Brooks went still for just a moment before finding the words "Thank you, I am as well." Then she kept walking, leaving the policeman puzzled he had been dealt with in such an off-handed manner.

She announced she had no intention of making any kind of statement; she wanted to go home. Then she took my arm and asked if I would walk her to the elevated.

I said, "Miss Dodson tells me there is a celebration planned at the salon."

"I did not want it. I told her I did not want it. She said, Miss Brooks, you aren't really going to deny all your friends and supporters the chance to welcome you home? She just wants to write the story."

"And you can't deny her that."

"Apparently, I can't. Some women will go where they mean to go."

When we reached the entrance to the train, I said, "You'll stay in New York?"

She smiled, surprised that I would think otherwise. "Oh, yes. I'm staying. In fact, I'm expanding. Mrs. Cross has a nephew with money he's not using as profitably as he might. I've agreed to advise him."

"But you won't neglect the hats."

"Never."

It occurred to me to nudge her toward kindness to Officer Nolan. He couldn't be blamed for not knowing what happened to Norman Brooks. That his fellow officers had looked the other way while her husband was murdered, or joined in the beatings, having decided they were Irish first and officers of the law second.

Then I thought, It wasn't so many years ago, and Officer Nolan was not a young man. Otelia Brooks remembered. Why didn't he? Why was he puzzled by her reaction? And why had I thought her wrong?

She took my hands. Pressed them gently. "Give my best to your uncle."

17

Two weeks later, spring decided to make its presence known. Crocuses began to peep out of the Tylers' window boxes. Trees exploded into bud. The air was kinder.

As I dabbed a mild soap on the edge of Louise's corset, I thought they really were hellish objects to clean. Maybe I would ask Mrs. Hirschfeld if Lord & Taylor—where she now worked—had taken her advice about bras. Louise might be shocked at first, but I had a feeling it would make us both breathe easier.

At the moment, Louise was in the parlor, engaged in her morning phone conversation with her mother. From the kitchen, I could hear her voice rising to a surprisingly high pitch of excitement. Then I heard, "Jane! Jane, come in! Quickly!"

Setting aside the corset, I hurried into the parlor. Face alight, Louise said, "You'll never guess! Mother says Charlotte is engaged. To a count! Is that better than a prince? I can't remember."

For a moment I stood gape-mouthed in surprise. Louise's younger sister had never been my favorite of the Benchleys, and

I was not sad when she went abroad. I did acknowledge she had shrewdness to match her abundant good looks. Still, even I would not have expected this triumph.

"I would think it depends on the count," I said, recovering. "When is the wedding? Have they decided?"

Louise shook her head. "Next year, I would think. Mother's sailing to Europe in order to meet him; Father is to follow. But she wants me to go with her, says she can't possibly travel on her own. I don't know what William will say, and we haven't learned nearly enough French. Oh! I just realized, I don't even know where he's from, this count. I don't know what they speak. What if it isn't French?"

It was with the word "we" that the possibility dawned: "we" might mean . . . me. If Louise Tyler was sailing for Europe, I was sailing for Europe. *I* was going to Europe.

"Everyone speaks French, Mrs. Tyler. He's a count, he must. Or even English. After all, if he's fallen in love with your sister, they must have managed somehow." At the very least, I thought, he knew the English word for wealthy.

"Oh, Jane, we have a million things to do. Mother's coming over in the afternoon. I must call Monsieur Lafitte. Lessons every day, don't you think?"

"I do."

"Every day, and you and I shall only speak *en français*."

"*Bien sur, Madame Tyler. Et n'oubliez pas les vetements nouveaux pour le voyage.*"

Louise hesitated.

"The clothes for the trip, Mrs. Tyler. We'll make a list. *Une* list."

★ ★ ★

Despite the Benchleys' happy news, I was finding it hard. I still woke up gasping for breath, Carrie's face freshly clear in my mind.

And I felt the strange need for confession, even though I did not believe in it. I imagined whispering to an unseen authority: I have sinned against Sadie Ellis for treating her like a fool because she was cruelly treated. I have sinned against Carrie Biel by putting her in harm's way. I have sinned against Otelia Brooks because I put her, too, in harm's way. I have sinned by not thinking about that which I should have.

When I met Michael Behan for a walk in the park to thank him for his articles, I asked, "Do you go to confession?"

"I do," he said warily.

"Do you find it helpful?"

He considered, as if the efficacy of the practice had never crossed his mind before. "Helps to admit it. Put it behind you."

"Do people put it behind them?" I kicked at the path. "Sometimes I think we just commit the same sins over and over."

"Still gives you a bit of a grace period. I can't imagine not doing it. Having years of . . ." He shrugged, reluctant to give his transgressions a name. ". . . hanging around your neck."

"Good Lord, Mr. Behan, what do you have on your conscience?" I teased.

"You're not a priest, Miss Prescott, so that is none of your business."

We passed by the zoo, where a line of excited children and weary parents waited to go in. I thought of my trip to the Zoological Society, now postponed, and everything else I had meant to do on my holiday.

Regret must have showed in my face, because Michael Behan asked quietly, "And how was your holiday, Miss Prescott?"

"I think I shall make different plans next year."

"Well, you started with the Armory Show. *Dropped Book*, there was your first mistake."

"*Nude Descending*. And it wasn't all bad. I went dancing."

"Ah, yes, the cotillion."

"No, at the Acme Café."

At the mention of the gangster's club, Behan frowned. "You should tell that milkman to take you to more suitable places."

"He wasn't a milkman." I paused. "He was a songwriter."

Behan took that in. "You'll tell me if it's time to weigh in with the silver fish knife."

"Oh, I don't think he's that sort. I probably won't be seeing him again."

"Does this fellow need a punch in the nose?"

I smiled. "He does not. But you could buy the fish knife for Charlotte Benchley. She's engaged to be married."

"May the groom make it to the altar in one piece," he said, alluding to the fact that Charlotte's first fiancé had not been so fortunate. "Who is it?"

"The Count Barkoczy of Austria-Hungary."

"The what of the who of the where?" I repeated the title. "So Miss Benchley joins the nobility."

"And I get to go to Europe."

"Europe."

"For the wedding. Mrs. Tyler is going, and I'm traveling with her and her mother, Mrs. Benchley."

"But you'll be back?"

"Oh, yes, of course. Although Mrs. Tyler means to spend some time in Europe—she's never been—so I don't know when we'll return. Not more than a year, I'm sure. Mrs. Benchley is deathly afraid of foreign anything. Even a countess for a daughter won't be compensation for long."

He nodded, a slow up and down, and said nothing. I had expected the obvious pleasantries. Or teasing. Disparaging comments about the English. But he was . . . disappointed, I realized, with a twinge of pleasure. When I gave my uncle the news, he had said our family were poor sea travelers and hoped I would fare better. Anna had just given me a long list of books and pamphlets to send her.

Michael Behan opened his mouth, then decided silence was the better course. I opened my mouth to ask what he had meant to say, then also decided silence was the better course. We rounded Sheep Meadow, where the sheep had just been let out to graze.

"I'll write to you, if you like. All the details about the wedding. I'm sure Charlotte wouldn't mind the attention, so long as you tell New York—repeatedly and in great detail—that she's made a spectacular match."

"Well, that would be kind of you," he said. "And I shall write you if the heir to the Behan fortune makes an appearance before you get back."

Gazing up at the trees, I thought how by this time next spring, Michael Behan might be a father. Charlotte would be a countess, and I would have been to Europe—a miraculous thought.

And only a month ago, Sadie and Carrie were both alive and would now never see another day, much less another year.

"He was there that day. At the Armory. Did you know that?"

"Who? Rutherford?"

"Remember the dead cat? You made a joke about it being the *Herald* critic. I think he did it. Dolly Rutherford said he took one look at the Cubists and left. She said he was offended." I thought of the Picasso I had found both thrilling and disturbing, the way it carved a woman's face into sections. "I think he was inspired."

"I don't care to enter the mind of George Rutherford."

I didn't care to either, but I felt we should. If it was possible, and I wasn't sure it was. The miasma of rage, grandiosity, and the will to destroy that some might dismiss as madness felt disquietingly resonant. I knew the pleasure of adjusting a woman's appearance, even radically, to help her show herself to new advantage. It had never felt arrogant to me before. I thought of Leo's mother, Mrs. Hirschfeld, the way her attentions made women worry less about what they did not have to offer and proud of what they did. But George Rutherford saw women as clay. The only thing he recognized in a woman was his effect on her. For a while, I had wondered how such a creature managed to run a business. Then I thought, Perhaps he had not run so much of it. Of the two Rutherfords, Dolly was the more astute. George had been primarily known for his advice. And, of course, the pageant. The police had already learned that two other American Beauties had met with unfortunate fates. I suspected there would be more.

And yet he was afraid, too. Outraged. That was the word he had used when he found me where I shouldn't have been: in his office. How many years had he stared at the women strolling the aisles of his store, so free and entitled? So, invent a contest. Show them exactly as you wanted. At the Armory, what would he have seen? I remembered the paintings, the woman on her back, frank and open. And the girls on the rooftop, carefree, washing their hair. Finally, those women at their windows, enjoying the night air. And the watching shadow figure who made their liberty seem like vain folly.

I gazed about the park. Couples strolling. An elderly woman in a chair pushed by a nurse. A child toddling after a pigeon. A policeman nodded to a gentleman sketching the ducks. In light of a George Rutherford, was it idiocy to think this was reality? And yet I didn't want to think of Michael Behan's fat-cheeked, happy baby-to-be in a world where only the cruel drives of George Rutherford held sway.

Michael Behan said, "I did say, those paintings . . . some of them could bring out an ugly side of human nature."

"I think they just reveal what's there. I don't think you can blame the paintings."

★ ★ ★

When the poor had nowhere to go in life, they ended up in the city's lodging houses or the streets. In death, they lay on Hart Island. During the Civil War, Hart Island was used as a prisoner of war camp for Confederate soldiers. For a time, it was a boys' reformatory, and many ill-treated boys joined the young men of the Civil War in their graves. So it was already crowded with the dead when it was purchased by the city and made into a potter's field to replace other mass burial sites such as Washington Square Park and Bryant Park.

In 1913, it became the final resting place of Sadie Ellis and Carrie Biel. They would be buried in simple wood coffins, lying in a trench alongside hundreds of other unknowns. Even the buildings were abandoned on Hart Island, the old barracks of the Civil War internment camp hollowed out behind windowless walls of red brick, roofs long since fallen and blown away.

We could not make the final journey on the barge up the sound to the Bronx with them, but that did not mean they had no funeral. Given the distinction of their wounds, the bodies of Sadie and Carrie had been held until the investigation was closed. Now they could travel together in a horse-drawn rattletrap truck, the boxes shifting and sliding with every bump in the road. But they were not alone. At dawn that morning, my uncle, Berthe, the other women, and I gathered to follow the truck on foot to the barge.

It was a warm enough day that we could wear only black shawls. Berthe and my uncle walked ahead. Walking behind them, I thought Berthe's place should be mine; surely I should be leading the walk at my uncle's side. But I realized I had a different place in the world. I didn't share the daily life of the refuge's residents. And so I should not be leading them. It didn't mean I had no place.

Anna walked alongside me. When I was recovering, she had come every few days, bearing more food from her aunts than one person could eat in a year, all of it soft, making me feel like a gorgeously spoiled infant. Now looking at the wreaths of dried roses, myrtle, and eucalyptus we had put on the coffins, she said, "Is it strange that we want to make death look pretty?"

This morning, we had laid Carrie's rope bracelet beside her, placed a crown of flowers on Sadie's head. I thought of how Otelia Brooks felt about the women whose hair she dressed. *You care for someone, you make them beautiful. Show the world what you see.*

I said as much to Anna, adding, "You don't stop caring once the person has died." Sighing, she took my hand and shook it, in her habitual blend of irritation and affection.

As I walked, I considered that Norman Brooks probably also lay at the City Cemetery. Otelia had no way to visit him, as we would have no way to visit Carrie and Sadie. They were lost to us. But not forgotten.

Our parade took a turn onto Baxter Street. The Duchess and several other ladies stood on the corner, waiting to join. The Duchess wore a black crêpe veil over her hair, and the ladies wore black armbands. As they headed toward the back, I said to the Duchess, "Miss Bullotte, perhaps you would like to walk with my uncle."

Startled that I had addressed her by name, or that I had addressed her at all, she assessed the meaning of my offer for a moment. Then smiled. "I would at that."

At the dock, my uncle read from the Book of John as the coffins were loaded onto the barge. "In my Father's house are many rooms. If it were not so, would I have told you that I go to prepare a place for you? And if I go and prepare a place for you, I will come again and will take you to myself, that where I am you may be also."

Then he began to sing "Amazing Grace." The women who knew the song well from Sunday services joined in.

Looking at the man who had appeared at the police station so many years ago and offered me his hand, I sang the echo: *And grace will lead us home.*

Epilogue

Shaking the newspaper out, I remember Ella Dodson's point to Michael Behan, that certain citizens were always described by certain newspapers by their race. That habit continued at the *Times* until 1946. "This may seem like a small thing," the *Times*'s editorialist wrote in a rather self-congratulatory piece. "The Negroes don't think so." I can imagine Ella Dodson answering, *Yes, we haven't thought so for a century.*

By the 1940s, however, Ella Dodson would not have been reading the *Times*. When President Wilson celebrated the fiftieth anniversary of the Emancipation Proclamation by segregating all federal workers—even going so far as to put a cage around one worker who could not be moved or fired—she decided matters in the capital needed sharper observation. And so she became the Washington correspondent for the Associated Negro Press. Ella became the reporter no White House press officer wanted to call on, not unless they had their facts and ethics in order, something more than a few have found challenging. In her late seventies, she became something of a celebrity as she lashed the Nixon White House, exigent and unbudgeable in the front row, cane in hand, splendid hat on her head. The hat that had finally arrived at her Washington home, after many years of good-humored nagging.

Few newspapers noticed when Otelia Brooks died in 1937. By then George Rutherford had been supplanted by killers even more flamboyantly cruel, and the passing of the woman who dispatched him excited little interest. But the *Times* wrote an obituary, as did the *Herald*. Both papers had reporters who remembered the Rutherford case and Miss Brooks. (Or if they had forgotten, they were reminded by those who had not.)

Those papers might have been astonished by the crowds that attended Otelia Brooks's service at the Mercy Street Baptist Church. I have been fortunate to see many ravishing things in my life, but the sight of hundreds of women, both celebrated and private citizens, gathered together in their Otelia hats is among the most memorable. Some I recognized—a well-known actress and a noted educator, as well as a stunning woman who brought her six-year-old daughter, who was wearing the very hat I had seen her mother wear so many years ago. Others Ella Dodson identified for me, such as Mary Kenner, whose invention she had to whisper given that we were in a church. At one point, she indicated a large flower arrangement and said if I looked closely, I would see they had been sent from the White House, the first lady having received a hat, but only after she supported Walter White's anti-lynching legislation.

"You don't know what I had to do to get her to make it," Ella complained after the service. "I called her over and over, saying, Just send it, it'll help. She said, That woman has a hundred people making hats for her. She doesn't need mine. She won't look right in it anyway."

"I imagine she was right about that."

"I said, I will keep calling you every day, twice a day, until you do this. She threatened to tear out her phone. Finally, she said, If I read in your paper that she's been helpful, I'll *consider* it. She never would let me write about her work. I think she only left that house to go to church."

It was true I had only seen her on very few occasions, although she had been kind enough to attend my uncle's funeral. "I think she was happiest in her workroom."

"I suspect it's where she felt safe," conceded Ella Dodson, adding with a roll of the eyes, "Surrounded by cloth and straw and all those things she could twist and bend to her will."

I looked out at the women still leaving the church, their hats creating a vast landscape of shape and color and movement. Acts of will, yes, even ruthless will. But joyous, generous, and celebratory. And so, so beautiful. Otelia Brooks might have avoided the world outside her workroom, but she had sent out the deepest part of herself.

During Watergate, Ella liked to call me to gloat over the *Post*'s triumph over the New York papers. Funny, remembering Watergate. Leo and I watched so much of that coverage. At the time, he was in rehearsals for *Days Gone By*, which was a showcase of his songs. He said the book was awful, the dancing worse, but the songs were fine. He let me watch one of the dress rehearsals, and we laughed over the costumes. "Pickle Barrel Rag" has long been forgotten, as has "Lady Lion Tamer." But the first act ended with a lovely rendition of "But on Fridays," which has been recorded by everyone from Sophie Tucker to Judy Garland and Barbra Streisand. The critics were divided as to whether the show was a charming evocation of America's past or shamelessly sentimental and crassly commercial. ("The second," said Leo. "Obviously.")

But they all agreed it was an effective showcase for the greatest American composer of the last hundred years. Which was, said Leo, the point.

There was a tribute concert to him at the time of the Bicentennial. He was invited to the capital, but he declined, and so we watched it from the living room, eating off trays. As it ended with flags and a vast chorus singing the song so famous most people have forgotten he wrote it, he said, "I'll say this for it. Unlike 'The Star-Spangled Banner,' it's a song you can actually sing."

"It's a great song."

"Not bad for a singing waiter."

"Not bad at all, Mr. Hirschfeld."

Scott Joplin died in 1917 at the Manhattan Psychiatric Center. Penniless, he was buried in a group plot in Queens. And my prediction proved wrong. The Marshall Hotel closed down in 1913.

Clementine Pickett ended her crusade against the sins of the flesh soon after George Rutherford's crimes were revealed and turned her considerable energies to outlawing the consumption of alcohol. Here she was more successful, becoming something of a national figure. She had learned a thing or two from Bill Danvers; prayers and hymns were all very well, but a more direct approach brought the press. She took to carrying a small axe, which she swung with great panache in saloons across the city as she railed against the devastation liquor had wrought upon American families. Through it all, her son was at her side, driving her to her many engagements and ejecting the more aggressive hecklers.

Bill Danvers washed up in the East River under the Hell Gate Bridge, then under construction. His throat had been cut, and nobody much cared to find out who had done it.

Dolly Rutherford had a change of heart about her husband's innocence when she realized that as the widow of a monster, she excited far more interest than she ever had with her salons. Once she was out of mourning, she was much in demand at dinner parties, where she regaled her fellow diners with tales of her life with the Beauty Killer. She professed suspicions I certainly never witnessed when her husband was alive and a terror that was quite out of character for her. But people seemed to prefer her version, so much so that she wrote a book, which was then made into a movie. Starring Lillian Gish, as a matter of fact.

Turning back to the front page, I try to read the article about the young man who wanted to kill the president over a vision of a woman who existed only in his head. But the memory of George Rutherford has made me tired and angry with this story. It's one I've heard too many times.

And so I turn to the bottom half of the paper to read that three men have been attacked by a mob in Brooklyn. The three men were black; white teenagers swarmed their car, stopping it in the street. They threw beer cans, smashed windows, broke a bottle over one man's head as he tried to escape. Two of the men did get away. But William Turks, a transit worker with a ten-year-old daughter, was dragged from his car and beaten to death. This is also a story heard too many times, and for a moment I am tempted to set it aside.

But then I turn my bad old eyes back to the account.